A PUSHED BIRD DOESN'T FALL FAR FROM THE NEST

By Jason LaMountain

This book is dedicated to my fiancé Keleigh. My last four years with her have been the best of my life and this novel never would have seen the light of day without her.

It is also dedicated to the memory of Bill Tapply, who was a great teacher, author, and man.

PART I
THE RESULT OF A
LETTER RECEIVED

THE HOUSE I WAS BORN IN AND THE
WOMAN RESPONSIBLE
(PROLOGUE TO PART I)

"Hey Ma," I came into her house screaming. "Are you home?"

I had spoken to her once that morning, filling her in on the most recent of the proceedings with Fred. Ever since then, I had been unable to get through. I was worried. There was a chance that she couldn't hear the phone, or that she couldn't find it, but I was still worried.

I started moving through the house I grew up in, sticking my head into the kitchen first. Every stick of furniture was exactly the same as it had been when I was a kid:

There was the kitchen table where we had our best fights over pork chop dinners; there was the fridge with the same blown out bulb from the time, not long ago, that my mother forgot to close the door for the entire day; there was the kitchen sink that my younger brother, Morty, had used to accidentally dispose of Mom's engagement ring when he was five.

"Ma?" I asked the empty fishbowl that always sat on the windowsill, miraculously unbroken after surviving three boys.

"Ma?" I asked the living room.

I walked upstairs and looked right, down to the end of the hall. There was the room I had lived in for most of my life; the room I had lived in with my wife Gen for a year and a half after we got married; the room that I brought my darling Cecilia home to after she had been given life.

"Ma?"

Down the hall from my room, there was no light coming from my brother Fred's old room. There was no light from my brother Morty's old room next door. There was no light from my mother's room, the room she used to share with my father Jackson.

•••

Once my mother's hair dried, I made the first of two phone calls.

Boop beep beep!

The other end of the line clicked. "Nine-one-one emergency."

"Hello?" I said.

"Hello, sir," the woman said. "What is your emergency?"

"It's my mother. She's dead. I found her—"

"—Alright, sir. Can I please have your name and address?"

"I'm Paul Morrison." I continued on with the address and everything else.

"And do you have any idea how the death occurred?"

"No," I said. "I found her when I came to the house."

"Ok," she said, "And where is the body?"

"Um…" I paused. "On her bed."

2

"Ok, sir, it looks like we'll have an ambulance and squad car out there in about fifteen minutes."

"Alright, come as quick as you can." I hung up the phone and stared at it. I asked it, "What have I done?"

Now what?

I checked the clock. Three. I picked up the phone and called my cousin Howie.

"Hey, Howie?" I said once he picked up.

"Hey Paul."

"Listen, I'm dropping the lawsuit. I don't want it to go to trial anymore. That's it, end of story, I don't want to talk about it ever again."

•••

When the police showed up, they began their investigation immediately. They parked two squad cars and an ambulance in front of the house, blocking the way to pedestrians with rolls and rolls of yellow caution tape. I was sitting on the curb next to my car, right in front of my mother's house. I had my face buried in my hands.

An officer came over with a small pad of paper. "Excuse me, Mr. Morrison?"

"Yes?" I said, looking up at him.

"Could I ask you a few questions, please?"

"Sure, officer."

He pulled a pen out of his utility belt. "Ok. Let's start out with the time. What time did you arrive here on the scene?"

"Oh, I don't know. About two o'clock."

He jotted. "And when did you find the body?"

"Almost right away," I said. I watched him write. "I found her on her bed."

"Mm hmm..." he said, writing more. "And then what happened?"

"I called nine-one-one."

He started talking while finishing up a sentence on the paper. "Mr. Morrison, it says right here that you called nine-one-one at five minutes to three." He stopped writing and looked up at me. "Are you trying to tell me that you arrived here at about two o'clock, found the body, and then

3

called nine-one-one right away?" He shook his head. "That doesn't add up. Where did that hour go?"

"...I don't know." Inside, I fumbled for words. Outside, I kept my cool. "I was in shock when I found her. I remember slamming the bedroom door shut as soon as I saw her. I was sitting on the floor in the hallway for a while. Maybe for an hour, I don't remember. Then I went into her bedroom to make sure, you know...that she was dead...then I made the call."

"Alright," he said, marking down a few last items. "Mr. Morrison, I'm going to have to ask for your address and phone number. There are quite a few discrepancies that I want to clear up here, but I can see that you have enough to deal with right now."

I gave him my information.

"Go home to your family, now. But don't go too far, ok? Try to relax and grieve and pull yourself together, because it's very important that you are ready to answer all of the questions I have for you."

•••

Three days later—today—they called me in. I wasn't ready to answer all of their questions. Everything that's happened, the last ten weeks have all come crashing down on me.

So when the officers asked me about the discrepancies they had found—my mother's hair was damp (apparently it hadn't dried all the way); my mother was wearing shoes on her feet without any stockings (she had stockings hanging in her closet, a lot of stockings); my mother had fingerprint bruises on her neck (I don't know how those got there)—I just wasn't ready to talk about it.

The good cop said, "We don't want to do it, Mr. Morrison, but until you are willing to tell us what happened, exactly, we have enough forensic evidence against you that we are going to have to try you for murder. You had the motive, you were at the scene of the crime, and you aren't telling us the truth. I'll be perfectly honest with you: I don't think you could kill, and I certainly don't think you could kill your own mother. So do all of us a favor. Tell us what happened."

"That's right, Mista Morrison," the bad cop said. "Do yourself a fay-vah."

I'm not doing anyone any favors yet and I'm still not ready to talk about what has happened. So for now, I'm locked up in a jail cell. I'm up for bail tomorrow, and my trial will start sometime after that. I decided that—to clear my name—I would write out what happened. A written deposition. A signed confession, if you prefer.

And so this is it: why my mother died, starting with Fred's decision to come back from the dead.

1.

BARTLETT'S FAMOUS QUOTES

Ten weeks ago, I was sitting behind the cash register of my small business. On a barstool. There were a few people standing in line, which made it an ok day. (I admit, I was a little disappointed that only one person was holding a used book. My original intention for the place was as a used bookshop that sold a little coffee and a few pastries on the side. But people started buying a lot of coffee and more pastries than we could handle baking. So, one thing led to another and we had to add "and Café" to the end of the shop's name.) I was good at what I did: I made friends with the customers and I made them come back again and again. I was good at what I did because I'd wanted it so bad for so long.

I had waited years for that—to look out and see people walking around my store, buying my books and drinking my coffee. I'd waited with my wife Gen—who was upstairs resting—for the day we could get off on our own and open my dream.

The phone sounded over the bustle in my bookshop and café. I told the next person in line to wait just a minute and I picked it up. "This is the Morrison Bookshop and Café. Paul speaking."

"Paul, dear, I'm glad you picked up." It was my mother. She sounded upset.

"What is it, Ma?"

"I got a letter from Fred today."

I waved to my eight year old, Cecilia and covered the mouthpiece on the phone. "Honey, come here and take over at the register for a minute." I smiled at the next customer while my girl made her way over and put up a finger to say, "She'll be with you in a second."

Then I gave the phone my full attention. So Fred finally got in touch with us again, after seven years of absolute silence. I'd wondered where he'd snuck off to, what hole he'd crawled in to hide, and I usually wondered at night while my wife was asleep in bed next to me. I don't know why, but there in the dark, I always had the sneaking suspicion that he'd found his way into the advertising business. "Where is he?" I asked. "What the hell is he doing?"

"He's in New York City. He's been married…"

"Ma?"

"Oh, I'll just read it to you. It's not that long."

She cleared her throat. "It says, *Dear Mom, Paul, and Morty. I am dropping this line to tell you of my recent successes. When I left, I moved down to New York City, and I have been living here ever since. The first couple of months were hard, but now I have a very good job as an editor at a publishing house. I also just recently asked a girl to marry me and the wedding date is sometime in the fall of next year. Otherwise, I am healthy, and I'm willing to come up to visit all of you if it is necessary.*"

If it is necessary?

"*My number at the Flatiron Building, where I work, is (212) 555-7763. Fred.*"

Even though I often thought about him late at night, I was doing fine without Fred in my life anymore. Why did he decide to get back in touch with us?

"Oh Paul," my mother said after waiting some time for me to respond. "I wish your father were still alive."

"Me too, Ma." It was inconsiderate of him to be dead, quite frankly. If he were still alive, none of this would have happened. Our family would still own The General Store, my mother would be taken care of, and while it's true that Fred probably would have moved either way, his departure wouldn't have been surrounded with so many emotional confusions.

Then again, maybe I wouldn't have owned the bookstore.

My father was the Elmer's that held his family—his wife and three sons—together. He was a good businessman with a keen interest in history. Whenever he had the time, which was rare, he would read non-fiction on anything from Sumerian culture to the Cold War. There were always a few books hidden away in one recess of his room or another.

He was also a fan of *Bartlett's Famous Quotes*, which could have been found under his bed, tucked into the corner made by his night table and the wall. When I was a kid, we would flip through the pages of quotes together after I took my shower, before I went to bed. Eventually, this turned into a game. He would ask me questions like, "What would Mark Twain say if he were here right now?" And I would have to think up a quote.

I have the distinct memory of sitting in my father's room at the hospital when I was 22. I was next to him until the end, and I couldn't help thinking: *If Mark Twain were here, he would have said, "The reports of your father's death were right on."*

"Well," I said, "what do you think, Ma? Do you want to call him?"

"I don't know," she said. "Preston said I shouldn't."

"Wait." Was she serious? "You talked to Uncle Preston about this before me?" I was livid. "I'm Fred's brother!"

8

"Well, I called my sister and he picked up."

"Ma, I don't want you talking to Uncle Preston about this," I said. "This is *our* family's problem, and we should keep it between you and us three sons. We can work it out among ourselves."

"Ok dear, you're right," she said.

I blew the stress out of my body like a horse whinnying. "I'm sorry I raised my voice."

"That's ok, dear." Mom paused on the other end of the line. "Oh, by the way. Morty is going to give me a lift to your bookshop on Saturday for the baby shower."

"Well it's not really a baby shower," I said, "but that's great!"

"What is it then?"

"It's sort of just a general celebration of the baby on the way, I guess. But I have to go now. I'll see you then and we can talk about Fred's letter a little more." I hung up and looked around the café. We had a lot of cleaning up to do before Saturday.

Cecilia was just finishing up with her second sale. "Here's your change, mister." A penny fell from the customer's hand during the exchange. "Oops! I'll get it."

"Oh, that's ok, don't worry abou—ok, thank you. Thanks a lot."

"Welcome," Cecilia said. She looked at me. "Next?" she asked.

I nodded. "Go ahead."

"Next!" she said.

2.

THE MECHANIC

Gen was almost eight months pregnant with our second child. She was getting big.

Two weeks earlier, we had been talking: "You know," she said, "my parents live so close and I never get to see them." So we talked about it and figured the baby was as good an excuse as any to throw a party and get Gen's parents to come visit. We decided to throw the party at our bookstore, in the back where the café was.

We had decorated for the event with paper streamers zig-zagging between the walls. The café tables were covered in blue and pink cloth—Gen's idea, not mine—and the café bar was stocked with food and alcohol.

It was a little too cold to open up the bay doors to the terrace at that time of year, but they provided a nice view of the patches of grass making a comeback from winter.

Gen's parents were the first to arrive. "Hi John," I said. "Hi Sally."

They nodded and waved their hands at me. John headed over towards the kitchen and Sally gave Gen a kiss on the cheek.

"Is there anything to drink around here?" Gen's father asked.

"Yeah," I said. "Check back there behind the register. There are a couple of bottles to choose from, or there's some beer in the fridge in the kitchen. You see 'em?"

"Yup."

Once more lively people began to arrive, the party started in full. Our guests milled about, grabbing food and drinks. Some of the guests were so bold as to tap their feet to the music coming from the speakers set up next to the food. Some sat down at the café tables, but most just stood around and talked.

Cecilia ran around everywhere and received the usual comments that an eight-year old girl would: "Oh my, you've grown so big!" "Just look at you, you're so adorable! I could eat you up." "How tall are you now? You must've just had a growth spurt or something, because the last time I saw you, you were only this tall."

If my father were here, he would have said, "Paul, get that child down to the butcher. She'll go for at least twice what you paid for her."

Gen spent most of her time around the door, saying hello to everyone that was arriving and accepting the gifts that they bore. I tried to stay close by—for moral support, I guess—but I ended up talking to Gen's parents for most of the party. They were telling me that my little Cecilia was so bright, beautiful, and talented that they just couldn't wait for their next grandchild to be born. I couldn't help but wonder why: they already had more than enough macaroni and glue slapped on their fridge.

My real problem with Gen's parents was this: even at this "baby shower" for their grandson-to-be, they couldn't pretend to like my family. They wouldn't "lower themselves" to speak to my mom. I remember Gen's mom once said to me, "I'm sorry, Paul, but I just think that your

11

mother is rather simpleminded. And as for your *brother*. Well! How could one speak with him and not stare?"

If Christopher Reeves were here, he would have said, "Fuck you, lady."

My brother Morty was, of course, in attendance. He had rolled over to the coffee bar to get some liquor in him as soon as he had arrived. Drinking was half of Morty's life. The other half was his job at the floral shop.

He was balancing his drink on one of his chair's armrests and putting Cecilia up on his lap when I came up behind him. "Whoa, now," I said. "I don't want you operating heavy machinery around my daughter. Especially not when you're under the influence."

He laughed and gently punched me in the arm. Or maybe he took a real swing at me and just grazed me, I just don't remember.

From across the room, I could hear an exaggerated kissing sound and then a loud, "Congratulations!" from Aunt Hallie, who was holding on to Uncle Preston's arm. I made eye contact with him by accident, and he started moving towards me.

"Oh Jesus, Morty. I guess I have to talk to Uncle Preston."

He laughed. "Well keep him away from me, anyways. There's a pain in the A-S-S that I don't need," he said, covering Cecilia's ears with his hands while he spelled it out.

•••

Now let me tell you a little something about my Uncle Preston: he is a real jackass. He's a mechanic and the reigning champion of all bullshitters. He would joke around with you when you were face to face, but the second you turned away, he would reach a hand into your pocket and take your wallet.

Especially if you were his customer. When a customer would pull up to his garage and ask to have the oil checked, Preston would pull the dipstick out and, rubbing some of the oil away with his thumb, go to the window to say, "Oh, it looks like you need a quart of oil."

12

The customer would say, "Ok, could I buy enough to fill 'er up, please?"

And he would say, "Sure thing," run inside the station, grab an empty bottle of oil, and use this to "fill 'er up." He would pocket the cash, of course. When times were running slow at the station he would tell people they needed new alternators, new spark plugs, new anythings, and charge them an arm and a leg for something they didn't even know was part of their car. But he was a professional con man, and he was good at what he did: he color-coded his parts so he wouldn't tell the same person they needed the same part replaced twice.

•••

My uncle was very good at what he did, however illegal it was, and a good con man can always spot a bad one. One time, a guy came into the station saying that he was having electrical problems. Preston told him, "The tricky thing about electrical problems is that they can take me a few minutes to find, or they could take me a few hours. And I charge by the hour. It could be expensive." The man said he understood, and agreed to have Preston fix it anyways. Preston was licking his chops. When a problem like this presented itself, he could charge almost anything he wanted. This was quite an opportunity. So he spent the time looking for the problem. After a couple of minutes, he found it: a wire running along the bottom of the car had come unplugged. That kind of wire could not easily come unplugged on its own, and Uncle Preston suspected foul play.

When the guy came back for the car, Preston said, "Listen. It took a couple of hours to find the problem, but all that happened was a wire came loose from its connection. So I'll tell you what. I want you to come back here as a regular customer. This one's on me." The guy thanked him and, two weeks later, Preston's garage was listed in the Globe Magazine as the only honest garage in the tri-county area. All of the other mechanics had charged the investigative reporter anywhere from eighty to one hundred and sixty dollars for the unplugged wire.

And this was the kind of bullshit I had the pleasure of looking forward to as he walked over.

"Paul!" he said. "How are you doing?"

"Just fine, Uncle Preston. How about you?" I asked. "How's the garage these days?"

"Times are good," he replied. "Howie just graduated law school. Last month, in fact. A semester early!"

"Really?" I said. "How about that. How exciting."

"Yes sir. But Paul," he said, taking a hold of my arm. "There's something I wanted to talk to you about." And there it was, his not so subtle and almost immediate cut to the chase. He had the bedside manner of a Dr. Kevorkian. "I wanted to talk to you for a second about Fred. I assume you heard about the letter he finally got around to sending home?"

I had.

"I figured as much. But listen. It sounds like he's been doing fairly well for himself lately." He slicked his hair back with his hand. "I spoke to Howie, your cousin, about the...situation surrounding Fred's departure, and he agrees with me that the case against your brother is just waiting to be filed. He could win your mother a nice settlement."

He had quite a pitch. *If Dr. Jack Kevorkian were here, he would have said, to me, "I can squeeze you in on Thursday morning, if you like." And I would have thought long and hard about it.*

"You're probably right," I said, "but I don't want to drag my family into the courtroom. What's done is done — we can't do anything about the store now anyway — and time makes me forgive. If we were going to do anything about it, we should've done it then, when the water was still boiling."

"Better late than never."

"Mmm, I don't think that's true in this case. What could we possibly accomplish?"

"We have to think about your mother," Preston said. "Couldn't she use the money, Paulie?"

14

The last time my uncle called me Paulie was when I was five and he would hold a sucking candy just out of my reach and make me jump and snatch it out of his hand like a dolphin at Seaworld.

"All right, Uncle Preston," I said. "Thanks for worrying about us, but I'm a big boy and I can take care of my mother just fine." I took a deep breath. "But let's not talk about this now. It's my wife's baby shower, or whatever this is. Why not go mingle with everyone?"

He turned to go. "We'll talk about this later, though, huh?"

"Sure, but please don't bother my mother with this now, ok?"

He nodded and started to walk off.

"Oh!" I said. "Don't forget to say hi to Morty."

I watched as Preston walked over to my Aunt Hallie, touched her on the arm, and whispered in her ear. Then I saw him turn and walk over to Morty. Morty immediately put on one of those fake smiles that would hurt his cheeks if he used it for too long.

When I was satisfied that Preston was successfully distracted, I went over to stand by Gen again. She had moved over to a table, sitting with her parents to rest her swollen ankles.

"Hey guys," I said. "Is everyone enjoying themselves?"

"Sure," Gen's mother said. "Why not?"

"It's a lovely party," Gen said, staring at her mother with furrowed eyebrows and a frown. "I'm glad we did this."

"Me too," I said. "It was a good chance to catch up with everyone." Just as I sat down, I noticed my mother, standing in a corner by herself. She was watching the rest of the party. "Excuse me for a minute, everyone." I stood up and walked over to her.

"Hey Ma," I said.

"Hello dear."

I noticed that her mascara had been running. Her eyes were red and puffy. Either it was allergy season, or she'd been crying. "Ma. Are you ok?"

"Oh," she said, looking at the ceiling and blinking her eyes to hold back more tears. "I'm fine. Really. It's just that these family get-togethers make me miss Jackson and Fred even more."

"Yeah, I know what you mean."

She pulled an old tissue out of her pocket and wiped her eyes dry, smiling at me. "Don't you worry about me, Paul—it's my job to worry about you."

3.

THE BABY RESPONDS TO SOUND IN THE WOMB

That night, after the party, Gen and I sat up in bed watching television. A black man and an Asian woman were telling us about everything that was going wrong.

Click.

"I'm sorry, sweetie," I said, "but I've had enough of that bullshit for one night."

"Paul, not in front of the baby!" Gen pulled the blankets over her belly to shield our unborn baby boy from the obscenity. "No bad language. Please!"

"Are you kidding me?"

"Well," Gen said, crossing her arms in front of her, "I read that babies respond to sound when they're in the womb. They can pick up on your harsh tone, and it will be a detrimental effect on their young, developing minds."

"Jesus, where do you read this crap?"

"Paul!"

"Ok, I'm sorry. You're right."

17

"I know," she said. "Sorry for yelling, though. This pregnancy is freaking me out much more than the one with Cecilia."

"Yeah," Rodney Dangerfield would have said, "your mood is swinging so fast that it should have three venereal diseases by now. Sheesh. I mean, it swings better than my nine iron."

"That's ok," I said. "You're allowed to freak out."

She smiled at me.

"Goodnight." I gave her a kiss.

"Goodnight, sweets."

I rolled over and closed my eyes.

"Paul?"

"Yeah?"

"Will you get me something to eat?"

"Sure."

I got out of bed and ran downstairs. I grabbed what I could out of the fridge and back upstairs, sliding back into bed. I gave her the food and smiled and gave her a kiss on the forehead. I rolled over and closed my eyes again.

"Thanks, Paul." I heard her crunch through a chip. "Is there any chocolate syrup downstairs?"

"No, you finished that last night, remember?"

"Damn it." She put one hand on her belly and the other over her mouth. "Oops!"

4.

COUSIN HOWIE PRETENDS HE'S ALREADY A LAWYER

The next day, in the early afternoon, I got a call from Howie. Uncle Preston's son. "Hey, how's it going?" I asked. I didn't care to hear the answer, but I wanted to prolong what I knew he would bring up.

"Pretty good, Paul. I just graduated from law school."

I'd heard.

"Listen, Dad asked me to talk to you about a few things. I'm sort of in the neighborhood anyway, so I figured I could swing by."

"No no," I said, "don't do that. I already know what you want to talk about, and I don't want any part of it. And neither does my mother. There won't be any lawsuit."

"Yeah, hold on a minute," he said. "There's an accident up ahead."

One minute passed.

"Oh by the way," he said, startling me from my blank staring. "I'm sorry I didn't make it to your party yesterday, but my parents told me all about it. Dad said he got to talk to you for a while. I would have come myself, but I was busy doing some work and trying to find more. You know, my bar exam is coming up soon, and—"

"That's fine, Howard," I interrupted. "No big deal."

"Ok," he said. "I guess I'll see you in a bit."

"Ok, see you later."

•••

"Hey Howie. How's it going. Come in. Let me take your jacket." I was thrilled that Howie had decided to stop by despite our conversation. I sometimes wonder if he heard a single word I ever said.

"Thanks, Paul."

In a lot of ways, Howie was like his father. He had slicked back hair like Uncle Preston. He had a curved nose like Uncle Preston. He had brown eyes so dark they looked to be all pupils. Just like Uncle Preston. He even had the same frumpy look as Uncle Preston, except he was able to achieve the look without a mechanic's jumpsuit—in fact, with a suit like the one he wore that day, I would have been surprised if he ever found work.

Father and son even shared mannerisms. Uncle Preston had the habit of pushing his hair back with his hand, a tick that Howie duplicated. Like Uncle Preston, he was aggressive. Like Uncle Preston, he would blindly push forward once he had decided on a course of action. And like Uncle Preston, Howie was a pain in my ass.

The one big difference between Uncle Preston and my cousin Howie, in fact, was that Preston was smart. Or, at the very least, clever.

I brought my cousin past the bookshelves in the front room and into the café. There were two people sitting with their coffee and reading, one with a copy of the *Massachusetts Messenger*, the other with John Irving's "A Prayer for Owen Meany" (now on sale in the Morrison Bookshop's used-books section for three dollars).

We sat at a table near the back, near the glass doors that looked out on the terrace.

"Thanks for having me over Paul," Howie said.

I didn't seem to have a choice, I thought. Instead, I said, "It's always nice to see someone from the family."

"It certainly is." He put his briefcase down on the table. "Listen. I came to talk about Fred.

"Paul," he continued, "I want you to know that, considering the situation, there is no way we would lose a law suit against him." He spoke to me, careful to maintain eye contact. "This case is very clear-cut, and I would like to file it with the court as soon as I pass the bar, in about one months ti—"

"—I already spoke with your father about this," I said, "and I'm sorry, but I haven't changed my mind. I don't want to sue."

"I understand that, Paul, but I spoke with your mother about it, and *she* said—"

"—You what? I will say this once more!" I said, loud enough to disturb the customers. I leaned in close to Howie and said, softer, "I don't want anyone bothering my mother with this whole fiasco. If there is something to consider, tell me about it and I will bring it up with her. She can't handle this, and she doesn't need to handle this. All right?"

"Ok, Paul," he said in a soothing tone. "I understand that now. But I already spoke with your mother and she said that she thinks we should go ahead and do what we think is best."

"She said that because she doesn't understand what the hell you're talking about." I threw my arms up in the air, exasperated beyond all belief. "Of course she would want you to do what you think is best! She has no idea what she's doing when it comes to this crap."

"Alright, Paul, I'm sorry you feel that way," he said, eyeing the customers. "I just thought you would understand that what Fred did was an affront to your family."

"I understand that perfectly well," I said. "No one understands that better than me. That store was going to be mine, all right? So don't give me that bullshit."

"Ok, ok."

"Now I have to go over and explain everything to my mother. So," I said while standing up. "If you'd excuse me please?"

"Sure thing." He fixed his tie and stood. "I'll just be on my way."

5.

UNCLE PRESTON IMPOSES HIMSELF ON A CONVERSATION

Ding-dong!

"Paul! What a wonderful surprise!" my mother said, opening the door to her house.

"Hey, Ma. How's it going?"

I stepped into the living room that I'd grown up in.

There was the TV my mother used to watch the tragic death of half of the Kennedy family.

There was the Lay-Z-Boy my father sat in every night after work, his indentation still visible even now, seven years later.

There were the doilies covering every otherwise blank space.

And there was the coffee table, the phone that gave us daily updates on Morty's condition placed beside a lamp.

"It's going well, Paul. Oh!" she exclaimed, "You'll never believe who took the time to stop by this morning!"

"Was it Howie?" I asked, already certain of the answer.

"Yes! He stopped by and had some tea with me. What a bright young man he has become." She sat down on the couch. "That was a very good guess," she said, obviously disappointed that I had been able to guess it right so easily.

"Did you talk about Fred?"

She looked down at her feet. "Yes." She shuffled one foot on top of the other. "I know you told me not to talk about it without you, but he just explained a few things to me."

"Now Mom, I said that—"

Ring! Ring!

The phone cut me off.

Mom stood up to answer it. "Just a second dear. Hello?" she said into the receiver. She listened for a minute. "Yes, hello! How are you? ...I'm fine, yes." She listened again, then looked over at me a couple of quick times out of the corner of her eye. "I can't talk about that anymore... Yes, that's right." She looked at me again. "Yes, that's what Paul said."

"Who is that, Ma?"

She covered the mouthpiece on the phone. "It's Uncle Preston."

"Give me the phone, I want to talk to him."

"Ok, hold on one minute." She took her hand off the phone and said, "Preston? Paul wants to talk to you... Yes, hold on one minute." She held the phone out to me.

"Hey Uncle Preston."

"Hey Paul." And then, before I could get a word in edgewise, he said, "Listen. Howie told me that you were very short with him when you two met the other day. Don't forget that even if you have different opinions, he's still your cousin."

"Well I was a little angry." I hated that I was already on the defensive. "He spoke to Mom about this thing with Fred after I told you not to bother her about it right now."

"I thought that 'now' meant at the party. You weren't very specific."

24

"'Now' means however long it takes us to cope with the fact that Fred finally got in touch with us. This is a stressful period of time. Let us handle it, ok?"

The other end of the line was quiet, but I could imagine Preston frowning into the phone and slicking back his hair. He didn't like being disagreed with. "Your mother is a grown woman. She can handle things for herself."

"Then she doesn't need your help, does she?"

"Put your mother back on the phone."

"There's no confusion this time?"

"Put your mother back on the phone. There's no confusion."

"Ok, talk to you later. Here you go, Ma."

She looked at me, surprised at my aggressive tone. I was surprised by it too.

"Hi again." She listened for a while, then Mom said, "Preston! It's fine. I'll talk to you tomorrow... Ok. Bye bye now." She hung up the phone and sat on the couch.

"Was he just talking about it again?"

She didn't say anything.

"Was he?"

"...No."

"Mom, don't lie for him."

She looked down at her feet. "He only brings it up because he cares about all of us. He just wants to make sure that we're all going to be ok."

"We'll be ok." I chuckled. "It's been seven years, now. We are ok." I sat down next to her. "Aren't we?"

"Yes." She shook her head. "Of course we are."

6.

THE BABY RESPONDS TO POSITIVE THINKING

I was lying in bed with Gen that night after I went to my mother's house. The round trip would have added another eighty miles to my odometer.

Luckily, my odometer stopped working about nine hundred miles ago.

We were watching the news again, but I had it on mute. "More news after the break on... Action 5," was the line they always said before the screen went dark and they cut to a Charles Schwab ad with two guys sitting down at a lunch table, joking about a bear and a bull market.

"I read that babies will grow up to be much smarter if you think positive thoughts."

"Oh yeah?" I said, half-listening and staring at the silent images running all over the TV screen.

"Yeah..." Gen looked at her stomach and started drumming her fingers next to her ousted belly button. Then she dropped a bomb on my head. "I've been attending Buddhist services for the past two weeks."

That got my attention. I looked over at her with a raised eyebrow.

"I just thought you should know," she said, fast. "The whole atmosphere is so calming. I can really center my ch'i there. I don't know what it is about the place where they hold the services, but it makes me relax." She was talking nervous, looking down at her stomach, like the revelation of her trips to the Buddhist services was something she had been dreading for a long time.

"Take it easy," I said, rubbing her arm. "It's no big deal. You can tell me about this stuff. I won't flip out." I wondered why she had kept the Buddhist services a secret for two weeks, but I figured it was none of my business. And as far as I was concerned, I had stopped questioning the credibility of her baby-rearing sources long ago. I may not have agreed with her, but I was more than willing to support whatever she felt would help the baby. "What do you do there?"

"Well, the services are held in the basement of a non-denominational church in Salsburgh, and we basically practice meditation."

Salsburgh was just over the border in Connecticut, which was a good half-hour drive. "I don't love the idea of you driving that far in the car by yourself," I said. "You could break down or lose control of the car. You know what a piece of shit it is."

"Language, Paul!" she reminded me by pointing at her stomach.

"Sorry, but my point is that the car isn't very reliable. Something could happen to the baby!"

"It'll be fine," she said. "Don't worry."

"I do worry. I can't help it." I slipped myself under the blanket. "So does this mean you've converted to Buddhism or what?" I knew she hadn't, but I asked the question sarcastically to hurt her feelings a little, I think. I wanted her to know that I didn't mind the fact that she was going to the services, but I also wanted her to know that I really dislike secrets, especially between the two of us.

27

"I just go to the services, Paul," she said, tired and a little pissed. She always picked up on the subtleties of my cadence. "And I do that much just to keep my mind clear and positive. You know I'm a devout atheist."

"Just making sure nothing's changed."

Click! I turned off the TV.

"Goodnight babe."

"Goodnight, sweets."

I closed my eyes and rolled over to sleep.

"Paul?"

"Yeah?"

"I'm sorry I didn't tell you earlier."

"That's ok. You told me now. And I guess that was harder than telling me right away. I'm glad you could tell me now."

She smiled at me. "Thanks, honey."

I rolled over and closed my eyes. I could feel Gen behind me, looking at me and getting ready to ask a question. "Anything else you want to talk about before we go to sleep?" I asked her.

"Yeah... Will you get me something to eat?"

7.

THE DEAD MAN IS RUNNING LATE

The day after Gen told me about her trips to Salsburgh, I went over to my mother's house to check up on her. She seemed to be a little slower than usual, even for her at her age. Over the phone, she had started calling me Fred, and when I told her it was Paul, she said, "My, you're sounding older. Soon you'll be a man."

"Yeah, Ma," I said, confused. I waited for a beat, then said, "I'm coming over."

"Yes, you should," she said. "We're having dinner soon."

"...Ok, I'll be right over."

I handed the reigns of the bookshop over to Gen and Cecilia and hopped in the Buick. Usually, I would turn the key and listen to the "rurr, rurr, rurr" of the starter catching the engine off-guard, but that time, the ignition caught on the first try. It helped that I had driven over to my mother's the day before. The beast was still feeling limber.

However, I still had to treat it like the monstrous baby that it was. I turned the car off and let it sit for a minute before turning it back on. The car and I went through this routine every time before we hit the road because if we didn't, the Beastly Buick would stall the first time I tapped on the brakes. The car was more emotionally delicate than a pregnant Gen.

I pulled out of my parking spot and headed down the street. I drove like I was driving on eggshells: I used my breaks early and often, and I used the gas only when I had to. Despite my care, there was a loud pop about halfway to my mother's house. I nearly had a heart attack. I pulled over to the side of the road and lifted the hood of the car.

Thanks to the steam escaping from my engine, it was easy to see what had happened. The coolant container had made the loud popping noise. Gen's secret trips to Salsburgh had thrown off my careful calibrations for the car, and I had let the level of engine coolant fall below the necessary amount. This caused the car to heat up way too much, turning what was left of the liquid blue in the engine's container into blue steam. More and more of the coolant turned to steam as the car was running and the pressure in the container built up to the point where the cap was shot off like a gun.

Obviously I had no reason to worry about Gen taking the car out on long trips by herself.

I filled the container to the line with engine coolant I kept handy in the trunk. I sat in the car on the side of the highway and listened to the snap, crackle and pop of my Rice Crispies engine while it cooled down enough for me to drive again. It was only another fifteen minutes before I was on my way.

I made it to the house at about six. The trip had taken an hour longer than it should've because I had to drive slow.

The living room smelled of lamb and I walked into the kitchen to find Mom in her plain, pastel-yellow dress preparing a dinner. There were five cups on the table.

Bent over with her head in the stove, my mother asked, "How was work today?"

30

"It was fine," I said. "Nice and busy." I paused, looking at the cups. "Are you having guests over for dinner?"

"No. Why do you ask?"

"Oh," I said. "I just saw all of the cups, is all." I sat down in the chair I used as a kid, my chair.

•••

I don't remember how it all started, exactly, but when I was a kid, my brothers and I would have battles over who got to sit where at the kitchen table. Somehow, all of us had decided that the chair closest to the living room door was best. So every night, us three brothers had a footrace to the "best chair" followed by a wrestling match in the kitchen.

Jackson always showed up ten minutes late for dinner, so it was up to our mother to try to stop us from fighting. We usually figured it out amongst ourselves before she could convince us to stop.

But then, there was that one time Jackson was home early. He was sitting at the table when Fred, Morty and I rolled into the kitchen, screaming and biting and pulling hair. He was silent for a moment while he watched Fred and me beat the living shit out of each other. Once we both turned our attention on Morty—who had slipped out of the fray and was trying to sneak the best chair away from us—Jackson felt like it was time to intervene.

"Hey! What's going on here?"

We all froze. "What?" Fred said.

"What do you boys think you're doing? This is the kitchen. It's no place for roughhousing. You'll get in your mother's way. Does someone want to explain to me what this is all about?"

We told him about the chair and how great it was.

"Well that's it. From now on," he said, sitting down in the best chair, "this chair is mine. Morty, you'll sit there, Paul, you're there, and Fred is next to me. Everyone got it?"

"Yes sir."

•••

31

So I sat in my assigned seat. "I'm sitting here, right?" Something still wasn't sitting quite right with me.

"Of course," she said. "I wouldn't let someone else sit in your chair. You're in a funny mood today."

"Yeah, I'm a little out of it, I guess." I watched her.

"When are the rest of the boys coming home?"

"Morty and Fred?" I wondered what was going on in her head. "I don't think they're coming tonight."

"Oh. Ok... will you clear two of the settings, then? Thanks, pumpkin."

"Sure thing." I was starting to get what was going on, and I was starting to get worried.

"I shouldn't really have expected Fred to come in the first place," she said. "I completely forgot about what happened. We must get around to suing him one of these days."

That last statement was different from what I expected. "What?"

"I just forgot what I had been talking about earlier," she said. "That's all."

"Talking about with who?" I asked. "Uncle Preston was here, wasn't he?"

"Yes, he stopped by for a while. He's looking quite old these days. You should really be nicer to him. My mother always said that each grey hair is a grievance and each wrinkle a worry." She pulled the lamb out of the stove. "So you help keep Preston young, ok?"

"Ok, Ma," I said. "What were you and Uncle Preston talking about?"

"Oh," she said, "a little bit about everything. My sister and how she was doing, mostly. She's good, by the way." Mom put a hand on my shoulder. "And we talked about you for a little while. I bet your little ears would have been red if you had been there!" She ruffled the hair on the top of my head and turned back to the counter to move the lamb from the pan to a plate. She brought it over to the table. "And we talked about Fred." She sighed. "I just don't know what to do with that one."

"Ma, listen to me, please. There's no reason to bring a lawsuit against Fred. The time has come and gone. That's it."

"All right, dear," she said, patting my leg. "That's just fine." She looked over at the clock ticking above the fridge. It read six fifteen. "Now where is your father? It's not like him to be this late for dinner. Ten minutes, maybe. But fifteen?"

Shit, shit, shit. I had to get my mother to a doctor as soon as I could.

PART II
SENTENCED TO LIFE
IN THE CHAIR

KETCHUP: MY FAVORITE VEGETABLE
(PROLOGUE TO PART II)

This is my second day in jail, my second day awaiting my trial, my second day writing this deposition. I hate this place, but I was denied bail earlier today. That means I have to stay here through my trial. My lawyer says that means about two months. When we got back from the courthouse, he tried to be cute and joke about it. "You might as well get comfortable," he said.

Ha ha.

It's not as bad as it could be, I suppose. I'm in jail, not prison, so I'm allowed to have guests as often as I want and the police officers treat me well. It's good to see Gen and Cecilia and the baby. They are the ones that keep me together through this. If I couldn't see them everyday, I would start to lose it. It's not as bad as it could be.

34

But the food! The food is bad. I once heard that the government served the same food at prisons and schools, but I figured the other elementary school kids were just complaining. But now I know it's true. When I got lunch today, the vegetable they gave me was ketchup.

They serve the food straight to my cell. The room here is very sparse. Other than the bed with sheets and a pillow, there's a toilet in the corner, a wall of bars, a wall with a barred-on-the-in-and-outside window, and two blank cinderblock walls. There isn't much room for fun. Even the sheets are nailed down to the frame of the bed so I can't use the lining to hang myself. Oh well.

I have another week to go before my trial starts. Seven days. But I don't have to stay here for all that time, thank God. My mother's funeral is being held in four days, and my lawyer has made arrangements so that I will be able to attend. I have to go with a police escort, but Morty will be there, and Gen will be there... and maybe Fred...

Mom died four days ago. That's a long time to go unburied. But the police needed to do a careful post-mortem examination for their case against me. My fingerprints were everywhere in the house and my hair and skin follicles were all over her body, even under her clothes. As the good cop said, "We have enough evidence to put you away, but come on, Mr. Morrison. You don't seem like the murdering type. Help us out and tell us what happened."

My lawyer agrees, and he told me that I'm going to have to come out and tell the police what happened for real. "No one believes that you found her in bed, Paul," he said. "Her skin was moist. What really happened? You can tell me, we have a confidential relationship."

But I don't want to talk about it. So I'll write it down here, eventually, once I get the courage and once I finish explaining why everything happened.

But in order to do that, to fully explain what happened to my family and to my mother, I have to jump back a ways, back to when Jackson — my father, our father — was still alive.

1.

THE HEIR-APPARENT OF "THE GENERAL STORE"

I was born and raised in a small, dumpy Massachusetts town, about an hour away from anything of any importance. And it's strange: I moved away from Mom and Marborough with Gen almost nine years ago, and I think about it now and wonder how I managed to end up in another small Massachusetts town only a couple of hours away.

For all of the first twenty-two years of my life, Jackson owned and operated his own store, so I suppose that small businesses run in the Morrison blood. Once I turned thirteen, I would head over there after school and work; over the summers I would work; on the weekends I would work; and whenever I wasn't working, Jackson would find some work for me to do.

The store didn't really belong only to my father, but I've never been particularly proud of saying that the store, in part, belonged to me. Our store sold general items that people needed, things like Goya beans and light bulbs and condoms. It served as a general store, and that was also its name: "The General Store." It was on Marborough's Main Street, the only store on Main Street that had a decent amount of open land around it. The store, with its few patches of grass, was found sandwiched between Billy's Pub and a Mobil station. All day, the smell of gasoline was nauseating and in the late afternoon, the sounds of happy hour made me wish I wasn't working anymore.

I said that I worked at the store, but to be fair, my "job" wasn't very strenuous. Ever since I'd started working there, it was my responsibility to stand around until a customer came into the store—which wasn't as often as you would think or my father would have liked—and follow them around as they did their shopping. No, I wasn't the acting security guard on the prowl for shoplifters: after all, in a town as small as Marborough, where everyone knows everyone, shoplifting is almost non-existent.

It was my job to make a note of whatever it was that the customer purchased, run into the "back room," and replace whatever-it-was on the shelves. For the first couple of months that I did this service for Jackson, my job was completely worthless and inefficient: what I did could have been done much later in the day at a much faster clip. However, after about a month, my job became very important. Since I had been putting the goods I replaced at the front of the shelves, everything behind it had begun to go bad. An analogy—I was to The General Store what software updates are to computers: without me, customers would be shafted with old items long past their expiration date.

While I performed my job like the one-trick-pony that I was, my brothers were being kept busy as well. Fred, when he was still working there, had been responsible for ringing up sales into the register. Our family worked on the principle of seniority: this was a cushy job for the oldest brother, complete with a chair and cup holder. He would "greet" the customers with a lifeless "Will that be all today" before ringing them up and sending them on their way.

You could tell, even then, that Fred would not be here in Marborough, Massachusetts for very long. He spent his free time at the store staring out the window with his mouth agape, drool pooling in the corners of his mouth. When I would ask him about the far-away look, he said he was thinking, but it looked a lot like he was trying to flip his brain's switch into the "off" position. However, he did what he had to because he saw The General Store as an easy way to make money for the rest of his life.

Morty was Fred's polar opposite down at the store and in life. He spent his time in the stock room, jumping off the walls and knocking shit over all of the time. He had never been very coordinated when it came to walking. Thankfully, he didn't have to worry about that any more.

It wasn't until I was older that I started taking anything seriously, but I've got to admit that I never took my job down at the store seriously. Like Fred, I didn't see myself staying in Marborough for very long. Certainly no longer than I had to. I had big plans for myself, and almost none of them involved The General Store.

When I started my junior year of High School, I started working every day. At that point, I was responsible for a little bit of everything that went on at the family business. It was also that winter when I supplanted Fred as the man behind the register, and he was pissed.

•••

I remember when Jackson called me out into the backyard for a meeting. It was the dead of winter, it was snowing, and my footsteps went crunch, crunch, like a candy bar beneath my feet. I was a junior in High School.

He said, "Sit down, Paul."

I looked at the chairs covered in snow and then back to my father. He gave me a look that shut me up before I even had a formulated complaint. I sat down and felt first the cold, then the wet soak through the seat of my pants. Jackson continued to stand over me and, from that angle, I could see the mucus freezing in his nostrils.

This had always been the "boardroom" of our General Store, this small plot of grass with one table and four chairs in our backyard. My brothers and I dreaded any meetings between the months of October and March.

As I sat, the snow continued to pile on my lap, and I felt first the cold, then the wet soak through to my crotch. Even at seventeen, I would have been hard-pressed to get an erection in those conditions.

"Paul," my father began as he tried to keep the blood in his toes. "Paul, you've done an excellent job for me down at the store as of late."

"Thank you, sir."

"Shut up and wait your turn," he barked. "I'm thinking about taking you off of shelf-stocking."

Shelf-stocking had been my life down at the store. It was straightforward and didn't involve too much thinking on my end. I stared out into the snow. Even before Jackson said anything more, I knew that I was cornered, that harder work was in my future, that I was being pulled further and further into the family business that I wanted no real part of in the first place.

"Paul, I'm thinking about taking you off of shelf-stocking and moving you to the register," he said. "I'm thinking that, one day, I want you to take over down at the store."

Uh-oh. I did not want to be the heir-apparent. I didn't want to be stuck here for the rest of my life. I wanted to get out into the world, open up a business of my own, open up a used bookstore...

But I didn't want to hurt Jackson's feelings, so I started to say, "Wow, Dad, that's—"

"—Don't go talking and change my mind now, ok? Ha ha. Come on, let's get back inside quick. I'm starting to get frostbite here because of you."

I got up and followed him inside. Jackson disappeared immediately, so I went upstairs to my room. Morty was sitting on my bed, reading *The Catcher in the Rye* (now on sale in the Morrison Bookshop's used-books section for one fifty). He looked up and said, "Oh, oh oh! You just had a meeting with Dad, didn't you! What did he say? Are you fired for that eight year old Poptart that got Mrs. Murphy sick?"

"Ha ha. No, you jerk. But get this: he's moving me to the register."

"Holy shit," Morty said. "Doesn't he think?"

"Shh!" I put my index finger over my mouth. "Not so loud! Come on man. Both Dad and Fred are right next door."

"I know, I know," he whispered. "What is he going to do with Fred now? You know how much Fred likes sitting on his ass all day."

"I don't know," I said. "I don't think he's talked to him yet. Knowing Dad, he probably won't feel the need to say anything at all. He'll just tell Fred to do something else and never mention it ever again."

Morty put a hand on his forehead. "Well Fred definitely won't say anything about it when he finds out. He'll just take it personally and keep on hating us."

I stared at the lamp next to my bed, considering whether or not to tell Morty the whole story. I decided to tell him once I started seeing bruises from looking at the light for too long.

"The register isn't all," I said.

"What? What else did he say?"

"He said he wants me to run the store when he retires."

Morty put his book down on the bed next to him.

If Holden Caulfield were here, he would have said, "I am definitely not ready for responsibility."

Morty said, "Wow."

"I'm never going to get out of here at this rate." I sat down on my bed next to Morty, shaking my head.

I felt, somehow, that I was personally responsible for cheating Fred out of what was rightly his, and I felt bad. But then I remembered Christmas.

•••

When we were kids, Christmas was a time of joy and loss. We would all run into the living room with the tree and the presents and the tinsel all waiting for us. There was the joy. But as we three sons opened present after present, Fred would offer "trades." Fred was four years older than

40

me and six years older than Morty, so when it came to negotiations, we were at his mercy. Once, he traded me his new bike for my new sleeper yoyo, a trade that I thought put me ahead: in a small town, the man with two axels and ten gears was king. Besides, you can't ride a yoyo anywhere. Of course, I went out to try the bike right away and, of course, the bike was way too big for me. "Fred!" I came back inside hollering, "The bike's no good."

"Oh, that's too bad."

"I wanna trade back."

"No can do, little buddy. A deal's a deal."

I chewed on my lip for a while. "Fine. Wanna trade something for the bike?"

And then I was at his mercy. Every year, he would get me right where he wanted me, and every year, I came back begging for more, a completely incompetent Pavlov's dog. I think I ended up trading his bike back for a pair of socks and a candy bar. Talk about your buyer's remorse.

After years and years of falling for the same tricks over and over again, I finally learned a hard lesson from Fred. Always look a gift horse in the mouth: if it looks like someone is giving you a good deal, they've probably stolen your wallet in the meantime.

•••

So never assume that the things you have can't be taken from you.

It was my first day on the register at The General Store, and Fred was pissed. While I sat in my new chair up front, I could hear him throwing some empty cigarette cartons in the stockroom. I could also hear him kicking them. And ripping them. And snarling at them. And biting them.

To say the very least, he was not at all pleased.

Jackson had stepped in the way of the register when Fred had shown up to work that morning. Without any fanfare, Jackson said, "Paul is going to start working the register from now on. I want you working back in the stockroom."

Fred's jaw dropped.

41

He stormed into the back room.

At least he didn't know that I was the heir-apparent at The General Store yet.

"Woah-ho! I wonder what Freud would say if he were here now?" Jackson asked me when Fred had first stormed off.

Freud would have said, "Freud wants to sleep with his mother and kill his father. Wait, I mean Fred."

•••

That night, Fred barricaded himself in his bedroom. He pushed his desk in front of the door to his room so no one could open it. By cracking the door open the inch that the desk allowed, I could see him. He was lying on his bed, surrounded by piles of books with less structural integrity than the tower in Pisa. He was staring at his ceiling. There was an open copy of Emily Bronte's "Wuthering Heights" (now on sale in the Morrison Bookshop's used-books section for two fifty) resting on his chest. The one thing that Fred and I had in common was our love of books.

"Hey man," I said, slipping my message through the door slit.

He noticed me for the first time. "What do you want?" he asked.

"I know you're pissed about today," I said, "and I wanted to say I'm sorry."

"It's not your fault," he said, "...I guess. But fuck, man! What the fuck."

"Hey, keep that language down," my mother said, coming up behind me. "What's going on here?" She tried the door. "Fred, why is your desk in front of the door?"

"I'm just moving some things in here, Mom," Fred said. "I'll fix it in a little while."

"Ok sweetie," she said. "Just make sure you move it soon. It's a fire hazard where it is right now."

"Alright."

Mom walked downstairs.

"I just wanted to make sure that there are no hard feelings between us."

"Well you could have told me what was going on ahead of time, for Christ's sake."

I walked away feeling bad for the way Fred had been treated. And thinking that maybe he was right to be pissed at me. I suppose I could have said something to Fred after Jackson and I had talked, but I couldn't make myself confront him. And I guess that is one thing that I share with every member of my family. All of us—in some way or another—were afraid of outright confrontation: Jackson preferred to gloss over confrontations; Morty would never get himself into any sort of disagreement; Mom would rather die than deal with conflict; and I couldn't even talk to Fred about the register.

And Fred! Well. I don't think Jackson even noticed when Fred wasn't at the table for dinner.

2.

THE BUTTON FOR EMERGENCIES ONLY

Fred and I have always had a competitive relationship. This is to be expected of brothers, especially when there are three, but we tended to take things too far. When we were little kids, I was always the most athletic of us three boys, but Fred was by far the oldest. So, whenever we had footraces, Fred usually won by a handy margin. When Fred was twelve and I was eight, he was in the prime of his racing domination. We used to race from school to The General Store, leaving the six-year-old Morty in our dust. (Morty tried to keep up, but he was too young and too uncoordinated to stay close enough even to keep within sight.) I remember one time when Fred let me catch up and pass him intentionally. I didn't know he had done it on purpose, and while I looked out onto the empty road in front of me, I felt like a king. We ran like this for a while, with Fred right on my heels.

Finally, he made his move. He kicked out at my right foot, sending it right into the back of my left. I tripped and fell to the concrete, bracing my fall with my forearm and getting some excellent raspberries on my skin for the effort.

If Tonya Harding were here, she would have said, "Why didn't I think of that?"

"Damnit, Fred!" I shouted, tears beginning to fill my eyes because I knew I had been cheated, that I had never really been winning in the first place. "That's cheating and you know it!"

"It was an accident!" he said.

"Was not!"

"Was too, dickfor!"

"Wait," I said, "what's a dickfor?"

"Peeing!" Fred said, then he started cracking up, bent over and holding on to his sides from laughing so hard.

It took me a while, but then I got the joke, too, and tried my best not to laugh and stay angry at Fred. "That's not the point!" I shouted. "You tripped me!"

"Did not!"

•••

Fred didn't really hurt me then, but I was in the hospital once when I was 18, almost a year and a half after Jackson had decided my future for me by naming me heir to The General Store throne. At the time, Fred still didn't know I was set to take over someday.

I'd been knocked out for a while, and I remember waking up in a sterile room. My vision was cloudy and I had no idea where I was or where I had just been before I woke up. I felt so bad that I just wanted to throw up. I wasn't even nauseous. My mother was in the corner, crying, and there was my dad right next to her, with a hand on her shoulder.

I tried to speak, but all I could come out with was, "hunhooooah," which meant, "I think there's a barbell on my chest, will someone help me get it off?"

My mother's face was streaked and red when she looked up. It was Jackson who spoke. "Well it's about time you woke up." Then to Mom, "Come on, Ruth, let's get back to the other room."

"We'll be back soon, Paul," my mother choked out.

And they opened the door and Jackson held it open for my new life, who walked right in as they left.

"And how are you feeling, sir?" she said. She had little spackles of paint in her hair, a touch of beehive-yellow highlights in her dark brown.

"Hunhooooah."

"Oh, that good, hmm? Now let's see what happened to you here," she said, picking up the chart at the foot of my bed. "Oh, not too bad, considering. One broken arm and almost all of your ribs are bruised. You should be out of here in no time at all. Nothing to worry about."

That made me remember how upset my mom was.

•••

I stayed in the hospital for four days, which was a little longer than they usually would have kept me but they wanted to be on the safe side, and my parents would have been around the hospital most of the time anyway. It was like being under the care of licensed and professional babysitters.

Three times a day, one of the nurses would come in and set a meal down next to me. I would nap when I was sleepy and other than that, I would do whatever I could think of to occupy myself, which meant that all I had to do all day was lie in bed and read. Now that I think about it, it was pretty similar to the situation I find myself in right now, with only two differences that I can think of. The first is that I write now, instead of reading.

The second was a buzzer at the head of my bed. It was a strange little thing and it looked like the kind of technology that would've been outdated before I was born. It was made up of a small rectangle (the button) on a circular base. The base itself was metal, but it had been painted over several times (I could tell because the paint was chipping). For all intents and purposes, it had the appearance of a doorbell. Except for the fact that, running vertically, down the face of the rectangular button, the word "EMERGENCY" was written in big red letters.

My favorite nurse was also the first one I met—Gen—and I had a feeling that she liked me, too. She always "forgot her pen" in my room that one time, or she was "doing rounds", or I "rang the buzzer to the nurse's station that was for emergencies only." No matter what, she always found some excuse to come into my room.

And whenever she came in, it was all, "How are you doing?" or, breathless, "Are you ok?" or, "That really is for emergencies only, Mr. Morrison." It was nice to feel cared about.

But I didn't even know that Morty was in the hospital, too, until my last day in that damn place, after my arm had been put in a cast and my ribs were less tender. And when I heard what happened, I didn't know whether to strangle him or coddle him. Here's what led up to my stay at the hospital:

3.

THE ALL-AMERICAN GENTLEMEN
ABOUT TOWN

I'd been working for pay down at The General Store for four years at the time, with a month to go in my senior year of high school. The whole time I worked, I saved up for one thing: a convertible. I didn't care what the make of the car was as long as I was allowed to pay extra for a roof that wasn't there.

The day I'd finally saved up enough money to buy my first used car was the best damn day of my entire life. Ever since then, it's all been downhill. That Buick was living, exhaust-spewing proof that if you worked hard, or worked at all, you could earn the right to pollute.

I bought the car from a lively old man named Mr. Willikers. He's one of the nicest men I ever met. Whenever he came into The General Store, he was always full of hello's and covered in sweater-vests. I'd mentioned to Jackson that I was looking for a car, and he dropped me off in front of Mr. Willikers' house a couple of days later, on a Saturday.

Mr. Willikers and I worked out the details in front of his house, and we shook hands.

"You just bought yourself a fine automobile, my boy," he said. "She has a few years and a few miles on her, but I'd be damned if she doesn't still float down the road."

"I appreciate how easy you made all of this."

"Don't even mention it, my boy. The wife's been pressuring me to get rid of her for years." Mr. Willikers rubbed the hood of the car sensually. From the looks of it, Mrs. Willikers wanted him to get rid of the car because she was jealous.

"Ever since I bought the damned thing," he continued. "The wife says it's too fast for someone my age." He knocked on the hood. "You got a lot of power under here."

Mr. Willikers took the keys out of his pocket and handed them to me. "You should be careful, Paul." He winked at me. "Now I know someone your age can't be stopped from speeding on the highway, but don't go speeding down these narrow streets, here. People jump out of nowhere, sometimes."

I took the keys out of his hand. "Thanks, Mr. Willikers. I'll be careful." I got in the car and started her up.

Mr. Willikers leaned in the driver's window. "Alright, my boy. You drive safe and take care of my baby. And say hi to your dad for me."

The first thing I did when I'd finished buying that car from Mr. Willikers was to drive it over to the bar. In retrospect, that may not have been the most responsible decision, but that's what retrospect is for. Morty and I wanted to pick up some girls, and a new used car was an easy way to do it. We figured that all we had to do was impress some girls enough that they would let us drive them home. Then, when they saw the car, they would fall in love with us. It was a good plan.

We made our way into Billy's Pub. (Morty wasn't old enough to drink, but he had come in here with Jackson before, and Billy knew us, and anyway, underage drinking was no big deal .) The bar was packed with High School seniors, so I started off with the advantage of knowing most people's names.

We looked around and made a beeline for the booth with two girls and two empty seats. "Hey Sonya," I said, "Patricia. How're you two doing?"

They smiled at each other. "Not bad," Sonya replied for both.

"Who's your friend, Paul?" Patricia asked. "He's cute."

"Oh, this is—"

"—I'm Morty," he said, extending a hand to her. She gave him hers and he kissed her knuckle.

She giggled. "An old fashioned gentleman. You know, there aren't enough guys like you left around anymore."

"Well," Morty said, "I do my best to keep up the reputation of the gender."

We sat around for an hour, talking about God knows what, having a few beers, and then Patricia said, "It's about time we got home. My Dad'll kill me for staying out this late. And if he knew I was talking to two real, live boys, he would kill me, then shoot me."

"Yeah," Sonya said, "I should get going, too."

And this was what Morty and I had been waiting for.

"Why don't we drive you ladies home?" I asked.

"That sounds good to me," Patricia said.

"Sure," Sonya said.

We walked out into a spring night in New England, the air a little blustery and the snow only a vague memory. I pulled out my keys to unlock the passenger side door. Morty and Patricia got in the back seat and Sonya in the front. I went around and let myself in.

I wouldn't have used the door at all, but it was a little too cold outside at night to be driving with the canvas roof down.

"Wow, Paul," Patricia said. "This is a great car."

"Oh," I said. "I know it is. A brand-new used car." I started the car. "So where am I dropping you off, Patricia?"

"It's just a block up. Make a left on Chandler, and I'm number 58." She leaned back in her seat and turned to Morty. "So what grade are you in again?"

"I'm a sophomore," Morty said.

"Really?" Patricia said, scrunching her eyebrows. "You look much older."

Morty frowned and looked sad and serious. "It's a medical condition, actually. Advanced aging. I'll be dead by the age of forty, and I'd rather not talk about it."

"Really?" Patricia put a hand on Morty's shoulder. His shoulders started heaving, and when he looked up he was laughing.

I stopped the car in front of Patricia's and turned to Sonya, thumbing towards the backseat. "I can't take him anywhere."

"So what are you two up to next weekend?" Sonya asked.

Morty grinned. "I'm pretty sure that's when we're having our date."

"That's a little presumptuous..." Patricia put a hand on the handle to the door. "...but I guess that sounds ok to me." She started to get out.

"Let me walk you to the door," Morty said.

Patricia turned towards Morty, smiled, and got out of the car, leaving the door open.

Morty started butt-shuffling towards the open car door. Before he got out, he grinned at me. "I'll walk home from here, Paul. See you later."

"So where do I drop you off?" I said to Sonya.

"Make the next left. I'm two blocks away." She turned to look at Morty and Patricia making their way up to her front door. "Your brother is something else."

"He sure is." I made the turn and nervously drummed my fingers on the wheel. "So you're up for the big date next weekend?"

51

"Wouldn't miss it." Sonya looked out her window and pointed at the glass. "That's me, right there."

I stopped the car and looked at her. She didn't move to get out. "Well, goodnight," she said.

"Goodnight." I leaned in to kiss her, but right before I closed my eyes—in my mind, at least—she looked like she didn't want to kiss me. So I pulled back and opened my eyes. She had already closed her eyes looking for the kiss, so I leaned back in quickly. Our faces collided nose first. It was an incredible two seconds, a gloriously awkward first kiss.

•••

Next Friday, I was sitting in the living room with Fred and Morty. I was explaining what had happened to Fred. "...and then Morty said, 'I'll walk home from here.' So what else could I do? I let him walk."

Then Morty whined at Fred. "But he drove right by me when I was walking home. He slowed down and waited until I put a hand on the car door before speeding off, for Christ's sake!"

Fred smirked. "Sounds like you got what you asked for."

"That's what I'm saying," I said. I gave Fred a high-five and we both started laughing.

"Well Ha-Ha," Morty said. "Listen, Mr. Smooth. I was the one who got us the date tonight."

"I wouldn't deny that," I said. "Thanks for that."

•••

I was getting ready for the date in the bathroom, shaving off the five o'clock shadow I had been growing for the past week. Morty came in and scooted me over to get at a little bit of the sink and mirror. He took some of my shaving cream and put a little on the right side of his face.

I rubbed the clean side of his face. "Are you kidding me? Did you see a patch of peach fuzz or something?"

"Shut up."

He started shaving. While he was working, he kept looking over at me.

Finally, I was forced to say something. "What?"

52

"What what?"

"What do you want?"

He looked at the floor, then said, "Could I drive tonight?"

"Absolutely not. No way."

And that wasn't the last of that. In the car to pick up the girls, Morty just wouldn't give up.

"I just don't get why you won't let me drive."

"No way. You don't have a license!"

"That doesn't stop Jackson from letting me drive."

I glared at Morty, trying to hint at the fact that he should drop it. I looked back at the road. "Whatever. If you crashed the station wagon, you wouldn't even be able to tell."

"Fine. Whatever."

•••

We took the girls to a movie and then to some cheap restaurant on Main Street. It was one of those places with a garbage dump's worth of crap on the wall. A waitress led us to our seats, and came back five minutes later with our drinks.

"That movie was terrible," Patricia said.

Morty brushed her critique away with his hand. "You're just saying that because you don't like Westerns."

"Of course I am. How could anyone like Westerns? It's just a bunch of tough guys strutting around."

Morty took a sip from his drink. "There is nothing better than two tough guys having a standoff on a dusty street. When that tumbleweed blows bye... man! You can just cut the tension in the air—" he said, cutting his pinkie through the air, "—with your pinkie finger."

Patricia laughed. "Whatever."

I looked around the restaurant, my eyes focusing and un-focusing on the A.D.D. décor. "Hopefully the fine cuisine here will make up for the movie," I said.

The waitress brought us our food and we had a fine time clowning around and flirting. I had a particularly good time, but by the end of the meal, I had had way more to drink than anyone else. When the check came and we all

53

stood up to leave, I felt the alcohol in my system rushing to my head, and I almost fell back into my chair.

Morty held his arm out in front of him. "After you, ladies." Sonya and Patricia headed for the door. When I went to pass Morty, he held me back with a hand on my shoulder. "Listen, man," he said. "Let me drive. You've drank way more than me."

I thought about it, then held the keys out to Morty. When he went to take them, I pulled the keys back out of his reach. "Remember, Morty," I said. "This isn't the station wagon."

I let Morty take the keys and we left the restaurant.

When we got outside, Morty jumped in the front to drive, and—even though it was a little too cold for it—we put the top down and let the freezing cold blow through our hair. Maybe she was cold, maybe she was drunk, or maybe she was just trying to be a good date, but no matter how you would explain it, Sonya found her way onto my lap in the back seat of the car. She was facing me, her legs on either side of my torso tucked under themselves, straddling me like the stallion I have always wished I could be in bed. We started making out, first gentle pecks on the lips between whispered nothings of a conversation, and then dropping the small talk altogether and really going at it. She had my full attention to say the least, so I barely noticed when things started to heat up in the front seat.

•••

And that was the last thing I could remember after sitting up at night in my hospital bed, doing my best to piece everything together, still not quite certain how I'd ended up there, a few miles from home with a broken arm and a rib cage full of bruises.

4.

THE LIVING PILE OF IV's AND CATHETERS

As soon as Gen, my nurse practitioner, had told me of Morty's condition, I ran from my room to his, banging my elbow on the door on my way out.

"Hunhooooah!" I screamed as the pain ran up my arm to remind my brain how awful my clumsiness could be.

Morty was just down the hall from me. This was before they moved him to another room in another wing of the labyrinth of white halls and coats. My paper shoes skidded all over the smooth, checker-tiled floor.

I found Morty buried, his head barely visible among all of the sheets and pillows he had been wrapped in by his own staff of nurses. There was an IV standing next to his bed, the pouch of fluid almost empty. His legs were elevated, casted, and disconnected from the instructions that his brain practically shouted at them. He looked exhausted, his eyes half-closed and his mouth agape, and I had seen that expression before: he, like Fred, was tired of his surroundings, and his brain was escaping into itself.

"Hey Morty," I said.

He turned his head as much as the pillows would allow him without completely blinding him. "Hey Paul," he said groggily, only one eye and his mouth visible to me. His pained expression confused me when he said, "I just wanted to say that I'm sorry."

"Morty, please! What could you possibly have to apologize for? I should be the one apologizing, and even that would just be out of empathy."

"Do you know what happened?" he asked.

"Not really," I said, "I've been pretty out of it. The medicine they've been giving me has been keeping me pretty loopy."

"Well I'm apologizing for what happened," he said. "Come on in, sit down for a while."

I took the folding chair next to his bed. "So what happened?"

"Well," he started, "we were driving home from the date. You and Sonya were in the back seat making out and having a good time."

"Yeah," I said, "I remember that much. I mean, how could I forget that part?"

Morty started to chew on his lip. "So yeah," he said, "you guys were in the back seat. Patricia and I were getting bored in the front just watching you guys make out, so we started to get a little touchy-feely ourselves."

"That's understandable," I said.

Morty gave me a look like my Biology teacher would: no more interruptions. "Anyway, she was leaning over in her seat belt, nibbling my ear, rubbing my leg, and I started getting into it, you know?"

I nodded.

"So I start rubbing her thigh. She reaches down and starts to undo my fly, and—"

"Jesus, Morty. Do we need all the juicy details for this story or can we just get to what happened?"

"Relax, relax," he said as loud as he could, barely above a whisper. "I'm there now. So she's undoing my zipper and I look over at her, down at my lap...the point is I took my eyes off the road for just a minute—a second!—and when I look back up, there's some guy, walking diagonal across the intersection of Brook Street and Maple. I swerved out of the way, and I missed him, but..."

"What didn't you miss?" I asked him.

"We hit that huge oak tree in front of Mr. Peterson's place. Pretty head on."

"So what happened to you?" I asked.

"When the front of the car hit the tree," he said, "the crumple zone didn't really live up to its name. The hood bent right in half, and the steering column crushed my legs." Tears started welling up in his eyes. "And that's only the half of it. They don't know if I'll be able to walk again. The doctors are saying that it isn't looking great. They're not sure if the bones will be able to heal up well enough to support me." He laughed a high-pitched squeak of a laugh. "But they tell me that at least all my equipment will still work."

"Wow, Morty. I'm so sorry. I don't even know what to say."

"It's ok. What can you say?" He looked out the window by his bed. There was a small playground across the street. Children were running around, running and sliding and climbing and... doing all the things that Morty could never do again.

"What about Patricia?" I asked the back of his head after a while. "And Sonya? How are they doing? Where are they?"

"I haven't heard anything about them yet," Morty said, turning back to me. "I just completely forgot to ask. I've been so out of it, I haven't been able to keep a thought in my head for much longer than it would take to say it. And whenever the nurse comes back in, she fills up this bag with more drugs, or water, or urine, or whatever else they can think of that my body needs. I think that pretty soon, they're just going to hook my catheter directly to my IV to save on costs."

It was good to see him joking. And I didn't want to spoil the mood. "Yeah, and soon they won't even have sponges for your baths. They'll just start rubbing you down with a sanitized stick. If you're lucky, there'll be some dead leaves on the end of it so they can really get that hospital dust out of your pores."

He turned to look back out the window. I could only see a tuft of hair and an ear when he said, "Paul." From his tone, I could tell that the smile was long gone. "I'm so sorry. I didn't mean to...I mean I shouldn't have—"

"Come on," I said. "There's no need to apologize. It was an accident. We made it out alive and I'm sure that I could work out a deal with uncle Preston and he'll fix the car."

"The car was completely totaled, Paul. It's finished."

"Well that's ok, too. You just worry about getting yourself healthy again, alright?"

5.

AND IT'S TIME TO GO WHEELCHAIR SHOPPING

I returned to my room after chatting with Morty for a little while longer. He was getting tired, and the babysitter who came in to plug the catheter into Morty's IV and administer the Brillo Bath told me that he needed his rest and that I should return to my room now.

I walked back cursing under my breath, trying to convince myself not to worry too much. "It's not like things could get any worse," I thought to myself.

Gen was there when I got back. I jumped into bed. "So what's the inside scoop on Morty? How is it looking?"

"Not terribly good, I'm afraid," she said. "You saw how he was set up in there, and while there is a small chance he can walk again, we don't want to get his hopes up."

"Yeah, that's pretty much what he said."

She wrote something on my chart and said, "Well this is probably your last day here with us, at least. You seem to be healing quite nicely."

"That's some good news."

"Yup." She fiddled with a chart for a minute. "Well I have to attend to my other patients now, but Doctor Horowitz should be coming in here to chat with you in a little while."

•••

A little while in hospital terms means an hour in real-life time. I had just given up hope of staying awake while waiting. A quick knock at the door woke me, and I opened my eyes.

Doctor Horowitz strolled in with a clipboard under each arm and a pen bleeding blue through the front pocket of his coat. He was still wearing a surgical mask when he said, "How are you feeling these days?" so I had a hard time understanding him.

"What? Oh, I'm feeling ok," I said. "I banged my elbow on the doorway before, but otherwise it hasn't been bothering me all that much."

"That's great," he said. "Well, Mr. Morrison, it looks like this will be your last day with us," he said, leafing through the clipboard that held my fate here at St. John's Memorial. "You'll be on your way in no time."

"Yup," I said.

"And your brother is doing great, despite everything," he said.

"Yeah, I went and checked in on him before. But I've been meaning to ask you. How are the other two passengers of the vehicle doing? Sonya and Patricia?"

"Patricia was the girl in the front passenger seat, correct?"

I nodded.

"Right. She sustained a concussion, and she was bruised and cut up, but other than that had no serious injury." He paused. "Sonya died."

I looked at the doctor, hoping to see something in his face to tell me that it wasn't true, that there was some sort of mistake. There was no mistake.

"I'm sorry," he said. "There's never an easy way to put it, so I just said it. When she came here, we placed her directly in the intensive care unit. She was almost stable, but we needed to transfer her to the Salsburgh Medical Center, in Connecticut. She needed to undergo a delicate surgery that we could not perform here." He sighed. "She died on the helicopter ride over there, the day after the crash."

But that wasn't the end of Sonya in my life. I wish it had been, and that I could have just moved on, but that wasn't the way it would be for my family and me.

•••

A few days after I had been released from the hospital, we got a call at home.

"Hello?" I said into the phone on the coffee table.

"Hello, this is Dr. Horowitz. Is this Paul?"

"Yes it is."

"How's the arm feeling these days?" he said.

I was only a few days away from having the cast removed. "Much, much better. Thanks."

"Oh great. Hey, is Jackson or Ruth there?"

"Sure, hold on a minute."

I climbed halfway up the stairs, carpeting filling in the gaps between my toes. "Mom!" I yelled. "Dr. Horowitz is on the phone for you!" I came back to the coffee table and told the doctor, "She'll be down in one minute."

"Great," he said.

"Paul?" my mom said, standing at the bottom of the stairs.

"Right here, Ma." I handed her the phone.

"Hello?" she said. "Yes, good. And you? What news? Oh, oh my." Her face grew ashen and she started to tear up.

Apparently, things were anything but "great."

"Alright doctor, thank you for taking the time to call yourself." She hung up the phone, trying to hold back her tears.

"What happened, Ma?"

"It's your brother." She started sobbing and couldn't speak anymore, though she tried.

I hugged her and rested my chin on the top of her head while she cried into my chest. "Are they sure?"

She took a few deep breaths and spoke to my t-shirt. "Yes, they're sure. The bones just won't... heal...right..." And then she was crying again.

•••

That wasn't the only time someone called about Morty before he got out of the hospital, and there was no good news from the second one, either. Jackson, Fred, Mom and I were sitting at the kitchen table, eating dinner. We had visited Morty earlier that day. I was feeling pretty good about myself because I had spent most of the day at The General Store looking through the newspaper, and I was looking forward to buying a new car with the insurance money.

"So you can drive me to check out a couple of used cars I saw in the paper today?"

"I told you," Jackson said. "Things are a little hectic right now with Morty in the hospital. Let's wait until he gets out and then we can worry about that."

"Fine, fine."

"So Fred," Jackson said. "Did you ever figure out what happened with that shipment of Coca Cola?"

"Yeah, I called 'em. They said it should've arrived already."

"Well it didn't."

"That's what I told them, and they said they would check their records and send someone out with a couple of boxes tomorrow."

"When I ask you to take care of something, I expect you to take care of it. We have a hard enough time making money on that place: we can't wait around for a shipment while customers are coming in and can't get what they want. Damn it, Fred, you have to be more assertive with the big corporations. I couldn't count how many times I've told you that."

The phone rang.

"Now who would call during dinner?" Mom asked.

Everyone kept eating, so I said, "I'll get it."

"Now Fred—"

"I get it, Dad! I know, I know..."

I picked up on the fourth ring. "Hello?"

"Hi, I'm Josh Weinstein. I'm calling on behalf of the Franklins. Sonya's parents?"

I instantly started sweating. "And what is this in regards to?"

"Is this..." I heard him shuffling through some papers. "...Paul?"

"That's me."

"Well then, as you know, you were all involved in an automobile accident almost a week ago. The accident resulted in Sonya's death, and there is evidence that the driver..." Once again, paper shuffling. "...Morty, was under the influence of alcohol. Anyway, the Franklins have decided—as is their constitutional right—to sue your family for emotional damages in the civil court."

"But that's not fair!" I said. "Sonya was drunk, too. She got into the car just like everyone else."

"I understand that to be true as well, but I have to tell you: you're lucky this is only a civil suit. The Franklins could have pursued charges of manslaughter against your brother. I think you should put your father on the phone and let me talk to him for a while."

"Ok, I think that's a good idea." I put the phone down and went back in the kitchen.

"...a question of integrity, Fred. You have to be able to go out there and get what you want."

"Dad?"

"Yes Paul."

"I think you better take this call."

Jackson got up from the table, grumbling. "Calling during dinner...who do they think they are?"

Jackson left the room.

"Don't let your father bother you too much, Fred," Mom said. "You know he just wants to help you get ready for the real world."

"Well I'm more ready than he thinks I am."

We ate in silence until Jackson came back into the room.

He sat down and started into his food without a word of explanation.

"Who was it on the phone, dear?" Mom asked.

"Some lawyer," Jackson said. "We're being sued by that girl's parents. What was her name?"

"Sonya," I said.

"Right. Well they're suing us because of the accident. Well really, they're suing Morty, but since he's a minor, I guess it's a family issue."

6.

THE SMASHED MIRROR: A MEMORY
OF FRED

Fred never, and I mean never, spent any of the money he would earn down at The General Store. When he got his license, he and Jackson split the cost of an excellent used Toyota, but other than that, he bought nothing. His only other possessions were his clothes (which Ruth bought for him) and his books (some of which were inherited from everyone he knew, most of which were flat out stolen from me). You could say that Fred was, in this sense, a simple man, who did just enough to get by and no more. He was not a man of extravagance by any stretch, but he did have extravagant (albeit passive-aggressive) reactions to the problems of his life.

This truism of Fred's life was never more apparent than the night Jackson took us all out to Cristina's Restaurant for my High School graduation dinner. It was almost three weeks after the car accident, and Morty had come home a few days earlier.

He had spent the last few days at home trying to cope with what he called his "life-sentence of sitting in The Chair." He was learning all of the basics, things like how to go to the bathroom by himself and how it was always important to lock the wheels on the chair when he wasn't going anywhere for a while.

We all crowded around a booth with a red-and-white-checkered plastic tablecloth. The cups were thick and tall, faux glass. The lighting was dim and the portions were large. This was about as "fancy" a place as my family would ever go.

We had just ordered our food and were talking about my graduation while we waited for our drinks.

"That whole ceremony today was just lovely," Mom said, "wasn't it?"

"Absolutely," Jackson said. "That kid who gave the speech was good. He was real good."

"Yeah," I said. "He's real smart. The valedictorian."

"Why the hell weren't you the valedictorian?" Jackson asked. He glared at me.

I wanted to say I wasn't the valedictorian because I was always working down at The General Store, but I couldn't say that to Jackson. And it was never a good idea to talk about the store in front of Fred. He was still sore over losing the register job even then, a full year and some change later.

"Anyway," Jackson said, "I really liked when he was talking about that manifesto shit."

"Jackson dear," my mom said. "Watch your language. We're in a restaurant!"

"Sorry," he said. "That manifesto crap."

The waitress came over with our drinks.

"Yeah, Dad," Fred said. "It was a great speech. Really entertaining."

"Young man, don't you take that sarcastic tone with me."

"And that principal of yours did a fine job of running events," my mother said, ignoring the argument that could have been between Fred and Jackson.

"Yeah," Morty said. "I loved it when he called up the Asian student. Eric Shen? Ha ha! Best name ever." It was good to see him laughing. Getting out of the house was doing him a lot of good.

"Hey, give him a break," I said smiling. "School must have been hell for that kid. One of about three Asian kids, and that's his name. Just awful."

"Ha ha!" Jackson said. "I missed that one the first time around. Ha ha. Eric Shen. That's genius."

"This isn't really appropriate table talk," Mom said with a frown.

Jackson held his Guinness high in the air. "A toast," he said.

We all raised our glasses—Mom raised her white wine, Morty raised his Coke, I raised my Miller Light and Fred raised his rum and coke.

"Paul," my father began, "today you graduated from High School. Now, the rest of your life is before you. I only see success for you, because failure is not really an option."

"No pressure, man," Morty said.

"Ha ha," I said with sarcasm.

"So, graduate," Fred said. "What are you going to do now?"

Morty chimed in with, "He's going to Disney World!"

Mom smiled proud. It was really good to see Morty being Morty again.

"He doesn't have any time for that," Jackson said. He winked at me. "Paul's going to be busy working down at the store and learning the ropes. Right?"

I looked down into my drink and didn't respond.

"I'm pretty sure he knows how to work the register by now," Fred grumbled.

"That's not what I mean," Jackson said. "Wait, Paul didn't tell you guys yet?"

"Tell us what?" Fred asked, looking at me.

"I just assumed he was so excited that he would have told you and Morty as soon as he found out. You really didn't tell them, Paul?"

I was frozen, completely petrified. I could tell it was coming, but I couldn't do anything to stop it.

"Well then this calls for another toast!" Jackson said. "Everyone lift up your glasses. Come on Paul, you too. Paul! Ok now. To Paul, who is going to be taking over down at The General Store when I retire."

Fred looked from one face to the other while this new information slowly sunk in. He put his glass to his mouth, finished his drink, and slammed it on the table. He turned to Jackson and said, "I can't believe this horse shit." Fred was looking into the future and he saw that his easy meal ticket was disappearing.

"Fred dear," Mom said, "you know better than that. Don't go taking lessons from your father here."

"I can't fucking believe this," he said again. Fred stood up. "Get out of my way Morty."

"What?"

"You're in my way, Morty. I can't get out of the booth."

Morty looked up at him, confused. "Where are you going?"

"Move!" Fred said, pushing Morty out of his way.

Of course Morty—that vigilant student of wheelchair safety—had remembered to lock his wheels once he was at the table. So when Fred pushed, Morty fell over backwards in his chair. Fred didn't even slow down to think about helping Morty back up, and walked out of the restaurant.

We all looked at each other with open mouths. I couldn't believe Jackson had told Fred that I was next in line and I couldn't believe that Fred had really just stormed out.

"Paul, what are you waiting for?" Jackson asked. "Help your brother back up already."

I lifted Morty back up to table level. "Is he coming back?" I asked Mom.

She shrugged her shoulders. "Who knows with that one."

"We'll see him at home if he doesn't come back here," Jackson said. "Let's not let Fred ruin dinner. That is exactly what he was trying to do, and I don't think we should give him the satisfaction."

The waitress came back with the food and put Fred's meal in front of his empty chair.

"I'm sorry," Mom said to the waitress. "Could we have that wrapped up? He had to leave."

"Sure thing."

We sat there and finished our meal. Despite Jackson's best efforts, Fred had ruined dinner.

When we returned home, we found the bathroom mirror smashed to pieces. Fred was gone with his car, his books (my books!), and his clothes.

7.

REFLECTIONS FROM THE PIECES OF SMASHED MIRROR

And when we came home to that smashed mirror in the bathroom, to that empty house, my mother started to cry. There was nothing that Morty, Jackson or I could do. She just kept saying, "My baby, my baby."

Pretty soon, Jackson decided it was time for bed. Even though I was already eighteen, a High School graduate, I was not about to question his authority. It could have been four in the afternoon and I would have been under the covers with my eyes closed within seconds of his command.

I was lying in bed, staring at my ceiling. I heard a hushed conversation between Mom and Jackson through the wall. I tried my best to ignore it, but I couldn't help but overhear what they were talking about:

"He'll be able to take care of himself," Jackson said. "He's our son and he's already twenty two years old. It's about time we pushed him out of the nest. We can't baby him forever, Ruth."

"I know that," Mom said. "Of course I do. But it didn't have to be like this, did it? He didn't have to leave so upset."

"Maybe he did. Who the hell knows. And besides, I'm sure we'll hear from him soon, no matter what happens. He'll need a little bit of help from us anyway. He'll need a little cash."

"I'm not worried that he's going to disappear," Mom said, "but you know that you made this much worse than it should have been, Jackson." There was silence through the wall for a moment. "I'm just saying that I understand why he was so upset."

"If you think a promise I made to Fred when he was two would upset him enough to make him leave, then maybe this really is for the best."

That was interesting. Jackson had never mentioned anything like that to me before. I guess I shouldn't have been surprised that Jackson didn't say anything about it before, considering the way he had handled the passing of the General Store up until then, but I was surprised. I had assumed that I was privy to all of the secrets. I put my ear up against the wall to see if I could hear anything more about this "promise."

There was some loud rustling from my parents' bedroom. It sounded like Jackson was pacing, which meant that he was about to deliver what he referred to as Words to the Wise. "Fred spent his whole life depending on us and he expects to be pampered all the time. In this world, you have to work for what you get. Fred never put in the work, and I don't think we would be teaching him the right lesson if I kept that promise to him. If you could even call it a promise. It was really more of an agreement of convenience between us, and he was only two."

"But Jackson," Mom said, "what are we teaching him if he can't trust his own family? It's our job to take care of him, isn't it?"

"That is one of our responsibilities as parents, yes, but our most important responsibility is to prepare our kids for the real world. What. Do you really think that school is enough for them? Do you think math will teach them how to rely on themselves and put food on their plates? Of course not. That is our job. And in certain situations, like this one, we have more than one responsibility and they may seem contradictory. But we have to remember what we're really here for: when they are young, we protect them, and when they grow up—and Fred is certainly grown up at this point—we have to get them out into the world. We have to cut that umbilical cord, Ruth.

"I just want him back here."

I decided I'd heard enough. These cryptic references to a promise were getting me nowhere. If I really wanted to know what was going on, I would just ask them about it later. I made some noise to remind my parents that you could hear anything through the walls. I got out of bed thudding and looked in on the bathroom. The mirror was everywhere under the sink, under the tub, and behind the toilet bowl. It was the only thing out of place. Even the radio, precarious on the edge of the sink and hanging over the tub, hadn't fallen over when the mirror smashed.

"Bang!" said the radiator.

I bent down to pick up some of the bigger pieces of silver-backed glass and twenty of me bent back up. I picked up a couple of the bigger pieces. The next time I bent, there were only eighteen of me.

One of the pieces cut me. "Ow! Fuck this," I mumbled to myself. I licked some of the blood off of my finger and went into the hall, closing the bathroom door with emphasis to remind my parents, again, that you could hear everything through the walls.

I walked into Fred's room. I sat on his bed and looked around. It had similar dimensions to my room, with one window facing the backyard like my room, the ceiling angled upward like my room. It was a depressing room, really, claustrophobic and filled with oppressive air. Even the window provided little consolation. Since it faced north, there was only an hour during the summer when natural light came in and a half-hour during winter. And since it faced the backyard—the backyard with its dying grass and fenced-in attitude—the view left much to be desired.

Fred had really succeeded in clearing out in the time it took us to finish up our meal. There were a few books scattered here and there, but otherwise it was the bed, the desk, the dresser, and the floorboards. I walked around the room and picked up a few of "his" books that belonged to me and sat on his bed, thinking about Fred as my brother and as my competition.

Competition in the modern sense, not in the classical Greek sense of the word. In ancient Greece, competition refered to two parties striving with eachother to be the best they could be. But Fred and I are not Greek. Today, we see competition as a struggle between two parties, with both trying to claim the upper hand. Thanks to Jackson, it seemed like Fred and I were already headed on a collision course with no winners.

8.

A LIFETIME OF CAR TROUBLE BEGINS
WHILE FRED IS AWAY

A lot of things happened in the time Fred was gone, and after a couple of days, with all of the distractions, I had completely forgot all about the agreement of convenience that Mom and Jackson had been talking about.

The first distraction was buying myself another car. I needed some way to get around after the accident with the convertible. The car I bought was a Buick as well, although I find it hard to believe that the two cars I owned in my life were made by the same company. That first car—my convertible—was a rock. I know I only owned it for a week or so, but it spoiled me. It ran so smooth that—aside from the Morty mishap—I never felt one bump in the road behind that wheel. Come to think of it, I don't remember feeling the bump of the accident, either. So naturally, it took me a while to adjust to the monstrosity that is, to this day, parked outside my bookshop.

I remember the day I bought it—or, to be more precise, the day it was dumped on me—a week after Fred had run off, a week after I had graduated. I went to the house of Jordan Mirth, whose name and number I had found in a local paper. The advertisement he took out was simple:

7-YEAR OLD BUICK
Good Condition
Call Jordan Mirth at...

And so I did, and we arranged a time when I could come over to look at the car.

Jackson dropped me off at Mr. Mirth's address and then peeled out while speeding off.

"Paul, right?" Mr. Mirth was sitting on his front step, waiting for me, with the 7-YEAR OLD BUICK already idling in his driveway. He smiled at me and exposed a gap between his front teeth that rivaled David Letterman's. He didn't speak with a lisp or anything, but the air rushing through the gap while he spoke gave his speech a unique quality.

"So," he whistled at me. "You want to see how this baby rides?"

"Sure," I said. I got behind the wheel and Mr. Mirth took shotgun.

He told me to take a right out of the driveway. "How far do you want to go?" he asked me.

"Just a short trip to get a feel for it," I said.

"Ok," he said eagerly. "In that case, make a right at the corner..."

I made the right. The car was a little bumpy, but nothing too bad for a car with seven years under her belt.

"...and a right at the stop sign..."

I was pretty happy with it as long as it wasn't too expensive. Besides, Jackson had left with his car and I needed some way home.

"...and a right at the traffic light..."

Yes, I had decided. If it was in my price range — under the sum the insurance company had given me for the totaled convertible — I would take it.

"...and a right up here. And just pull up in front of my house."

The car came to a stop. "So," he whistled. "What do you think?"

"It rides well enough, but how much does it cost?"

He leaned back in the pleather seat and sighed like he was doing me a favor. "How does four hundred dollars sound?"

It was my turn to whistle. "I don't know… That's a little steep. I was thinking more along the lines of two hundred fifty dollars?"

"Three hundred is as low as I go," he said, sounding like fingernails on a chalkboard.

I cringed. "Deal." I gave him the money and drove my "new" 7-YEAR OLD BUICK home. On the way, I was pulled over by a police officer, who gave me a ticket for a broken taillight. No wonder Mr. Mirth made me take all those right-hand turns.

If Letterman were here, he would have said, "And that is number one on the 'Top ten ways you know this guy ripped you off' list."

•••

A few days after I bought the 7-YEAR OLD BUICK, I gave Gen a call. I had gotten her number during one of my last visits to Morty before he was released into The Chair, but I hadn't had any time to call her since Fred ran away. And besides, I didn't feel comfortable asking her out on a date if I couldn't pick her up in a car that I didn't own.

"Hello?" a woman's voice said. Maybe Gen's mother.

"Hi, this is Paul. Is Gen there please?"

"Who is this?"

"Paul."

"And *how* do you know my Gen?" the female voice asked, now almost certainly belonging to a mom.

"I—uh—met her down at the hospital. Could I speak with her please?"

"Very well, don't get all excited. Hold on a moment."

76

The female voice had put me on edge and the longer I waited for Gen to get to the phone, the more nervous I got. I didn't really know her that well. What if she just gave me her phone number because she felt bad for me? And it had been almost a week and a half since she had given me her number. What if she'd forgotten who I was already?

I was debating whether or not it was too late to hang up when Gen said, "Hello?"

I didn't say anything.

"Paul?"

Shit. The woman/mother who picked up had told her who was on the phone. Too late to back out now. "Hi Gen. How are you?"

"Good. I was beginning to think you weren't going to call me."

"Sorry, I've been pretty busy. Morty just got back home a week ago, and things have been pretty crazy around here."

"That's ok. I know how it goes. I'm just glad you called. Sorry if my mom scared you when she picked up the phone, by the way. I know how she talks to people she doesn't know."

"Yeah, it was a little scary."

She laughed and I was starting to relax a little. I figured that was as good a time as any to ask her out. No reason to beat about the bush. "Well anyway, I was wondering if you wanted to go out to dinner with me sometime?"

"I would like that."

"Great! How does Friday sound?"

"That would work for me. I'm not working at the hospital that night."

"Ok. I'll pick you up at seven?"

"Seven sounds perfect."

•••

I picked Gen up at seven thirty. I was late because I couldn't get the 7-YEAR OLD BUICK to start for a while, but we were finally on our way. We were driving to Hartford and we had dinner reservations at eight.

77

Gen was dressed in a red skirt and a white top, with a black jacket thrown over her shoulders, and high-heeled boots. I could never forget what she looked like on our first date. She was the picture of perfection. She had always been an artist first and a nurse second, and on that night she had a dab of dried and cracking sky-blue paint in her hair.

I was dressed in pants and a collared shirt, nothing too fancy. I never felt comfortable in fancy clothing. Even collared shirts bothered my neck, but I didn't want Gen to think that I wasn't trying to look my best for her.

About halfway between Marborough and Hartford, there was the sound of a gunshot from my hood. A few seconds after that, the hood started steaming so profusely that it was blocking my view of the road. By some miracle, we made it over to the side of the highway without hitting another car, and I put on my hazards while I went to investigate this new problem with my car. I waved the steam out of the air in front of my face and looked at the engine. It was obvious that the gunshot sound had come from the engine coolant container attached to the radiator, which meant that my car had overheated. But I had just put more coolant in the car earlier that week. So why didn't I have any engine coolant left?

I looked closely at the container, careful not to touch the hot engine that warmed my fingers. And there it was: a little crack near the bottom that had left just enough coolant for the hot engine to turn into steam. Once the coolant steam had built up enough pressure, the cap to the container had blasted off, firing a warning shot at me. I got back into the car.

"I think I have to walk to a gas station to get this fixed," I said. "I think we have to get the car towed. I'm so sorry! This is a terrible first date." I looked at the clock. "And we're probably going to miss our reservation."

"It's ok, Paul." She smiled and put a hand on my forearm. "You're real nervous, aren't you? You must really like me."

She always could read me like a book. That hand of hers on my forearm made my stomach flutter like I was about to throw up, but I never wanted her to move it ever again. I looked over at her and she looked at me and we had a moment there where I was convinced we were about to kiss.

Just then a cop pulled in behind me.

"Oh thank God," I said to Gen. "Now I won't have to walk at least."

I got out of the car to meet the police officer.

"Thank you so much for stopping," I said to him. "I could really use a hand here."

"I only pulled over because I saw your hazards were on," he said. "I'm going to have to give you a ticket."

"What?" I was flabbergasted. "Why?"

"Well, sir," he said. "Were you aware that your left taillight is broken?"

•••

Two weeks after our first date and a week and six days after our first kiss, I drove the 7-YEAR OLD BUICK to visit Uncle Preston and Aunt Hallie. Their house was no more than an hour away from our house in Marborough, an hour tops. And I'd been on the highway for maybe twenty minutes when my entire car started to rattle. The wheel was jumping around in my hands and I could barely keep the car in my lane.

I started to pull over and almost hit the car in the lane next to me, a car that had been conveniently positioned in my blind spot. I swerved out of its way right before there was a loud thump and my car fell towards the front right tire. I could see some sparks flying by the passenger side windows. After that, the car next to me gave me more than enough room to pass in front of him.

I got out and examined the tire. I could see where there was a small rip in the tire that had been the initial problem, but once the tire blew out, the hub of the wheel had fallen to the pavement entirely, taking on all of the weight of the car. The hub sliced straight through the tire, leaving two flopping rubber halves, and it was the metal of the hub on the blacktop that had created the fireworks.

After more than two weeks with this car, I was used to problems like this, and I kept the trunk of the car well stocked in all forms of car maintenance and repair items. I was more prepared for a car incident than the little shopping mart at a Shell Station, so I had the tools to quick-fix almost any problem I could come across.

I pulled out an Allen wrench, a car jack, and the spare tire and got down to it. It took a good thirty minutes, but I was pretty proud of the job I had done. The tire was on, anyway.

So I continued on to Uncle Preston's. The whole breakdown was annoying, and it was made no better by my destination: I never had any real desire to see my uncle. My aunt I could live with, but my uncle? He knew how to push my buttons without even trying.

But I continued the drive anyway. The car continued to lean forward and to the right because my spare was smaller than all of my other tires. After a little while, this started to worry me a little bit. The spare was clearly taking on more than its fair share of the car's weight, and I didn't want to put on another fireworks display, especially now that I was out of spare tires. So foolishly, I decided to drive to Preston's really fast. Once I was there, he could give me a new tire (he was a mechanic, after all) and I could drive home without even worrying about it.

Five minutes from my exit, there are blue lights flashing in the rearview mirror. Damn. I pulled over and rolled down my window.

The police officer—no doubt loving this display of authority—took his sweet time getting out of his cruiser before walking up to my door. "Sir, do you have any idea how fast you were going?"

"Yes, officer," I lied, hoping to avoid a ticket for my broken speedometer.

"You were fifteen miles over the limit, according to my radar gun. Unless you have a good excuse, I'm going to have to give you a ticket."

"Well," I said, "my tire did just blow out on this drive and I'm riding on my spare. I was going fast to make sure I got to a garage in time to get it replaced."

"I suppose that is a good excuse," he said. He began to write something down on his ticket pad. He ripped it off. "I guess I will let you off on the speeding ticket. Here you go."

"Well then what's this ticket for?" I asked.

"I gave you that because your left taillight is out. You drive careful, now, and get yourself to that garage." With those words of advice, he got back in his cruiser.

"Great," I mumbled to myself. "Thanks for nothing." I waited until the policeman pulled back onto the highway before I did the same, and soon, I was in front of Preston's house.

"Hey Paul," he said. "We were expecting you a while ago. What happened?"

I told him the story.

"Oh, that's too bad. Hey, you want me to put a new tire on for you?"

"Yeah, I was kind of hoping you would," I said.

"Ok," he said. "Just pull it into my driveway and I'll get right on it."

I did that, and then headed into the kitchen, where Aunt Hallie was sitting and having some tea. I poured myself some hot water and sat down next to her.

"So. Paul," she said, patting my knee. "How is everything?"

"It's going good," I said, dunking my teabag.

"Good. And how's my sister?"

"She's good."

We sat in silence for a while, and that is what I always liked about my aunt: she could tell when small-talk was dying, and she simply let it die. I could see Preston working through the kitchen window. He was on his back, looking under my car for God-knows-what reason.

Aunt Hallie was looking too, and when she turned back to me, she asked, "And how's that girlfriend of yours?

I've only heard a little about her from your mom. Give me a little gossip."

"She's doing well," I said. "We started seeing each other a couple of weeks ago—you know, going on dates and stuff. It's good. I like her a lot."

"Good. What's her name... Gen?" she asked. "I thought so. And you met at the hospital?"

"Yup! She was my nurse while I was there with the broken arm."

"Well that's a good, clean story to tell the grandkids one day," Aunt Hallie said. "Preston and I aren't so lucky. We met at a bar when his friend grabbed my ass. I yelled at him because he was the one laughing hardest, and go figure! Now I'm married to the guy." She shook her head. "But you're dating a nurse."

"Well yeah, she's a nurse. But really, she's an artist. I haven't seen any of her stuff yet, but whenever we go out she has paint in her hair."

Through the window, Preston was getting up and brushing himself off. He saw me looking at him and gave me the thumbs up. He came into the kitchen and washed the grime off his hands.

"All finished!" he said. "That'll be forty-five dollars."

I laughed.

"And if you want me to fix that taillight," he said with all seriousness, "it'll be another sixty."

I pulled out my wallet when I finally realized that he wasn't joking and I paid the bastard. "Do you have change for sixty?" I asked.

"Yeah, hold on just a minute. I'll grab it from upstairs."

When Uncle Preston went upstairs, Aunt Hallie turned to me and smiled, shaking her head. "You'd think he was never a student himself," she said, reaching into her purse. She gave me three crisp twenties. "Keep the change."

"Thanks, Aunt Hallie."

9.

FRED'S NOT-SO-TRIUMPHANT RETURN

Fred came back, over three weeks after he left. I heard a car door slam in our driveway at one in the morning and I went downstairs to investigate. I looked out the front window and there was Fred in the driveway, staring at nothing, halfway between his car door and the door to the house. He stood there for a few minutes, speaking to himself. I couldn't hear the words, but his lips were moving like he was a radio broadcaster announcing a horse race.

He picked up the bag at his feet and headed for the door, where I was waiting on the other side to greet him.

"Hey Fred," I said as he gently closed the door behind him.

He jumped. "Jesus H., you scared the shit out of me."

"Sorry about that," I said. "Where have you been?"

"I was living in New York City for a while, but I ran out of funds." He sighed. "I had to come back."

•••

Fred told me he'd come back to the house that night from my graduation dinner in a really pissed-off mood. When he left the restaurant, he was bent on leaving home forever. He didn't have any particular compass direction to head for, but he needed out.

He made a few trips between his room and his car, packing up everything that he wanted to take with him to start his life over. Before he left the house, he went into the bathroom and looked himself over in the mirror. He thought about what he had been confronted with that evening, namely that Jackson was leaving the store to me. Trying to slam his fist against the wall, he told me that he accidentally caught a corner of the mirror and smashed it to pieces, cutting his pinky finger. He left the house quickly after that, driving off in his Toyota.

He didn't leave town that night, however. Instead, he went and stayed at the motel on Main Street, just a few blocks down from Cristina's Restaurant. In fact, if we had been paying attention on the car ride back home, Jackson, Mom, Morty or I would have been able to see his car parked on the street. Instead, we were all lost on our own trains of thought.

Jackson was thinking about what he had to do tomorrow.

Mom was thinking about her little baby, and how angry he had been when he had left Cristina's.

Morty was thinking about The Chair.

And I was thinking about the rest of my life, a little concerned that this small, dumpy Massachusetts town was where I would probably end up dying.

Fred paid fifteen dollars for the motel room and, in the morning, he headed over to the bank and cleared out his account. Fred had managed to save up a little over six hundred dollars while working for our father. That was no small feat considering how little Jackson paid us.

("I pay you in room and board," is what he would always say to us when we complained about our salaries.)

Fred took his books (my books), his clothes, his savings, and his Toyota south on I-95 and found himself in

84

New York City by three o'clock in the afternoon. The first thing he did was find a bed to sleep in for the night. Fred, being the man he is, looked for something as cheap as he could find while still satisfying his needs for comfort. That turned out to be twenty-five dollars a night at the Hilton, a fairly pricey room. With a room for that price, his stay in New York already had a timeframe on it unless he could have found some work.

Which he couldn't quite pull off. Two weeks went by and he had already blown well over half of his money on the room, food, and gas. But it had been worth it: after two weeks, he had finally been offered a job, albeit a job as a waiter. The bad news was that he was promised a job that opened up in two more weeks' time. He tried his best to wait it out. He stayed in the hotel for three more days, and then started sleeping in his car to save on money.

He lasted another week in New York City, sleeping in his car. The first night he slept in the car, he was woken up early in the morning by the sun. From then on he covered his face with a newspaper. The second night Fred slept in the car, he noticed a small hole through which he could see the night stars. The third night he slept in the car, it rained, and he discovered that a pool of water—dripping through the Toyota roof—had formed in the backseat he slept on. Fred, who was running low on money, ate a piece of broccoli that he found—of all places—under the shotgun car seat. On the fourth night he slept in the car, Fred was woken once again, this time from sunlight reflected off of the rearview mirror, sunlight from a sun that was just coming over the horizon. On the fifth night he slept in his car, Fred woke up to find that the tree above his car was filled with birds. ("The one tree in New York City and I had to be dumb enough to park under it.") His car was covered with bird shit. On the sixth night Fred slept in his car, a police officer woke him up with a nightstick tapping on his window. Fred drove around the block and went back to sleep.

On the seventh night, Fred drove back to Marborough in his makeshift home to get a good night's sleep.

10.

PINK: THE SCARIEST OF COLORS

A couple of things changed in the weeks after Fred came back to the smashed mirror he left for us. For starters, Fred got himself a new job as soon as he could. He worked over at Billy's Pub as a buss boy. He did mostly nights and weekends, cleaning dishes and tables. It didn't pay terribly well, but he got a share of the tips at the end of the night, and it was still more than Jackson was paying Morty and me.

Another big change was with Gen. I was sitting downstairs in the living room with Morty and Fred. Fred and I were on the couch and Morty was in The Chair.

"I'm just saying," Morty said, "that this Alicia girl is pretty hot."

"Stop talking about it and start doing it then," Fred said. "Ask her out."

"Well maybe I will," Morty said.

"Well maybe you should," Fred said.

"What about you?" Morty asked Fred. "Are there any special ladies on the horizon?"

"Let me give you some brotherly advice," Fred said. "In my experience, girls are crazy. Nothing they do or say makes any sense. But I do know one thing: girls will ruin your life, one way or another. Either they drive you crazy with their talking, or you wake up one morning and can't remember the last time you went out and it wasn't with her. Don't ever tie yourself down with a girlfriend."

Morty laughed. "Look at me, Fred! You think there are any girls, let alone more than one, who want to get with a guy like me who's stuck in The Chair? I would love to tie myself down with a girlfriend, with any girl who is willing to put up with a man with dead legs."

"Yeah, you make it sound so bad, Fred," I said. "It's fun to have a girlfriend around. Girls don't ruin your life. The reason you can't remember the last time you went out without the girl when you are in a relationship is because you want to spend all your time with her. You just haven't found the right girl for you, is all."

Fred rolled his eyes at me. "Cornball, total cornball."

"I know it sounds corny," I said, "but it's true."

The phone rang. We all looked around at each other and on the fourth ring, Morty said, "Ugh. I'll get it."

He picked the phone up off of the coffee table and said, "Hello? Yeah, just a minute." He put the phone back down on the table and said, "Paaaaaaaaaaul," in a singsong voice. "It's for yoooooou. It's your giiiiiiiiirlfriend."

"Shut up and give me the phone. Hello?"

"Hey Paul," Gen said. "It's me."

"Hey sweetie, how's it going?" I asked.

"Hey sugar pie, hey love muffin," Fred and Morty said, mocking me.

I put my hand over my ear to drown them out.

"Paul, can you come over here?" she asked. "There's something important I have to tell you."

"Can it wait a while?" I asked. "I was just shooting the crap with Morty and Fred."

"No Paul," she said. "You will come over now."

"Ok, ok," I said, "I'm on my way."

●●●

Sally, Gen's mom, opened the front door for me after I rang the doorbell. The doorbell was one of those Big Ben chimes, meant to impress houseguests. *Bing-bong bang-boong, boong-bong biiiiiing-bang.*

"Hello, Paul. Come in. Gen is upstairs waiting for you. I don't know what you did to her, but she seems very upset."

"I, uh... hmm. Ok."

I climbed the ballroom stairs in Sally and John's house to Gen's room. This was only my second time in her house, and I felt very uneasy there. Aside from Gen's mom putting me on edge, the house was so big and everything looked so expensive that I was terrified of breaking something just by walking too hard.

Gen was on her bed crying. "What is it, sweetie?" I said. "What's wrong?"

She kept sobbing, so I laid down next to her. I put my arm around her and rubbed her back. I kissed her forehead and wiped the tears and the hair away from her face.

She made little whimpering sounds that were so sad I almost started crying too.

She nuzzled her snotty nose into my neck and started to calm down.

She laughed nervously. "Sorry about all of the mucus."

"That's ok," I said. "Now what's going on? What's wrong?"

She turned away from me and let me spoon her on the bed. "Well...this morning, I felt awful. I was throwing up and everything."

"Mm hmm," I said.

"So..." she said. She took a deep breath. "Do you remember that time when we went for a ride in your car...we ended up pulling over on some back street?"

"Yeah," I said. "I couldn't forget about that. I've been thinking about it ever since." I smiled. "That was hot."

88

"Right," she said. "Well...we didn't have a condom..."

I put my arm under her neck and leaned over her while she rolled onto her back, and I looked into her puffy eyes. "So," I said. "Are you...?"

"I took the test right before I called you," she said. "And it came out pink."

I looked at her blankly, not knowing what pink meant.

"Yes," she said. "I am."

Our lives were about to drastically change, that much was certain. Maybe Fred was right, I thought, although he presented it differently. I felt very tied down right then, and I didn't like it one bit.

11.

CHICKEN WINGS, TORTILLA CHIPS, AND CHOCOLATE SYRUP

Eight months later, I turned to Gen and started rubbing her belly. Occasionally, I could feel my little girl kicking.

"My back hurts," Gen said.

"Mmm…" I said, closing my eyes.

"Paul?"

"Mmm?"

"Will you get my heatpack for me?" she asked. "I think I left it down in the kitchen."

"Mmm-k," I said. I rolled out of bed in just my p.j. bottoms.

As I reached for the door, Gen said, "Paul?"

"Yeah."

"Will you bring me back some food, too?"

"Sure," I said. "What do you want?"

"Whatever's in the fridge," she said.

Which, in pregnant talk, meant everything in the fridge.

I brought the heatpack up to Gen, along with a smorgasbord of food.

We had been married about five months previously, due largely to the fact that Gen was three months pregnant, and we were living in my room. Mom and Jackson had chipped in to buy us a larger bed that took up most of the space. The rest of the room was consumed with Gen's art and brushes and paint.

We had been living with Jackson, Mom, Morty, Fred and little Cecilia on the way, and things had become cramped.

•••

This is what the average dinner conversation sounded like:

Me: So what did everyone do today?

Jackson: Well, Paul, as you know, we worked today. You were there with me.

Me: I know, Dad. I was asking the ladies.

Jackson: You shouldn't have asked everyone then.

Me: Fine. Mom, Gen, what did you two do today?

Mom: Oh, well Gen and I went to her Lamaze class today and we learned—

Jackson: Pass the peas, Fred. And the pork.

Mom: —and the regular breathing serves to—

Fred: Pass that to Dad. And pass me the mashed potatoes.

Mom: —and I think that's fascinating. I wish they had that when I was pregnant with
          you boys.

Jackson: Yes that does sound fascinating, dear. Oh, and Fred. I need you to come down
          to the store with me tomorrow to clean the front glass.

Gen: It was so much fun. There were so many people there, though, so many couples.
          Paul, you should come with me the next time.

Fred: I don't even work there anymore, Dad. Come on.

Me: Ooh, I don't know, honey. I've been awful busy lately, and I don't see things letting up anytime soon.

Mom: Oh come on, Paul. Of course you can make some
         time to go to the class with your wife. It's the least
         you can do. You have no idea how much it hurts to
         give birth. (*Turning to Gen.*) But don't you worry
         about a thing.

Jackson: But you live in this house, and as long as you do,
         you'd better damn well
         believe that there are certain responsibilities that you
         are going to have to take on. (*Shouting now.*) You
         are coming to the store tomorrow, and I don't want
         to hear any more about it.

At that point, we would all turn in shock towards the corner
of the table where Jackson and Fred were sitting so close
they were bumping elbows while they cut their turkey.

•••

When I made it up to the room, Gen began to pick at
the apple slices, cream cheese, baby carrots, ice cream,
chocolate syrup, tortilla chips and chicken wings. On my
way to the bed, I stepped in a puddle of green, which Gen
must have spilled before by accident.

"You know, Paul," she said, "we can't stay here at
your parents' place for much longer. We need our own
home soon. And I just happened to notice that there is an
apartment available on Main Street, right above Dave's
pharmacy. And since I don't work down at the hospital
anymore..."

"I know, honey," I said. "I need to ask Jackson for a
raise. I'll do it soon, I promise. I want to save up enough
money to start up that bookshop one day anyway, but I've
just been nervous to talk to him about it."

"Well get over it."

I rolled over and went to sleep while Gen crunched
through a chip.

PART III
DEATH IS NO EXCUSE, BOYS

DOING WHAT I CAN
(PROLOGUE TO PART III)

Morty came by to visit me this morning. He drove himself. Thanks to new technology, he was able to buy a car with hand brakes and gas a couple of years ago. He's practiced enough to get good at climbing in and out of the car by himself, and even at packing his wheelchair into the shotgun seat. It was good to see him. Aside from this writing, prison has gotten pretty boring.

Since he was the only visitor, I wasn't brought to the visiting room where I met with Gen and Cecilia and the baby when they came by. We met with a plate of glass between us, a phone call's distance away. We each picked up a receiver while one of the policemen watched from the doorway on my side of the partition.

"Hey Morty, how are you?"

"Better than you, from the looks of it."

It was true. My time in jail had not been kind to me. I wasn't eating very much and I was sleeping even less. Thankfully, I didn't have a mirror in my cell, so I could only imagine how I looked.

"Thanks, jerk," I said with a smile. "So how's life on the outside?"

"Wow, look at you using the prison vocabulary. You'll be a seasoned criminal by the time you get out of here." He paused, perhaps wondering just how much he was allowed to joke about my situation. "Things have been going as well as they could, I guess. Life at the floral shop is the same as ever, and I've been going over to the bookshop to help out whenever I can."

"Thank you so much, Morty. I really appreciate it." And then I couldn't hold it back any longer. I started to cry. All the frustration of being in jail, knowing my family was left out there alone, had built up so much in the past couple of days and I let it all out. I couldn't talk to Gen about it when she came to visit because she came with the kids. I didn't want to scare them, but I knew Morty wouldn't get scared by my tears. "I have to get out of here, Morty. This is driving me crazy."

"Don't worry Paul, this will all get sorted out soon. In a week, they'll figure out that you couldn't kill anyone and they'll let you go with their apologies."

"This is my life we're talking about. All the apologies in the world can't give me back my time spent in this shithole."

"You have to hang in there for everyone."

"I know, I know. And I will, of course. But it's so hard sometimes. Being in here for something I didn't do is the most helpless experience I've ever had. My life depends on people outside jail and, if it comes down to it, it will depend on twelve people I've never met before. It's a very scary truth that's a little hard for me to swallow right now."

"Yeah." Morty chewed his lip. "But the people you know are people you can count on. They will do anything to make sure that you don't have to stay here any longer than it takes to clear this whole mess up."

So I guess I'll keep on writing, if only to give myself the illusion that in some small way I can depend upon myself to get out of here. My mother's funeral is only three days away now and I can't stop thinking about it. So I suppose its only fitting to write about Jackson's death—and how Fred did what no lawsuit could ever undo—starting up one year and one month later.

1.

ONE YEAR AND ONE MONTH LATER, WE STILL LIVE WITH MY PARENTS

We were all at Cecilia's first birthday party, a collection of family members in the backyard of our house.

There was the conference room, with its one table and four chairs.

There were the few patches of living grass, mostly green.

There was the wooden fence surrounding the plot of land.

For Cecilia, we had all pitched in and paid for a clown. This was not my idea: the thought of a clown in my backyard, first and foremost, gave me the creeps. That foam nose—the one that looks like it was dipped in a bucket of blood—and the makeup so you can't identify them later and that hair which should be an offense in and of itself! Clowns were not my idea of fun, and I didn't know how my little one year old, my darling baby girl would react to the sight. I had read *It* (now on sale in the Morrison Bookshop's used-books section for three dollars), so my opinion was already tainted, but all the color and excitement could scare the girl. And worse still, who was this guy we were introducing Cecilia to? He could be a pedophile for all we knew. He could have a collection of fingers in his party van. I mean, who was to say?

Clown issues aside, the day had been going pretty well. Preston was there, and he was talking to me about marriage and the married life.

"So tell me," he said in his best imitation of sleaze, "Do you still get laid every once in a while?"

"Jesus Christ, Uncle Preston," I said, shrinking into my collared shirt. "Isn't that a little forward?"

"So is that a no?" he asked.

My natural male tendencies kicked in and I said, defensively, "That is not a no. In fact, I certainly do still 'get laid.'"

"You lucky dog you," he said. "Me and your Aunt Hallie haven't exactly been teenagers for the past few years, but just recently, we started going at it like dogs in heat. It's the darndest thing, really."

"Woah, woah, woah," I said. "I really don't feel comfortable talking about this."

"Oh come on, Paul. You're a man now. And men talk about sex all the time." He paused and scratched his chin. "Sex and sports. Don't really know what we'd talk about without that stuff, come to think of it."

"So how about them Whalers, then?"

"I wonder what guys talked about before sports?" Preston wondered out loud. "Well there was always sex, of course."

"I really think they might win the Stanley Cup one of these decades," I said.

"What?" he said. "Oh, preposterous. Everyone knows that the Whalers won't ever win the big game. Now the Bruins, there's a hockey team to be proud of. It's only been about fifteen years since they've made the playoffs, and that's not bad." And the conversation continued on and on like that, both of us feeling comfortably in autopilot.

97

The clown showed up and started his act, jumping around in a self-deprecating manner, squeezing all of the laughs that he could from the act. What a ham.

Perhaps not so coincidentally, the first spot of trouble at the party started up shortly after the clown arrived. I walked over to where Gen was quietly arguing with her parents. Before I move on, let me tell you a little bit about Gen's parents.

2.

DON'T YOU KNOW? THIS IS A
FORMAL OCCASION

Gen's mother and father were both born into rich families, real East Eggers (*The Great Gatsby* now on sale in the Morrison Bookshop's used-books section for four dollars and fifty cents). Her mother's family — the Brydmoths — was in the shipping business and her father's family — the Laffidilys — was in the brokerage business, helping people out with their investments. When Sally and John first met, they could both smell the sweet stench of money on the other. The first time one met the other was at a formal ball for Christ's sake. It was a fundraiser for a Republican Senator-to-be. After The Senator gave his speech, the dancing commenced. Both Sally and John were there with other dates, out on the floor when they saw each other. They gave each other the once over, starting with the patent leather and high-heels and ending with the carefully combed hair and the expensive perm.

They both made their way over to the same corner of the room, each losing their dates with excuses of bathrooms and open bars. I have no idea what they actually said to each other, but I imagine it went something like this:

John: Hello.

Sally: Hello.

John: You know, my family is quite wealthy.

Sally: I am wealthy as well! What an absolutely lovely and perfect coincidence, the two of us meeting here, at an expensive ball to support a republican senator.

John: Quite. Well then. Shall we away together this eve?

Sally: Indeed.

They each went off and spoke to their separate dates. John said, "I'm sorry, Tina, but this simply isn't working out for me. I don't see us going anywhere. Oh, and do me a favor. My aunt sends her regards to your cousin. Be a doll and pass that along for me? Thanks."

Sally said, "Richard, you've been nothing but rude to me the whole night. Constantly disrespecting me! Just look at that suit. What are you doing in a suit. Don't you know this is a formal occasion? I'm just glad that Mummy and Daddy aren't here to see this." (A quick note: Sally is by no means of British descent, yet she did say certain things like "Mummy," and "take away" instead of "take out" that had an odd British ring to them.) "I would have died from embarrassment. Get out of here, Richard. Get out of here forever."

3.

WHEN I MET JOHNNY AND SALLY

The first time that Gen brought me home—after we had been dating for almost a month—was a complete disaster. By the time I stumbled out of their house, I didn't know which way was up.

I remember that they greeted me in their foyer, John with a glass of scotch on the rocks and Sally with a snifter of brandy in one hand and the bottle in the other.

"Well hello there," Sally said. "Paul, is it now?"

I shook hands with John and he spilled a little of the scotch on his sleeve. "Gen's in the kitchen. Follow me to the living room, would you? We'll sit for a moment and just relax while the girls get to the dinner."

And we sat in his living room, surrounded by the comforts they had not yet lost to the bank:

A wall-to-wall carpet that was soft enough to sleep on.

Thick, velvet window drapes that kept in the heat or the cold.

A Mondrian hanging over their maple mantel.

A couch so soft it could eat a man whole.

And the chair I was sitting in, a wooden number that was anything but comfortable.

We didn't say a word to each other for a good five minutes, during which time I heard Gen ask from the kitchen, "Mom, did you have to start the drinking so early today? You knew we were coming, I know you knew. Everything's all laid out and everything."

I started to sweat and went into an early panic. "So," I tossed out there towards John. "How's business been lately?" And that was the wrong question to ask. I didn't know it then, but only three months before, his company had gone under, a series of bad investments in commodities sinking the ship once and for all. For the past three months, he had been putting a serious dent in his retirement fund with his drinking.

He mumbled the words, "Shot to hell," and chuckled at his feet. He chuckled like a fighter pilot would have if he was going down, spinning towards Earth below and above, like he was chuckling because what else could he do.

So I reverted to what I had been doing best. I shut my trap and stared at the pretty things spackled all over the room. John stared down into his booze, maybe looking at his reflection, maybe reflecting on himself. Hell, maybe he had just blacked out for a minute or two from all the drinking. But that's when Gen spared me by coming in and saying, "It's dinner time!"

We moved into the dining room with its formidable wooden table and chairs.

"So Paul," Sally said, while bringing out food and laying it on the table. "What do your parents do for a living?"

"Why don't you sit down and have Ann Marie bring the food out?" John asked Sally.

"Because we let Ann Marie go almost two weeks ago," Sally said with a sharp cut produced by her vocal cords. "Where have you been?"

John averted his eyes to his scotch.

I cleared my throat and said, "We own a general store."

"Oh really," Sally said, completely deadpan. "Isn't that...cute. And what will you end up doing?"

"Oh," I said, "I'm set to take over the business when my father retires, but I'm hoping to open up my own bookshop one day."

"Mm hmm..." Sally said. "I see." She continued to duck in and out of the dining room.

"Paul's family's store is pretty successful," Gen shouted after her, into the kitchen.

"I'm sure it is," Sally said. "Darling, will you come in here for a minute please? I need some help. With the bisque."

"Coming," Gen said.

And then, once again, there were two. John continued to look into his cup.

"So," I said to break the silence, "how long have you been living here?"

John realized that his cup was empty and went to fill it. "Oh, I don't know," he said as he walked over to the bottle. "About thirty-some-odd years. A few years after Sally and I were wedded in the Caymans. You know, we used to have a house down there."

"Wow," I said, "I bet that property sold for a pretty penny."

"We didn't sell it."

"Oh."

The ladies came back in with the soup. They sat down and we started.

"So Paul," Sally said.

And I preemptively cringed. "Yes?"

"Where do you and your family live?" she asked. "You do still live with your parents, I hear?"

"Yes I do," I said. "We live on the other side of Main Street. On Crest Drive."

"That figures," Sally said as a matter of fact.

"What figures?" I asked.

103

"That you'd live there. I had you pegged all the way as coming from a middle-class family that just recently clawed their way up from the lower-middle-class."

"Mom!" Gen gasped.

"I was just stating what I noticed," Sally said, raising her hands. "I have a very good eye for money, is all. Or at least I used to think so," she said, turning to John.

John got up and poured himself a glass of wine, not offering any to anyone else, and placed the wine bottle next to his glass on the table.

"I'll be right back," Sally said. "I have to go grab the lamb. Myself." She shot another glance at John and exited through the kitchen door.

Gen leaned in towards me and whispered, "I am so sorry."

"It's not your fault," I said, "but get me the hell out of here soon."

"Ok," she said, and kissed me on the cheek.

I squeezed her leg under the table and smiled at her. Gen was a lucky girl. I would only sit through that dinner for one person.

•••

There were very few things that Gen had in common with her parents. One was an appreciation for art. She could look at the Mondrian hanging in the living room of her parents' house and see more than the outcome of a haphazard tenth-grade geometry class. She loved art so much that she spent most of her free time painting. She experimented with brushstrokes all the time. She would say, "I'm trying to make the viewer confront my work with a clear understanding of what it was that went into it."

Gen had set up a studio on the second floor of her parent's house, near the back. John and Sally said that they set up the studio so far from the front door so that Gen could work in quiet, but the truth was, they didn't want their friends seeing the state of disarray that the room was always left in. The walls, which had been a uniform light blue, were splattered with colors from Gen's pallet. She tended to keep

104

a brighter selection of colors, so walking into the room was like being surrounded by a Pollock painting on Prozac.

The first time Gen brought me into her studio — after that painful first dinner with her parents — my brain felt overloaded. On top of the dismal redecoration, there were paintings with mismatching themes hung everywhere, with no regard given to feng shui. There was a study of a bowl of fruit, painted with broad sweeping motions. There was a portrait of a crying ballerina that looked to be a strange cross between Degas and Picasso's blue period. Leaning against the wall was a huge canvas with a human figure beginning to take form from a hodge-podge of tropical colors. And on the easel was a portrait of a man who looked like he could be Gen's father's fifth cousin.

"Do you like it?" she asked.

"Yeah," I said. "I like it. Who is it?"

"Well, it's not done yet, but when it is done, it should look a little more like Dad. He's a pretty sad figure. That's why I used the bright colors. An Edvard Munch knockoff, I guess."

"Oh," I said. I took a closer look at it. "Yeah, I can see him in there. Unfortunately, it looks like some other guy jumped in the way."

"Shut up." She punched me in the shoulder and laughed.

"Seriously though: I don't know anything about art, but it's looks good, especially considering that you didn't get a formal art education."

"You think so?" she said. "I don't know. There's certainly more of a future for me as a nurse."

"There's no denying that," I said. "Even the best artists die hungry." I thought about it for a second. "Or crazy, I guess." I pulled her in to me. "But I think you'll do ok for yourself."

"Hm. Thanks."

We kissed.

4.

JACKSON, CAN YOU SPARE A DIME?

"So what's the problem over here?" I said while the clown set up his table of fun by Cecilia. Gen and her parents had been at the fringe of the party for a while now, and their hushed tones indicated a barely controlled argument.

"Oh, it's nothing, Paul," Gen said. "We'll join everyone else in a minute."

"No I most certainly will not," Sally said.

"What the hell is the matter with you, Mom?" Gen asked. "Why can't you just talk to Paul's family for a little while?"

"Because conversing with them brings me great discomfort," she said. "I'm sorry, Paul, but I just think that your mother is rather simpleminded. And as for your *brother*. Well! How could one speak with him and not stare?"

I smiled that smile you use when you know you can't hit someone. "Oh come on, Mother," I said, trying to be cute. "Give it a shot for Cecilia, at least."

She paused, thought it over, and said, "No."

106

So I played my Ace: "There's an open bar on the other side of the yard."

"Why didn't you say that in the first place," John mumbled as he shuffled away.

But Sally still didn't move. "I will not be bribed! I will not!" she shouted.

"Mom!" Gen said in a stage whisper. "Keep your voice down! This is my little girl's first birthday party. Don't start a big thing here."

"Fine," she said, "but I WILL just stand over here."

"We'd really appreciate it—me, Gen, my family, everyone—would love it if you would just pretend to mingle," I said. "Just stand with John over by the open bar. You don't have to talk to anyone."

"But knowing your family," she said, "they will try to start up talking with me! I'm fine here."

"At least go over and talk to Cecilia for a while."

"Just send her over here, Paul," she said. "She's much younger than me, you know."

"You know what?" Gen said. "Fine. Stay here. Paul, I'm not going to waste my time arguing with my mother on such a nice day, so just let her do what she wants. I'm going to see how the clown is coming along with his setup."

•••

Long after the clown left, after we had eaten the barbeque and we were all sitting around with some drinks, Jackson noticed Sally standing off to the side with John. They were quiet, John looking at his drink and Sally softly scolding him for his multiple life errors. So he walked over, good host that he was, to make sure they were doing ok.

"Hi," Jackson said. "Sally and John, right?"

"Yeah, thas sus," John said.

"So how are you two enjoying the party?" my father asked.

"Is's great," John said. He hiccupped.

"Well, miss," Jackson said, "your husband seems to have enjoyed the open bar. But how about yourself? Are you having a good time?"

107

"Marvelous," Sally said.

"...Good," Jackson said. "Tell me if you need a ride home or anything like that."

"Remember what it was like to have a driver, John?" Sally asked as Jackson walked away. "We didn't have to worry about drinking or anything? Now we may have to take a ride home with him."

My father sat down next to Cecilia and me at one of the tables. "So, you little ragamuffin," Jackson said to my daughter, "did you like the clown today?"

"Mm hmm," she said, violently shaking her head up and down so her hair fell in her face.

"Yeah," Jackson said, "I thought he went over pretty well. It was funny when he got you in the face with a squirt of seltzer, wasn't it? Remember that, Paul? When he squirted you in the face?"

"I remember, I remember," I said, putting my hands up in surrender. He also scared the shit out of me when he shook my hand with one of those buzzing, electric shock contraptions. My whole right arm went completely dead for a few seconds.

Cecilia ran off to find Gen. Jackson looked out over the party, all of his guests. "Paul," he said. "When do you plan on taking over down at the store?"

"I've been meaning to talk to you about that."

"What's on your mind?"

"Well, you know I have a family now—I didn't really plan on having a family quite this early, but that's what happened—and we both know how crowded the house is right now."

"It's not so bad."

"Cecilia is sleeping in the living room right now. It's ok because she's only one now, but what happens when she gets older? She needs a room. So here is what I was thinking: I will work at The General Store for a few more years and save up. Then Gen and Cecilia and I need to move out on our own. And I want to start a bookshop, start up my own business."

Jackson was eyeing me, deciding whether or not to be offended or just hurt. He had chosen me out of three sons to take over the store and now I was saying that I didn't want to do it anymore.

"It's nothing personal, Dad. Its just something I've always wanted. But for this to work... I mean, I guess I was wondering if, until I did move out, if I could get a raise."

My father looked at me, smiled a kind, giving smile, and said, "Paul. Son. You know I won't do that."

"Really?" I said, a little surprised. "Why not?"

"Because we work at a general store," he said. "How much money do you think I actually make? With all three of you boys working—well only the two of you now—it's already hard enough to make money on the place. I just can't afford to give you a raise. But don't worry, you'll take over in five or six years." Apparently, he had chosen to ignore everything I said.

My father patted me on the leg, stood up, and walked away. He got about five steps before he fell to the ground on one knee. He grabbed at his left shoulder and slumped over.

5.

DAMN YOU, MARK TWAIN, FOR ALWAYS BEING RIGHT

The ambulance showed up about fifteen minutes later and carted him off to the hospital. One of the paramedics told us that it sounded like Jackson had a heart attack from what we were describing. And no one could say that early how well he would recover from it, or if he would even recover from it at all. The paramedic told us that they were taking him directly to the ER, and that we should go to the hospital's front desk to get information on Jackson's condition.

I pulled the car around and helped Mom into the front seat of my car, and then I helped Morty out of The Chair and into the back. Fred got in the car on his own. The drive to the hospital was quick and silent. No one wanted to say anything, one way or the other. Our plan was simple: we would go down to the hospital and see what arrangements needed to be made. We would do everything we could to help, but we expected that to mean staying out of the way of the doctor.

The woman working behind the front desk at St. John's Memorial Hospital told us to please wait for a few minutes in the chairs in the lobby. She had called a doctor working on Jackson, and he was going to come down to tell us what was going on.

In the lobby, healthy people were briskly walking in to visit the ill while the occasional bandaged man or a woman on crutches would walk out to freedom from recirculated air. We took a seat among the middle ground, patients waiting for appointments they had planned months before.

A doctor came out from behind a pair of free-swinging doors and headed in our direction. "Hello," he said, "are you the Morrisons?"

"Yes," I said. "That's us."

"Well," he said. "I have some good news. Jackson is in stable condition right now. He had a heart attack. We managed to get his heart pumping again with a defibrillator, and right now he is asleep. You should be able to go upstairs and visit him within an hour. You can follow me to the waiting room, and I'll have a nurse let you know when you can go in to see him."

•••

The nurse brought us in to see Jackson once he woke up. We filed into his room. He was buried under a pile of tubes. He looked over at us when we came in and smiled.

"Hey," Morty said. "How are you feeling?"

"Like a million bucks," Jackson said. "I'll be out of here in no time."

"What happened?" I asked. "Did the doctors say what went wrong?"

"It was a little heart attack," he said. "No big deal."

"I don't think a heart attack is 'no big deal,'" Mom said.

"I'm fine," Jackson said. "You guys don't have to worry about me. I'm still strong." He thumped on his chest. "My heart is still strong."

"They had to restart your heart!" Mom said. "Don't you treat this like nothing's wrong. You have to take better care of yourself, starting now."

"That's absolutely right," a doctor said, stepping into the room. "Hello, everyone, I'm Dr. Joe Don Daniels, M.D. And Mr. Morrison, your daughter is absolutely right."

"Oh," Mom said, blushing. "I'm not his daughter, I'm his wife."

"My you look young," Dr. Daniels said with a wink. "Well I'm glad I could catch all of you while you are still here. As you all know, Jackson here did indeed have a heart attack and he is in stable condition as of now. However, his future health is of great concern to me." Dr. Daniels took a clipboard from the end of the bed and looked it over. "Mr. Morrison, you have to start looking very carefully at what you consume. While you are in stable condition now, your heart has been weakened by a spasm caused by artery blockage. This artery could become blocked again."

Mom raised her eyebrows at Jackson and frowned.

"Basically," Dr. Daniels said, "you need to avoid any foods high in fat and cholesterol. If I were you, I would steer clear of eggs."

The doctor left us alone with Jackson. It was getting pretty late and Mom was noticeably drained from the entire ordeal. "Listen," I said, pulling Fred aside, "why don't you take Mom and Morty home in my car. I'll stay here with Dad for the night and someone can come pick me up in the morning."

"Ok," Fred said. "Come on Mom, let's get you home."

"I'll stay with Dad," I said, "so don't you worry about it."

"No one has to stay with me," Jackson said. "I'm fine."

"I think that's a good idea," Mom said. "We'll come back and see you two first thing in the morning."

"Morty has to open up the store," Jackson said. "We can't miss out on a day of business."

"I'll do that, Dad," Morty said.

They filed out of the room and I sat in the chair next to Jackson's bed. He smiled at me and said, "You don't need to stay. You should get the hell out of here."

"I know I don't have to, but Mom would worry if no one was here."

"You're right," he said. He nodded his head at me. "You're a good boy, Paul." And with that he drifted off to sleep.

The chair I was sitting in wasn't very comfortable and I kept moving around, struggling for a position where I could find sleep as well. So I'm not sure whether the rapid beeping of the heart monitor woke me up or snapped me out of a daydream. Either way, I leaped from the chair and looked at the clock. It was midnight.

A nurse barged through the door just as the rapid beeping flowed into one, continuous beep. She called for a doctor. The hallway was filled with the rapid squeaks of rubber on linoleum. A doctor appeared behind the nurse and said, "Grab the defibrillator!"

I watched from a corner of the room as the nurse grabbed the machine and injected a needle into my father's arm.

I watched as the doctor rubbed the two paddles together and said, "Clear!"

I watched as Jackson's body jumped from the electric stimulation.

They did this three more times, then I watched as the doctor pulled the sheet up and over Jackson's face.

If Mark Twain were here, he would have said, "The reports of your father's death were right on."

And then it wasn't long before Gen, Cecelia and I had to move.

6.

BOXING UP MY FATHER

Our "decision" to move came about one week after Jackson's funeral. The funeral itself had been a nice affair, held in the church before things moved over to the graveyard. The pews were filled with family and friends and people who had been shopping at The General Store for decades.

Reverend Sommers stood at the front, of course, and told everyone in attendance about how great my father was. "And now is the time in the ceremony," he said after a solid twenty minutes, "where I would like to ask some family members to come up and say a few words about the deceased. We will hear first from Morty, Jackson's third and youngest son." There was no handicapped access to the stage at the front of the church, but Fred and I helped Morty out with an improvised ramp of two-by-fours.

"I wanted to start by thanking everyone for coming down here today," he said, reading from a piece of crumpled paper held in his hands. His wheelchair stood next to the pulpit, so Morty was only visible to the pews on the right side of the church. But he spoke loud and clear, so I could hear him, even if I couldn't see him.   "My father—Jackson—was a good man, as everyone here in attendance knows. He was a shrewd businessman, a good person, and above all, a good father. Today, I will speak a little about that last title he held because that is how I knew him best.

"Jackson was never the kind of man who would come up and hug you."

Fred grunted an "amen" from his seat in the audience.

"But he was the kind of man who would support you as best he could," Morty continued. "I remember when I was in third grade. I was never a good student, and my grades did a bad job hiding that."

The audience chuckled.

"Once, I got a particularly bad report card sent home. Jackson wanted to have a talk with me about it." Morty smiled. "God, that was terrifying." He put a hand over his mouth. "Oh, Jesus. Can I say that here? God?"

The priest nodded for him to continue.

"Ok. Jackson took me out into the backyard, where we had all of our important talks. He sat me down and said, 'Son, now I know that you're smarter than this.' He showed me the report card I had brought home. 'So that's why I'm doing this,' he said as the thick paper ripped in half.

"'What I'm trying to tell you here, kiddo,' he said, 'is that grades don't matter to me. What bothers me is when I know you can do better and you just aren't applying yourself. So Morty, just take some time and think about what's important to you here. Try your best, put in the time, and it doesn't matter what kind of grades you get.' It looked like he had wrapped up his speech and I stood up. When I started to walk away, he said, 'But don't come back with any more shitty grades, you hear me?'"

The audience laughed again.

"But more to the point when you are trying to describe Jackson is what he said to me later that night when he was tucking me in. He said, 'Morty, just remember: I am always on your side. When teachers and their work get you

115

down, I'm with you all the way.' And he always was. I'm paraphrasing here, but that's the general gist of what he was getting at. My father would always be behind you one hundred percent, for better or worse."

Morty rolled off the stage.

"The next speaker," the priest announced, "is going to be Paul, Jackson's second son."

"Thank you, Reverend Sommers," I said from behind the pulpit. "And thank you everyone, once again, for coming here and supporting my family in this trying time."

I looked out over the crowd. My mother was in the front row, her chin held high, proudly displaying the stains on her cheeks from where her mascara had run. The seat on her left was empty—that's where I had been sitting—but Cecilia was sitting on her lap, Fred was on her other side, and Morty was right up front in the aisle (as usual, he had brought his own chair). Right behind her were Uncle Preston, Aunt Hallie, and their son—my cousin—Howie. Hallie was leaning over the pew to rest a hand on my mother's shoulder. My mother grabbed Hallie's hand and held it tight and she began to cry again, her chin still pushed out and up, defying anyone to say something to her in ways of comfort.

"My father has always been my hero," I said, a finger following my place on a piece of paper. "When I was young, he taught me how to be tough. He taught me that no one should be able to push me around. If I got into a fight at school—which only happened a couple of times—he wouldn't stand for any crying or complaining. Instead," I said, caressing the next line on the paper with my finger, "he taught me how to throw a punch.

"Jackson was not a man to promote violence, but he was of the opinion that a boy should know how to fight just in case the situation called for it. He would hold out two open hands and let me use them as punching bags, teaching me to keep my wrists straight and to punch through the target. He taught me to keep my hands up and never let my guard down, and he taught me that the first punch was

116

usually the last in most fights. 'Aim for the nose,' he always said, 'and the fight won't last for very long at all.'"

I cleared my throat and looked out at my audience again. Gen was there in the pews, of course—front and center to support me—but I was surprised to see that her parents had come to the services as well. John and Sally sat near the back with those members of the funeral party from town that were there because they felt obligated to attend. These were people that knew Jackson well enough, just barely well enough, that it would seem like an insult if they did not show.

"My father," I continued, "wasn't just teaching me how to defend myself. He was teaching me about the importance of being able to fend for myself. He was a parent who understood that you couldn't just wait around for the time when you had to push your baby birds out of the nest. He did a fine job of preparing his three sons for the real world out here, and I would be lost without his wisdom. I only hope that I can do as fine a job for my little girl, Cecilia."

Cecilia waved at me from her seat on my mother's lap.

"Yes," I said waving back. "Hello, sweetheart."

The audience laughed.

"I know this is short," I said, "and there are volumes more I could speak about my father. But I would like to leave you with that thought. And to all of the parents out there—whether you are a new parent like me, or a grizzled veteran like my mother—remember to always prepare your children and yourself for when that time comes and your child leaves and is out there on their own."

I stepped down from the stage.

"And finally," the preacher said, "we will hear from Preston, Jackson's brother-in-law."

Preston stood up and shuffled past Hallie and Howie, his wife and son. He took his place behind the pulpit without any paper or cue cards. He looked out over the crowd and began his speech.

"Ladies and gentlemen, Reverend Sommers, thank you all for coming today. In these most difficult of times, it is a great reminder that there are so many that we hold close and that there are so many that will hold us up when we stumble."

Preston cleared his throat before he dove right in. "Jackson was a man who was easy to respect. He was a fair man; he was a kind man. He was a man who always did his best to put you at ease.

"The first time I met Jackson was the first time I met his in-laws, Hallie's parents. I was nervous and shaking like a leaf on a tree. After we were introduced, he put an arm around my shoulder and said, 'Don't worry. Hallie's parents are pussycats. You'll get along with them fine. Just don't rub them the wrong way.' He then took it upon himself to introduce me to everyone else and made sure that I was comfortable and had everything that I needed."

Preston grabbed the pulpit with both hands. "Above all, Jackson was a provider. He was there to make sure that his family was taken care of. Now that he is gone, I will proudly take over that responsibility and make sure that his three sons and his wife, Ruth, always have whatever it is they may need."

Uncle Preston, short and sweet. As ever, he was his best public relations agent.

At that point, the closed coffin was carried to a Hearst, which carried it to the graveyard where, upon arrival, a few of us carried it to Jackson's final resting place. The spot was nice enough, right near a grouping of trees, and the church had arranged it so there were flowers piled up around the plot. The headstone was minimalist, with the inscription reading, "Jackson Morrison. Loving husband and father." It's probably what he would have wanted.

When everyone settled down, the preacher said a few more words, finishing up with the obligatory "ashes to ashes, dust to dust." The coffin was lowered into the ground with a series of belts and two-by-fours, at which point my mother was the first to throw a fistful of dirt in the hole.

Everyone in attendance followed suit, one at a time dropping a handful of dirt on the wooden box.

Reverend Sommers said, "Thank you, everyone, for coming."

And that was that.

7.

WHAT FRED DID

But now, back to why Gen and I had to move.

I feel that every little bump in the road, every inconvenience in my life, can all be traced back to one moment; one move of treachery and deceit that came at the hands of my brother Fred.

After Jackson's funeral, the six of us—my mother, Fred, Morty, Gen, Cecilia and I—came back to the house. We sat down for dinner, our first time eating together at home without Jackson's presence.

"Thanks for the salmon, Ma," I said. I sunk my fork in and took a bite. "It's delicious."

"Of course, dear," she said. "I think we deserve to spoil ourselves a little bit."

"Absolutely," Morty said.

"So," I said for the sake of routine. "When are we going to open up The Store tomorrow?"

"Well take a look at the big shot!" Fred said without looking up from his plate.

"Come on, Fred," I said. "Take it easy."

"You know, we all own The Store. It doesn't belong to you any more than the rest of us." Fred looked around the table. "Except you, Gen."

"I know," I said. "I wasn't trying to say that. I was just saying that we—all of us—need to keep it running."

"Boys, this isn't table talk," my mother said. "We can talk about all of that later."

"No," Fred pressed on. "I think that is what you were saying. Dad wanted you to take over when he retired and that is exactly what you are doing, isn't it?"

"Well yes, Fred," I said. "But I'm not trying to screw you out of anything. The Store is there to make sure that we all have some food on our plates."

"Yeah Fred," Morty said. "Take a chill-pill, man. Paul's just talking shop, he's not claiming ownership."

"But this is how it all starts, Morty," Fred said. "First he starts making sure that everything is running smoothly, then he starts telling us what to do and the next thing you know, Paul has the store all to himself. I put just as much work as anyone else into that place!"

"I'm not saying you didn't!" I said. "Jesus, Fred! I'm not saying anything. I'm just making sure that The Store keeps running."

"Fuck that!" Fred shouted.

"Fred!" Mom said.

"Hey!" Gen said. "Watch your language. Cecilia's right here."

"All I'm saying," Fred said in a calmer volume, "is that I'm not going to let you take my fair share of the pie."

"And all I'm saying," Gen mumbled, "is you better watch your goddamn language around my daughter."

"Mixed metaphors aside," I said, "I have no intention of doing that."

"We'll see," Fred said.

We sat quietly around the table after that outburst, everyone concentrating on their food. Finally, when we were all finishing up, Cecilia asked, "When's Grandpa coming home?"

•••

121

Morty and I went to The Store early the next morning. We opened the doors and took down the sign that said, "Closed due to a death in the family. Will re-open as soon as is possible." That sign had hung on the door for almost a week now.

If Jackson were here, he would have said, "Death is no excuse, boys. Get back to work!"

Being closed, it was easy to tell, had hurt business. Our regular customers weren't sure that we'd be open, so they took their business to the K-Mart a few towns over. It was a slow morning and only a few people came in, which was fine. That gave Morty and me a chance to talk.

"I can't believe Fred," Morty said. "What was he trying to accomplish?"

"Who knows, Morty. This is a tough time for everyone, though. We should try to cut him some slack. I guess we should talk about it in a few days when he calms down a little bit."

"Yeah, but to yell like that in front of Mom, when she's having such a hard time, too?" Morty said. "I don't know about that. He better tone it down at the table tonight, or I'll have to pull out my guns." He kissed both of his biceps. The Chair provided him with an excellent upper-body workout on a daily basis, and he liked to show it off.

"Fred is who he is," I said. "He's passive-aggressive, and that's just the way things come out when he has a problem. Who knows what's really bothering him? It could be that I'm supposedly in charge of things down here, or it could be something else entirely. The point is," I said, fingering the register's buttons, "he could be mad about something that happened months ago and it's just starting to come out now because of everything that's going on."

"Well either way," Morty said, "he's still being a huge baby."

"Ain't that the truth," I said.

●●●

Being a baby was always Fred's way. He would always assume that he would get whatever he wanted and when he didn't, he would get upset. One time when we were

122

little kids—and I do mean little, like Fred was eight and I was four—we went shopping with Mom.

When we were little, she always took us to department stores and made us try on shirts and pants and shoes and she made us wait while she did a little shopping for herself and Jackson, too. We always misbehaved, so Mom got the idea to make a deal with us.

The deal we always had when we went out on these little weekend road trips was that—if Fred and I were good and didn't complain or cry—we would get to pick out a toy from the toy store and Mom would buy it for us. Free toys always sounded like a good bargain, so Fred and I tried our best to be little angels throughout the trip. We tried on everything she wanted us to and smiled when she told us to "Wait right here," but that was always the hardest part. When Mom left us in the clothing department in Sears and told us to "Wait right here," Fred and I were faced with temptation. It was so easy and so fun to climb between the dresses hanging on the circular clothing racks and hide out inside, surrounded by cotton-walls. Sometimes, Fred and I would play hide and seek with each other. Sometimes, we would play hide and seek with our mother (a game she detested).

And sometimes, like on the trip I'm thinking of, we would make it. We had been good enough to get our reward, and we ran through the aisles like kids in a toy store and each picked out one toy. I picked out a blue rubber Spalding and Fred picked out a game. We brought our prizes over to Mom, who was waiting by the front of the store.

"And what did you guys pick out today?" she asked.

"I got a ball!" I said.

"And I got Rock 'em Sock 'em Robots!" Fred said.

Mom took each toy and examined the price tag. "I'm sorry," she said, turning to Fred. "This toy is a little too expensive. You need to pick something else out, ok sweetie?"

"No!" Fred said. "That's the only thing I want."

"I'm sorry honey," she said, "but I can't afford this. It is way too much money for some plastic toy that'll

123

probably break before we get home. Go ahead, you can take some time to find something else."

"I don't want anything else!" Fred said. "I want the Rock 'em Sock 'em Robots!"

"Watch your attitude," Mom said. "That almost sounds like complaining, to me. If you keep this up, you won't get anything."

"But Paul got what he wanted," Fred whined. "It's not fair!"

"That's just the way it works, honey," she said. "Sorry."

"No, no, no!" Fred said. "It's not fair!" He dropped to the floor and started screaming, banging his fists and kicking his feet.

"Alright, that's it. If that's how it's going to be..." Mom picked Fred up off the ground by his ear in an amazing feat of strength. "Paul, here is a dollar. Stand in line here and buy your ball. I'm going to take Fred to the car."

And that was the last time we went to the toy store after shopping with Mom. Fred had ruined it for us both.

•••

A week after Jackson had died, I woke up in a cold sweat. I had a bad dream. Frank Sinatra was chasing after me with the intent to kill me. He controlled a pack of rats that had cornered me on the roof of a building, and I was deciding my fate—whether I should jump or face the wrath of the rats—when I woke up.

"You ok, honey?" Gen asked me without opening her eyes.

"Yeah," I said. "I'm fine. I just had a bad dream. Go back to sleep."

I looked over at the alarm clock. Six twenty-nine. I rubbed my eyes and put my feet on the ground. The electric clock flipped its numbers to six, three and zero and shouted, "Beep! Beep! Beep!" I smacked it off and went into the bathroom for a shower.

The warm water ran over my shoulders and smoothed out the tension created by my dream. I was not the type to have nightmares, but since Jackson's death,

124

nightmares had become part of the routine. That was the fifth day in a row that I'd woken up terrified. And it was always a minute before my alarm went off. No day goes well when you wake up a minute before your alarm clock.

I turned the water off and wrapped a towel around myself before leaving the bathroom. Fred's door was closed, as was usual at this time in the morning.

I threw on some clothes and went downstairs. I could hear Morty's alarm going off through his door. I snuck past Cecilia, sleeping in the living room, and I banged on his door. "Wakey wakey, sleepy head!" I said. "Time for a big day at work!"

He groaned and threw a pillow at me. I noticed empty beer cans spilling from under his bed.

Mom was already in the kitchen making pancakes.

"Good morning, sweetie," she said as she dropped a few on my plate.

"Morning, Mom," I said. At heart, I was not a morning conversationalist. But after twenty-two years, I had grown accustomed to my mother's morning meetings.

"How are you feeling this morning?" she asked. "How did you two sleep?"

She was referring to Gen and me.

"We slept fine," I said. "I'm ready for a big day with Morty down at the Store." I slopped some syrup on my plate. "How are you doing?"

"Fine," she said. She poured more batter in a pan for Morty. "I'm still not used to that big, empty bed."

"That'll take some time," I said.

I heard Morty's wheels squeaking across the living room and past Cecilia's bed. He came into the kitchen still asleep,.

"No shower today?" I asked.

"Nah, I just put a hat over it," he said. His eyes were bloodshot.

"Good morning, sweetie," Mom said as she dropped a few pancakes on Morty's plate.

"Morning, Mom."

"And how did you sleep?" she asked.

"Ugh," Morty said. "I feel like I didn't sleep at all."

"Oh, poor baby," she said, facing the stove with her back to us at the table.

"Oh, poor baby," I whispered while I kicked him under the table. I gave him a look.

Morty gave me half a smile. "So Paul," he said with a mouthful of pancake. "What kind of showing should we expect today down at the store?"

"Well," I said, "I think that word of mouth has finally let everyone know that we are officially back in operation. There have been more and more people coming down every day, so we should be back to business as usual in no time. If not today, then soon."

"Sounds good to me," he said. "It's about time."

"I know."

I ate my last few bites and ran upstairs to grab the keys to my car. I gave Gen a light kiss on the cheek.

"Mmm..."

"Honey?" I said. "Will you get up and keep Mom company? I think this is going to be a rough day for her. I'm just getting that feeling."

"Sure," she said, stretching her arms high over her head. "Yeah, I'm getting up."

"Thanks, sweets." I gave her another kiss and headed downstairs.

Morty was waiting by the door. "Come on, champ," he said in his best imitation of Jackson. "It's a quarter to seven, we don't want to be late!"

"Don't you give me a hard time," I said. "You're the reason God invented the snooze button."

We left the house just as the sun started to light the sky. It was that kind of early morning glow that lasted for the time it took the sun to come over the horizon. It was that early morning glow that made everything look, or at least feel, like it was moving in slow motion.

"God damn, its cold!" Morty said after I put The Chair in the trunk and slid behind the wheel.

We drove the few blocks to the store and got out of the car. I pulled the ring of keys out of my back pocket and went to open the front door. I tried one key a few times before I realized I had the wrong one.

"Woops," I said to Morty. "My brain doesn't function this early in the morning."

"Just get the door open before I freeze to death," he said.

"Next time you'll know to bring a sweatshirt," I said. "Just because it's summer doesn't mean it'll be warm in the morning."

I found the right key and clicked the lock open. I pushed in on the door, but it wouldn't budge.

"What the hell is going on here?" I said.

And that's when I actually started processing the details of my surroundings. There was a padlock keeping the door closed, a padlock on the door at eye-level, a padlock that had never been there before.

"What the fuck?" I said. "Morty, check this out! What is this shit?"

"Uh, Paul?" he said. "You'd better come check this out."

He was standing in front of a sign on a post that had been hammered into the ground. I hadn't noticed it when I was walking up to the door because I had been fiddling with the ring of keys, but the sign was pretty tough to miss. It read, "Future Sight of K-Mart, Bringing Convenience to Your Neighborhood."

"What do you make of this?" Morty asked.

"I don't know," I said. I noticed a number for K-Mart's executive offices at the bottom of the sign. "But I think we'll be giving the folks over at K-Mart a call."

8.

THE SKYING BLOB IS SORELY MISSED

Morty and I went back to the house after our unsuccessful attempt at opening up the Store.

"What are you two doing back so soon?" Mom asked us.

"We're experiencing some technical difficulties," Morty said as way of explanation.

"Yeah," I said. "Is Fred upstairs? We have a lot of phone calls to make and I want him to be in on it."

"Yes," Mom said. "He hasn't come down for breakfast yet."

"That lazy bum," Morty said. "Well get him and tell him to come down, Paul."

I climbed up the stairs while Gen came in the room. "What are you two doing back here?"

I knocked on his bedroom door. "Fred? Get up man, there's something screwy going on down at the store."

There was no answer.

I banged harder. "Fred! Come on man, get up!"

128

I opened his door a crack, just enough to slip one eye through the slit.

The room was empty. Fred was gone. Just like last time, there were a few books scattered here and there, but otherwise it was the bed, the desk, the dresser, and the floorboards. I walked in and looked around for any hint at what had happened. It looked like Fred had just up and disappeared.

There was a piece of paper left on his bed, folded in half. I sat down and looked at it.

"Oh, crap." This wasn't what I needed.

I brought the note downstairs. "There's some real bad news," I said.

I gave the letter to Morty and he read it out loud. "*Dear Mom, Paul and Morty,*" it started. "*I can't take life in Marborough anymore. I've left, I don't know where I'll end up.*"

I looked over at Mom. She had covered her eyes with a hand and was looking down at the floor. Gen went to her and put a hand on her shoulder.

"*I suppose I will try to get in touch with all of you at some point,*" it continued, "*but don't wait by the phone or anything.*"

"*Also,*" Morty read, "*I have sold the Store, and the land around it. I need the cash to move on with my life. Fred.*"

Morty reached for the table to put the letter down, but he wasn't watching what he was doing and he dropped it on the floor.

He looked as shocked as I felt. Fred was our brother—yes, we'd always had our differences, and yes, we didn't always get along—but he was our brother, bottom line. I'd always been there for Fred if he had a problem to talk about or if he needed me to help him out. Fred helped me with my math homework when it got too hard for me. We took care of each other.

"I guess I'll call K-Mart and see what the story is," I said.

129

I ushered everyone into the kitchen before picking up the phone and dialing.

•••

"I came over as soon as I could," Preston said.

We were all in the kitchen—Mom, Morty, Gen, Cecilia and me—just staring at each other, aside from Cecilia who was drawing with her crayons.

When I'd called the K-Mart executive office to figure out what was going on, I had explained the situation to someone and they put me on hold.

"Hello, sir?" the man on the other end said when he returned to the line.

"Yes?"

"I looked into the purchase, and everything seems to be in order. The man who made the sale—um...Fred Morrison—had his name on the deed to the property, so everything was done by the books."

"I understand that," I said, "but don't all people on the deed have to agree to the sale?"

"Yes, sir. His was the only name on the deed."

"What?" I almost dropped the phone. "Only name on the deed? How is that possible?"

"I'm sorry, sir. His was the only documented name on the deed."

"I think we're going to have to bring some lawyers in to figure all of this out."

"I'm sorry to hear that, sir," he said, "but I understand. You do realize that there is nothing you can do from a legal standpoint?"

"We'll see about that," I said.

"Ok. Good luck. And I'm sorry about your loss."

And I guess that somewhere in all of the somewhat subdued confusion, Mom called Aunt Hallie, because here was Uncle Preston to add to the mess of a day.

"So who have you called so far?" Preston asked.

"I spoke to the folks at K-Mart," I said. "They said that there was nothing we could do. I was trying to figure out what I could do in terms of hiring a lawyer."

130

"I think the best place to start," Uncle Preston said, "is by finding Fred."

"Uncle Preston," I said, "I think that's a little easier said than done. Let's be honest here: he could be anywhere at this point. And I certainly don't have the time to walk around the country hoping I run into my brother."

"It's worth a shot," Preston said, "and I think it might be our best chance at actually getting the store back. At the very least, you could sue Fred for lost income."

"Why don't we let the lawyers decide what we can and can't do," I said.

Uncle Preston sat down. "Ok." He grinned, big and stupid. "Other than that, how is everyone doing?"

Cecilia piped up once no one else did. "I'm good! Look at this!" She held up a picture of six blobs standing in front of a box and two blobs at the top.

"Wow," Uncle Preston said, slicking his hair back with his fingers. "What is it a picture of?"

"It's us right outside. This is Momma," she said pointing to one of the blobs. "Daddy, Unca Morty 'n Fred, Gramma, and me. And this one up here," she said, pointing at one of the blobs at the top of the picture, "is Grampa."

With that, Mom burst into tears.

9.

GREAT BARRINGTON

After Uncle Preston had gone home; after I had spent the entire afternoon consoling my widowed mother because her oldest son had run away and sold the family's livelihood; after I had been on the phone with three different lawyers about the case with K-Mart and some paperwork had been processed; after all of that, it was bedtime. I was lying in bed with Gen. Cecilia and Morty were asleep downstairs and my mom was passed out a few rooms away, exhausted after all of the emotion of the day. I was having a hard time falling asleep myself, so Gen was humoring me and stayed up talking.

"...and Fred probably doesn't even care," I said. "He probably hasn't looked back over his shoulder once since he left." I let out a sigh.

Gen turned towards me and rested her head on my shoulder. "Paul," she said. "Where do you want to move when we're old and retired and bored of each other?"

"I'm not going to get bored of you."

"Sure you will," she said. "Someday, you will. I won't take it personally, but it happens in all relationships after a while. It certainly happened to my parents."

"I didn't see that happening to my parents."

"That's true," she said, "for the most part. But they were lucky enough to have three boys that stuck around the house for so long that they never had the time to get bored." She smacked me in the face with a pillow.

"What," I said smiling. "Are you implying that I'm too old to live with my mother?"

"I was," Gen said. "Seriously, honey, we've got to get out of here before your mom starts relying on us too much. Because if we stay long enough for that to happen, then we can never leave." She started playing with the little chest hair that I had, twirling it with a finger. "But that's not what we were talking about. Where do you want to end up when we're old and bored?"

"I'm telling you," I said, "I won't get bored of you."

"Humor me then."

"Alright," I said. "Give me a second to think about it."

And I took that second and thought about it.

•••

I knew right off the bat that the city life wasn't for me. I had only been to a couple of cities a handful of times, but they always struck me as hectic and way beyond my control. Every time I went to Hartford or Boston as a kid, my parents always dragged me along by the hand, leading me everywhere. And I got the feeling that was what city life was like: always being dragged along by outside forces, jostled and pushed around like dice at a craps table.

And the one time Gen and I had gone to Boston together—the one time I went to a city without my tugboat parents—my opinion of the city life was solidified. We drove my car in for a daytrip on a Sunday. (It was the used-car that the insurance money from the accident paid for, the Buick—just barely alive as always.)

Gen and I had been together for a few months when we took that summer daytrip to Boston. We planned to sit out on the commons and soak in the sun for most of the day and maybe drive over to the harbor and walk around a little bit, but the whole trip turned into a day of disastrous directions. After asking five different pedestrians—who had five different answers, all ending with "you can't miss it"—for directions to the largest park in the city, it took us five hours before we were sitting on the grass. At that point I was already fed up, so we just spent an hour there and then spent a few more finding our way out of that hellish labyrinth of one-way streets.

Give me a decent-sized town with a Main Street that reaches end to end and I'm happy. All of my favorite trips had been to towns like New London, Connecticut and Great Barrington, Massachusetts. When Gen and I went to New London, I had a great time walking along the boardwalk. We strolled down Main Street and stopped in any of the thirty used bookshops—which I instantly fell in love with, of course—and we even sat down for a cup of coffee at one of the larger ones.

And Great Barrington. Don't even get me started! I love it so much. It has a beautiful main street with amazing alleyway entrances to great restaurants. Every time I went there, I fell in love with it a little more.

•••

"I guess I wouldn't mind ending up in Great Barrington," I said. "It seems like a good place to get old and die."

"Don't be so cryptic Paul," Gen said.

"It's hard not to be right now," I said. "I just had the rug pulled out from under me. I don't really know what we should do from here."

"Let's just take what money we have and start over."

"That would be nice," I said.

"So what's holding us back?"

"Well, I don't know," I said. "I guess part of the problem is what am I going to do for a job now. You can always go back to work as a nurse, but I have no backup."

"Don't look at this as a setback, Paul," Gen said. "This is the chance to do what you've always wanted.

134

There's nothing stopping us from going anywhere. We can always get a loan or something."

"We do have a chance to start something new..." I said. "You're right. We should move to Great Barrington, maybe give a real shot at opening up that bookshop. You're right, honey. This is a great opportunity."

•••

Over the next couple of days, we tried to get down to the nitty-gritty of the move. Eventually, we found the building that currently doubles as both our residence and the Morrison Bookshop and Café; and eventually, we moved in, but that only came after a very difficult trip to the bank. A few days after Gen and I talked about it, I drove over to the First Federal Reserve Bank of Marborough, Massachusetts. I dressed up for the occasion with my only suit (a hand-me-down) and a striped tie.

When I got to the bank, there was someone pulling out of a spot right in front. I was feeling lucky. I went up the stairs and into one of the four front doors I had to choose from.

Whenever I walk into a bank, I always get a feeling of being completely overwhelmed. I mean a certain kind of bank, of course, the kind of bank that the First Federal Reserve Bank of Marborough, Massachusetts was—all cavernous marble with columns thrown anywhere they could be fit in, the kind of pre-Depression bank that says, "Look at us! If your money isn't safe here, then it isn't safe anywhere."

I did my best to look confident and walked right up to a woman sitting at one of the desks hidden between a mess of columns. I sat down in the chair across from her.

"Hello sir, how can I help you today?"

I looked at her desk: scattered papers somehow arranged to appear neat, some pens, and a placard that read, "Cindy Rosenblatt."

"Hi, Cindy. I'd like to take out a mortgage so I can buy this building." I slid a picture and a piece of paper with information about the building in Great Barrington. "The price is right there on the paper."

"Yes... I see it..." She looked everything over. "I'll go talk to the bank manager about this for a moment, if you'll excuse me."

"Of course."

"Alright, just wait right here, sir."

"You got it." When she walked away, I realized I had been sweating. I looked around—no one was watching—so I wiped my forehead with the palm of my hand and rubbed it off on the felt of the chair I was sitting on.

I waited, and waited, and waited. And the longer I waited, the more it felt like there was a jury of two somewhere out there in the vaults of the First Federal Reserve Bank of Marborough, Massachusetts, waiting to give me my sentence. And contrary to real life, the longer this jury took, the worse my chances were of getting the verdict I wanted.

So I waited some more, and I sweated some more. I was thankful for the suit jacket, for how well it hid my pit-stained shirt underneath. Cindy finally came back while I was trying to circulate some air into my shirt by pulling it away from my chest and stomach. I stopped and pretended I was adjusting my tie when I noticed her.

She was standing with a sixty-something-year-old man with a gray toilet seat's worth of hair hugging the sides and back of his head. I tried to make eye contact with Cindy, tried to get some idea of what the verdict was. She wouldn't look at me, and I figured that was the verdict in and of itself.

When I returned, disappointed, to my car, I saw that I had a ticket stuck under the wiper. I guess it's not as lucky to catch someone pulling out of a spot when they were probably just waiting for someone inside, sitting in a no-parking zone.

•••

So we were unable to take out a loan, no thanks to the stiffs down at the bank. But with my mom's help, we took out a mortgage on her house. She was more than willing to do it for us. She said, "Of all of my sons, I would

136

never worry about you missing a mortgage payment." She pinched my cheek. "You're just like your father. You have a knack for success."

So we got the money we needed and Gen and I got boxes and started piling everything that belonged to us from my mother's house. In our room, there were piles on the bed, in the closet, on the floor in front of the dresser and the door, under the bed; in Cecilia's room (which was commonly referred to as the Living Room in most traditional households) there were piles on the couch, on the mattress on the floor, on the floor; and basically there were piles everywhere.

Moving is no easy task, and it is made even harder when a two-and-a-half-year-old girl is involved. Gen and I would pile clothes as we would, getting it ready to be thrown in a box, and Cecilia would come along and burrow into the cotton clump. Our little Inuit would then refuse to exit her igloo. I pulled the top of the pile off of her, but then I looked down and saw that—even though she was playing and horsing around—Cecilia was terrified over the thought of moving.

"Hey!" she said.

I dropped the clothes back on top of her and said, "Ok. We'll pack this stuff up last."

"Don't hurt any of Mommy's clothes," Gen said. "Ok, dear?"

"Ok," Cecilia said.

10.

THE CARTOON ELECTRICIAN WIRES
A NEW LIFE

And we started over. Uncle Preston was paying for the lawsuit against K-Mart, and we spent most of the money from Mom's mortgaged house on the bookshop.

"Take a look at this place!" Gen said. She waved her hands around like she was in an ABBA music video. "We're getting somewhere!"

I was standing with Gen in the middle of the construction zone that would become the Morrison Bookshop and Café. We had moved into the building in Great Barrington a week earlier, a fairly large brownstone that we bought for a decent price. The top two floors were livable, with a couple of bedrooms already furnished, but we had to completely transform the first floor for the purposes of business.

We left Cecilia over at my mother's house so the sawdust and asbestos flakes flying around wouldn't bother her young lungs.

And so, behind the married couple, us, was a man with a mallet, walking around and indiscriminately smashing holes into the exposed sheetrock walls. He called himself an electrician, but he looked like a demolition enthusiast.

"How much longer are we looking at here?" I asked him.

"Hmm..." the electrician mused, resting the cartoon hammer on his shoulder and rubbing his five o'clock shadow. "I still have to get some wires over to where the coffee bar is going to be. We also need some juice over by the far wall, if you want to have an outlet or two for lamps or whatever."

"Yes, I definitely want some outlets over there," Gen said. We walked the electrician from the café to the bookshop through the widened doorway the carpenter finished the day before. "And I also want a couple more hanging lights in the bookshop here," she said, pointing to a spot on the ceiling. "We need to make sure this space is well lit for title-browsing. No need to make people strain their eyes."

There, at the front of the brownstone, was a man with measuring tape. He was making notes on how to install the plate-glass window that would look out on the street and look in on the shelves of books that were on their way.

"Mmhmm, mmhmm," the electrician said. He leaned forward on the mallet. "Well I would just be guessing, but I would say that this job should take a month more, give or take a few weeks." He nodded his head as he looked around, self-assured.

"You're really going out on a limb with that guess, there," I said. "Anywhere from a couple of weeks to a couple of months?"

"I would lean towards one month exactly," he said, "but I do like to hedge my guesses a little. I don't want people complaining when I don't finish the job on time."

"When?" I said. "You don't plan to finish the job on time?"

"If," he corrected himself. "If I don't." He went back into the café to continue playing whack-a-mole with our walls.

"Oh Paul," Gen said. "I'm so excited. This whole disaster is going to work out for the best, I think. Just look at this place!"

So I looked at the place. It was a shit hole, with piles of dirt everywhere, but it did have potential. The trial with K-Mart was always on my mind, but I had to admit I was excited about the new start I was handed.

I sighed, and wished it hadn't been a father's death and a brother's betrayal that was making my dream come true.

•••

The whole disaster wasn't working out so well for everyone, though. Morty was still stuck in the house with Mom.

After the construction workers and electricians left my house for the night, I drove to Mom's house to pick up Cecilia.

When I stepped through the door, Morty was just finishing up a phone call. "No no," he said. "I understand. That's the way these things go...well thanks for getting in touch with me so quickly. No...thanks. All right, goodbye. Argh!" He slammed the phone down into the receiver. "I give up." He picked up his beer where it had been sitting next to the phone.

"Job hunting isn't going too well?" I asked.

"No way, man," he said. "That was my third rejection in the past two days. From McDonalds. Can you believe that? Even a fast food joint won't hire me."

"Oh come on," I said. "You'll find something soon." He rolled next to the couch, so I sat down.

"I don't know, Paul. Every interview I've had, without fail, the first question's about the chair. They're all like, 'what happened?' and 'were you in the war?' I swear to God, they don't even care if I'm qualified or not. And what the hell war would I've been in anyway?" He smacked the side of the wheelchair. "It doesn't matter what kind of

140

head I have on my shoulders: as long as I'm in The Chair, they send me walking."

"Not the most appropriate cliché, Morty."

"Ha ha."

"Well where else have you applied for a job?" I asked.

"I've talked to every moving company in New England," he said, "but none of them want me."

"Morty, of course they won't hire you for a job! There's all those stairs and lifting."

He rolled his eyes. "I was joking, Paul."

"Oh," I said. "I get it."

"But seriously. What am I supposed to do?"

"Well, if you think they're that hung up on the wheelchair, maybe you should start doing interviews on the phone. That's an easy out."

"Yeah, that's not a bad idea," Morty said. "But this is driving me crazy. I had no clue it would be this hard. I hate this fucking thing, even if it does help me get around." He finished his beer and pulled a glass and a bottle of Jack Daniels from The Chair's undercarriage, pouring and drinking.

"Just hang in there, tough guy," I said. "There's no rush for you to get a job. At least you have enough money to get by for a while. Be thankful for that much, I guess."

"Paul?" my mother said from the kitchen. "Is that you?"

"Yeah Ma."

"Well come in here and see what me and Cecilia have been doing all day," she said.

I walked over to the kitchen. The first thing I noticed was the mess. On every surface of the kitchen, there were cracked eggs, empty boxes, and enough flour to make it look like Mom was giving Cecilia a lesson in forensics ("today, we will learn how to dust for fingerprints…").

"Look, Daddy!" Cecilia said. "Brownies!"

If the little girl from the Shake 'n' Bake commercials were there, she would have said, "And I helped!"

"Wow, it looks like you two have been having a lot of fun," I said.

"Sure have," Cecilia said. "Gram-ma let me be the official taste-tester."

"And tell Daddy how our brownies did," Mom said.

"They got an A-plus!"

"That good, hunh? I guess I'll have to try some of those for myself."

"They're not ready yet," Cecilia said. "They still need..." She looked at an egg-timer on the counter. "Thirty minutes before they're done."

"I'm not sure we can stay long enough to wait," I said to Cecilia after looking at my watch. "Mommy needs us back at the house soon for dinner."

"That's ok," my mom said. "I'll take them out of the oven and we can have them when you come back tomorrow."

"That's a good idea," I said. "Why don't you go grab your jacket."

"But I need to help Gram-ma clean up."

"I'll take care of that too, sweetie. Now go on and get your coat."

Cecilia ran off to the living room. I could hear her stop along the way to talk to Morty.

I took the opportunity to ask a question that had been gnawing at me for some time. "Mom?"

"Yes dear," she said. She was sponging all the surfaces in the kitchen. She and Cecilia had really made a mess of the kitchen.

"Do you remember a while ago, back when Fred ran away that first time after my graduation?"

She kept her back to me, but she stopped sponging. "Yes."

"Do you remember you and Jackson were talking for a while after I went to bed?"

"You heard?"

"Of course I did. The walls in this house are so thin."

"Well we were just having a disagreement. We weren't really fighting." She started sponging again.

"I know, I didn't say fighting. I wasn't worried you guys were getting a divorce or anything." I listened, and it sounded like Cecilia was still talking to Morty. "But I heard you guys talking about a promise Jackson made to Fred when he was younger, and I've been wondering what that promise was."

"Oh." Mom put her sponge in the sink and turned to me. "Paul, there's something you have to understand about your father. He was a great man, but he would sometimes say things and make these deals without thinking about the other people involved in his decisions."

"I kinda figured that out for myself when he didn't say anything to Fred about me taking over at the register."

"Right. Well..."

Cecilia came running into the kitchen with her jacket on. "All ready!"

Mom looked at me.

"Great," I said to Cecilia. I looked over at Mom. She looked like she still wanted to talk, but didn't want to do it in front of Cecilia. "Ok Mom, we'll talk about this some other time."

PART IV
MADNESS LOVES
COMPANY

DADDY, WHEN ARE YOU COMING
HOME?
(PROLOGUE TO PART IV)

This morning, when Gen came for her daily visit, her third in a row, she brought everyone with her. Everyone was Cecilia, the baby, and Gen's parents. One of the police officers led me into the room where my family was waiting, then closed the door when he left. There was a silent click when he locked the door.

The visiting room was bland—a table and chairs in a green room, with one barred-over window. The walls used to be white, I had been told, but they had been repainted because of a man awaiting trial. His girlfriend had come to visit him and managed to sneak a small knife inside the visiting room, which the man had used to slit his wrists. I guess he didn't think his chances of being acquitted were so good. But the blood sprayed everywhere, and the room had been repainted green because that was the only color that could cover the blood with one cost-efficient coat of paint.

"Hey sweets," I said. I gave Gen and the baby a kiss on the forehead each, and then gave my little girl a hug. "Hello, John. Sally." I gave each of them a nod of my head and sat down. Cecilia came over and sat on my lap. "How's everything at home?"

"Things are going," Gen said. "Mom and Dad have been real helpful with the bookshop and the kids. I don't know what I would do without them."

I gave John and Sally a tired smile. "Thanks, guys."

"Anything to help our daughter," John said. I could tell he had been drinking already when he opened his mouth. Even across the table I could smell the whiskey on his breath. At ten thirty?

"Well I do appreciate it anyway," I said.

"Morty came by again yesterday," Gen said. "To check in on us, make sure everything was ok. He stayed and helped out a little, too. And a good thing he did: yesterday was a very busy day. So many people in and out!"

"Yeah," Cecilia said. "I taught him how to use the register."

"Well good for you!" I said, the proud father. "And tell me. Are you enjoying your summer break?"

"Yeah, but I can't wait to get back to school." Wow, a child excited to get back to school. That girl was a rare find, a real gem.

"That's good," I said, "but in the meantime, you make sure you help Mommy as much as you can at home."

"I will," Cecilia said. She squirmed around on my lap to face me. "Daddy, when are you coming home?"

"Soon, sweets," I said. "Soon."

Hopefully, I can go back home as soon as I finish writing out what happened. I'm going to jump ahead, now, back to the point when we had already received Fred's letter. This is when things—and people—started to get a little crazy.

1.

SHARP AS A TACK AND TWICE AS SMART

I was lying in bed with Gen, about two weeks left to go in her pregnancy with Little Jack. "You know," she said, "I just read an article saying that, on average, the more sleep a child gets as a baby, the bigger he will grow up to be."

"Honey," I said. "If that were true, Cecilia would be huge. She slept all the time as a baby."

"Well, she's not done growing yet."

"But she's really tiny for her age."

"The study said 'on average!'" Gen screamed.

And that shut me up.

•••

The next day, I took my mother to see a doctor at St. John's Memorial Hospital.

"Hello Dr. Horowitz," I said. "It's good to see you again. How are you doing?"

"I've been great," he said. "Thanks for asking. Now, Mrs. Morrison, I'm going to need you to sit up on this table here... great." He picked up the chart that the nurse, who showed us in to the examination room, had left it at the end of the table.

I felt bad about leaving a very pregnant Gen alone with Cecilia and the bookshop, but it was only for a couple of hours. And besides, Cecilia was actually getting to the age where she could help out around the store. On Saturdays, she would sit on my lap at the register and do all the math herself, giving the customers the right change more often than not. I'll tell you: she was better at math at the age of eight than I was at the age of eighteen.

Dr. Horowitz turned to face me, and said, "Can I talk to you outside for a minute before we begin?"

"Of course."

"Great."

He grabbed my shoulder when we stepped outside the room and said, "Now Paul, what was it? A couple of days since this incident or whatnot?"

"It's been a week," I answered.

"That's right." He notated. "And what exactly happened when you went to your mother's house?"

"She was there making dinner," I said. "When we continued to talk, it became clear that she was waiting for my dead father to come home for dinner."

He jotted a couple of notes down on the clipboard. "Ok, great," he said. "Is there anything else that has given you cause for concern?"

"Except for that one time, she's been sharp as a tack."

"Great." He finished jotting. "Well I'm going to run some tests, but if I don't find anything physically wrong with her, I would suggest that you either take her to see a psychologist or even suggest that she be put in a nursing home."

I thought about how that would fit into my financial scheme. I decided it wouldn't, at least not without some serious sacrifices.

"Well let's run those tests."

"Great, I'll just get started then."

He drew some blood from my mother, then Dr. Horowitz spent the next two hours checking in on us while nurses performed CAT scans and MRIs.

●●●

That night, Cecilia, Gen and I were sitting around our kitchen table, eating dinner.

"Oh, Gen," I said. "This chicken is delicious. Job well done."

"Well thank you darling," she said.

Cecilia was just pushing around the food on her plate with her fork. "Do I hafta eat the green beans, Mom?" she asked.

"What do you think?" Gen asked.

"Fine," Cecilia said, stabbing one of the vile veggies straight through.

"So how was school today, kiddo?" I asked.

"It was good."

"What did you do?" I asked. "Anything fun?"

"Yeah," Cecilia said.

"Well what did you do?"

"I played jump rope at recess," she said, "and we had an assembly."

"Good," I said. "And what did you learn?"

"We learned about rocks," Cecilia said. "Sedminitary layers and stuff."

"Sedimentry," Gen corrected.

"Sedimentry," Cecilia repeated to me.

"Actually," I said, "it's sedimentary."

"Yeah, it's sedimentary, Mom."

"Are you sure?" Gen asked me.

"I wouldn't bet my life on it," I said, "but yeah."

I finished inhaling my food between sentences and leaned back from the table. Gen made a move like she was going to get up to clear my plate away. "I'll get it, honey," I said. "There's no need for you to get up with that belly you're lugging around. Stay off your feet as much as you can. That's what the doctor said, remember?"

148

"Where was that attitude when I was making dinner?" she asked, folding her arms across her body in a way that helped to support her swollen breasts.

"Why don't you go relax upstairs? Maybe lie down for a while. I'll take care of everything down here, and put this ragamuffin to bed." I rubbed a hand on Cecilia's head, ruining her hair.

"Daaaaaaaaad, quit it! You're making my hair all poofy."

"That sounds like a good idea to me," Gen said. She made her way up the stairs slowly, holding her lower back and the railing.

"Alright, kiddo!" I said to Cecilia. "Are you ready for some serious dish work?"

"I guess."

"Woah now, what's with the attitude?"

"I don't have attitude, Dad. It's not like I have to be excited about doing dishes."

"But you used to love doing dishes with me!"

"When I was six, maybe."

I took a look at my "little girl." She was still a short kid, even then when she was in the middle of a growth spurt. Knobby knees and elbows connected her lanky framework together. Her long, knotty brown hair would always be "poofy," even when I didn't mess it up. Everything about her indicated a child of eight, but when she opened that mouth, I could have been talking to a twenty year old, for all I knew. She spoke so smart and proper, qualities that must have come from Gen's side of the family. Luckily, Cecilia hadn't quite received the snobbish aspect of their speech, even if it sounded like it sometimes. It wasn't a snobbish quality that I confused with attitude, it was just my girl becoming a teenager before her time.

"Sorry, you're still my little girl. You bring the dishes over from the table and I'll do the washing. Deal?"

Cecilia grabbed dishes off the table and handed them to me lifelessly. I understood that part of being a premature teenage girl was hating everything, but I still wanted Cecilia to have a little fun with us at home. So I turned around with the retractable nozzle from the kitchen sink and sprayed her real good.

"Oh!" She was completely surprised for a second. In that second, I could see the gears working in her head. She was trying to decide whether to be angry or not. "You are TOTALLY going to get it."

She picked her cup up off the table, still half-full of water. When she splashed me in the face with it, I remember being happy that she could take herself less serious sometimes.

We finished cleaning up the dishes, cleaned the mess we had made, and then went upstairs. Cecilia went through her bedtime routine, and I said, "Ok, fifteen minutes of reading, then you have to turn your lights off. Don't tell Mom, she'll kill me." I winked while I closed her door.

"So what did the doctor say about your mother?" Gen asked me when I came into the bedroom.

I walked over and rested my cheek on her belly, listening to our little baby boy rolling around in amniotic fluid just on the other side of Gen.

"The good news," I said, "is that she doesn't need to be hospitalized." I picked my head up from Gen's warm skin. "Actually, the doctor said it would probably be best if we kept her in as much of a normal routine as possible. So she should continue living in her house."

"Well it's good that she gets to stay home," Gen said. "Right?"

"Yeah. Because it only happened once, the doc said he wasn't too worried yet."

"Did he say what caused it?" Gen asked.

"He said that it could have been a couple of things," I said. "This kind of mental breakdown is usually associated with stroke victims." I was happy for the chance to talk about my mother's problem in terms of the science behind the issue. It was actually the only way I could talk about her problem without breaking down. "Basically what he said was that when a vein in the brain pops—when someone has a stroke—the blood pools and builds up pressure in the skull. This damages the...shit, what was that called? Some sort of sensory system or something like that...and that damage will often cause people's memories to move backwards."

"In the case of my mother," I continued, "after doing a couple of tests on her, the doctor said it looked like it was likely that one or several of the veins going to her brain became inflamed. They didn't burst, but it is possible that — if the veins were somehow irritated and expanded — they could put just enough pressure on the inside of her skull to...hmm...confuse Mom's sense of time. This kind of thing could be caused by stress."

I started to burrow my way under the covers. "If you ask me," I said, "I think this whole thing happened because Uncle Preston was giving her a hard time about what to do with Fred. I don't think it's a coincidence that he talked to her earlier in the day. That's enough pressure for all of us."

"Well don't worry about it," Gen said. "It sounds like your mom's going to be fine. We just have to keep her away from the Fred thing, and make sure nothing upsets her. And if she has to, she can always move in with us for a while. She can have the baby's room and we'll just keep the baby in here with us for a little while longer than we did with Cecilia."

"Thank you so much," I said. "You're the best. Goodnight, sweetie."

"Goodnight, Paul," Gen said.

I closed my eyes.

"Oh, Paul?"

"Mmm?"

"Will you get me something to eat?"

2.

BOXING UP THE LIVES OF JOHN AND SALLY

Gen's parents called us soon after we woke up the next day. They said there was a problem and they needed us to come over. So we closed the bookshop for the day, dropped Cecilia off at school, and made the drive.

When we got to the house, both John and Sally were waiting for us. They were sitting on their front steps with their heads in their hands. The grinding of my Buick's wheels on the asphalt grabbed their attention. They brought their heads up, squinting as if they had been looking into their dark palms for so long that their eyes had to readjust to light. Sally waved at us—well, she waved at Gen, anyway—and John nodded his head in our general direction.

"Hey guys," Gen said while moving up the walkway to the house. "What's up?"

"Oh, nothing," John said. He smiled at his daughter.

"Nothing?" Sally said. "Ha! That's good for a laugh. We're ruined! That is what's up."

"Keep your voice down," John said. "Or even better, let's move inside, shall we?"

"Yes," Sally agreed. "Let's."

Gen and I followed them inside. Their foyer was filled with boxes of all sizes. Apparently, corrugated-brown was "in." With Gen's parents leading the way, we sidestepped the brown into the kitchen. John and Sally took their chairs at the head and foot of the table, so Gen and I sat next to each other somewhere between them.

"So what's going on?" Gen asked.

"Well…" John said.

"The bank is foreclosing on our house," Sally said.

"What!" I said.

"Why?" Gen asked.

"To put it simply," Sally said, "there was a series of unfortunate investments." She stared, but was not looking, at John. "We owe money and have nothing to pay with except for the house." She pointed a finger at John. "This is like the Caymans all over again!" she shouted.

"Take it easy, Mom," Gen said. "We'll figure something out."

"Yeah," I said. "You can always stay with us for a while."

"I think we have to," Sally said. "You'll help us move our things, right Paul?"

My jaw dropped—and I mean fell so hard it almost broke off—and Gen had to kick me under the table to pull me together. "Of course I will," I said.

•••

The first step in the moving process was securing more boxes—lots and lots of boxes. Gen and I were driving home to collect a good thirty of the thousands of boxes we had been holding on to at the bookshop, waiting for the time when we were feeling proactive enough to go recycle them. Most of the boxes we had flattened and put in the backyard—letting them sit in the rain and snow until they had congealed into corrugated blocks, rendering them useless—but we also had a backroom filled floor to ceiling and wall to wall with brown. The rest of the boxes we had

153

acquired over the years had been thoroughly destroyed by the playing of Cecilia.

We drove for ten minutes without a word to each other when Gen turned to me and said, "It was nice of you to offer them a place, but how are we going to do this?"

I drummed my fingers on the steering wheel, feigning deep thought. "I don't really know," I said. "All I was doing was being nice. I didn't really think they would take the offer." Trees whizzed by on the side of the road and we passed a man pulled over for a bathroom break. "I guess they'll take the baby's room for now," I said, rubbing her stomach with special attention given to her new outie bellybutton.

"What about your mother?" Gen asked. "What if she can't take care of herself for too much longer?"

"We'll figure something out," I said. I gripped the wheel a little tighter, turning my knuckles white like I used to do when Jackson took me driving as a ten year old. "Maybe we'll start looking into a few nursing homes for her or something."

We got back with Gen leaning her head against the window for the rest of the trip, staring at the passing view with the heel of her hand shoved into her cheek. We got out of the car and we were all business, carrying boxes out and putting them in the trunk. We did, after all, have experience with moving.

•••

"Be very careful with that!" Gen's mother yelled at me. "That vase is a priceless Brydmoth family heirloom!"

"Don't worry," I said. "I have it under control."

This was the fourth carload I was packing that day, and most of their stuff had been picked up earlier on by a storage facility that I was helping them pay for.

I thought they would be too proud to even consider moving in with us. If I had known they would take me up on my offer, I never would have suggested it. I still had my own mother to worry about, and her situation was more dire than theirs was.

154

But I stuffed the priceless Brydmoth family heirloom into the back seat between the ottoman and the box of fine china.

"Paul, please!" Gen's mother said when she heard the clink of porcelain on porcelain. "Be careful. This is all we have left." She turned and walked back into the house, and I could see that her shoulders were heaving on the way in, as if she were crying, as if she had the ability to cry.

If Frankenstein's monster were here, he would have said, "If she can express real emotions, then I must have the capacity for feelings, too!"

I closed the car door on the next to last load. Carload number four. I walked towards the house to tell John and Sally about load number five.

"Hey guys?" I said, poking my head into the house.

"Yes?" John said.

"I'm going to take this last trip over to my house and then I'm coming back to get you two, ok?"

"Sounds fine," he said.

3.

I BET MY DEAD FATHER WOULD LIKE A SCREWDRIVER, TOO

John and Sally were making life at the Morrison Bookshop and Café a living and breathing hell. They had only been living with Gen and me for about a week and already I had had enough. And I know that I give them a bad rap, and they aren't as bad as I make them out to be, but I had taken all I could. Unfortunately, there was nothing I could do and the best defense was to curl up in a ball and shut up and take all of their abuses.

"Paul!" Gen's mother screamed from the kitchen.

I was sitting at the register behind the coffee bar. The few people sitting with books and drinking coffee looked up when they heard the yell.

"Yeah?" I said. The customers went back to their business.

"You don't have any orange juice left," she said, "and I wanted to make a screwdriver."

This caught the customers' attention again.

"Make John go get some," I said.

156

"Paul!"

"Fine," I said. "Will you send Gen out here then?"

"Just a miiinuuuute," Sally said in a sing-song voice.

Gen came out and I told her I was running to the deli real fast. "Watch the register for me?" I asked. "I'll be back soon."

"Sure thing, darling," she said. She gave me a kiss on the cheek. "You are so good to my parents."

"Well I'm also this close to killing them," I said. I held my thumb and forefinger up, as close together as I could without actually having them touch.

•••

When I got back with Sally's orange juice, Gen told me that my mom had called while I was gone. "She sounded real far away," Gen said, "but it may have just been a bad connection."

I tried to call her. The phone rang and rang. There was no answering machine, so I let it go on ringing for a while.

"I'm going to drive over there," I said. "She's not picking up."

"Ok," Gen said. "If you have to go, you have to go."

I hung up and pulled my jacket on again. I hoped Mom had just gone out for a while.

•••

I pulled into Mom's driveway. Her car was in its regular spot, so she was probably home. Maybe she just hadn't heard the phone. There was water coming out from under the front door and I started to panic. I fumbled with my keys and finally opened the front door. "Hey Ma," I came in screaming. "Are you home?" With my first step inside, I hit water. There it was, slowly cascading down the stairs and pooling by the doorway.

There was no answer for a minute. "Ma?"

"Hello, Paul," she said. "I'm in the kitchen!"

"I'll be there in a minute!" I walked up the stairs and found the water coming from under the bathroom door. I opened it up and I could hear the deafening rush of water before I saw the bathtub overflowing. I turned the water off and tiptoed my way through the water, into the kitchen.

I walked over and stood by the table. Mom was busying herself in front of the stove, making some rice to go with the lamb in the oven. She was hunched over her work, wearing her plain, pastel-yellow dress. "Honey?" she said.

"Mom, did you know that the tub—"

"Will you be a dear and set the table for us?"

"Sure thing," I said. "Did you know that you left the tub on?"

"Oh my goodness, I completely forgot. You know, I was going to take a bath ten minutes ago, but then I remembered I had already started dinner. I must've forgot to turn it off."

I grabbed a couple of plates out of the cabinet by the stove, maneuvering around my mother, and put them on the table. She was busy stirring the rice.

"I'll go clean it up in a minute," I said. "So how's everything going? Gen told me you called the bookshop looking for me." I pulled a couple of forks and knives from the drawer under the sink.

"Oh, I did," she said. "I wanted to know when you would come over for dinner."

I put the silverware down on the table. "Well," I said, "here I am."

"Here you are," she echoed. She pulled something off of the spice rack and gave the rice a healthy dose.

"Did we make plans to have dinner tonight?" I asked.

"Ha ha," she laughed. "You're joking, right?"

"Yeah," I said, "I guess I forgot. Things have been pretty hectic lately with Gen's parents."

"What do you mean?" she asked.

"Nothing, Don't worry about it." I didn't want to upset her. "So what did you do today?" I took two glasses from the cabinet closest to the fridge.

"Well," she said. "This morning I went to the library for a little while. I found this fascinating book called

158

Coming to America: The Story of Immigration. This Betsy Maestro wrote it."

"Never heard of her," I said. I put two napkins on the table and sat down again.

"Well I think it's meant for younger kids," she said. "Morty might like it."

"Ha ha, yeah," I said. "He's still reading at a fourth grade level."

"Now don't you give your brother a hard time," she said. She moved the rice from the active burner and switched the stovetop off. "My parents must have had a real tough time making the trip to this country."

"Yeah," I said. I picked up my fork and played with it, poking my finger with one of the tines. "And what else did you do today?"

"This afternoon," she said, "after I called you, I went to the supermarket to do a little shopping. On the way back, I decided to stop off at your Aunt Hallie's house. It was a little out of the way, but I was glad to talk with her for a while."

"Oh," I said. "I was a little worried when I called you back and no one picked up. I thought something might have happened."

"No," she said over her shoulder. She scooped the rice into a bowl. "I was just out and about. Nothing to worry about. Everything's been going fine. I feel fine. The tub was just a mistake."

"That's a relief to hear," I said. I spoke too soon.

She turned towards me to put the rice on the table. "Paul," she said. "When I ask you to set the table, I want you to set the table for everyone. Don't be lazy and just put dishes out for you and me."

Damn it. It was time for Mom and me to take another trip to Dr. Horowitz's office at St. John's Memorial.

159

4.

ANOTHER TRIP TO DR. HOROWITZ'S OFFICE AT ST. JOHN'S MEMORIAL

I took Mom home with me after her relapse because I was afraid to leave her alone. We came through the front of the bookshop and the chimes over the door banged together. "Ding! Ding! Ding!"

"Paul?" Gen said.

"Yeah, it's me, honey." I lead my mom through the aisles of used books, past the copies of Kafka and Chekhov.

"How's your Mom doing?" Gen asked from behind the register in the next room

We stepped into the café. "I brought her over to spend the night," I said. "I guess Mom'll take Cecilia's bed and Cecilia can sleep with us for tonight."

"Oh," Gen said. "Hello, Ruth. How are you doing?"

"Fine, dear," Mom said.

"Cecilia?" I yelled.

"Yeah Dad," she said from upstairs.

"Come down here and take Grandma to your room," I said. "She's sleeping over tonight."

"Ok." Her little feet came tromping down the stairs. I never understood how one little girl could make so much noise just walking.

"Hey Gram-ma!" Cecilia said. "You're staying over with me tonight?"

"No," I said. "You're going to sleep with me and Mommy tonight so Grandma has enough room. Your bed wouldn't be big enough for both of you."

"Come on, Gram-ma," Cecilia said. "I wanna show you the art I did in school this week."

"Ok, ok," Mom said. "I'm coming. Slow down, I can't climb the stairs as fast as you can."

The two girls disappeared into the kitchen and went upstairs, leaving Gen and me with the cash register.

"What happened?" Gen asked. "Is everything alright?"

"Mom had another one of her dinner episodes," I said. "She was cooking for five with no one else home again. And when I got to the house, the tub was overflowing and made a mess of the house. I spent an hour and a half cleaning it all up."

"Oh no," Gen said.

"I'm taking her to see Dr. Horowitz again tomorrow," I said. "I already made the appointment."

"Paul, what are we going to do if she can't live by herself anymore?" Gen asked.

"I don't know," I said. "I guess I'll start looking into nursing homes or something. We sure as hell don't have any space here."

"Language, Paul," Gen said.

"Sorry, I forgot."

"It's ok. Just be mindful of that around the baby," she said, rubbing her belly.

•••

"And this is the second time that your mother, um, slipped into the past?" Dr. Horowitz asked.

"Yeah."

161

"Alright," the doctor said. "Great." He made some notes on his clipboard. "Well, after examining your mother again, I found nothing conclusively wrong with her. I can only assume that whatever triggered the episode was, once again, stress-related. Do you have any idea what could have caused her to feel the sort of pressure needed to inflame a vein leading to the brain?"

"I really have no clue," I said. "She said she went to the library and had a visit with her sister, but that was all she did. It didn't sound like a stressful day at all."

"Mm hmm, mm hmm," Dr. Horowitz said. He rubbed his chin and looked over his notes. "Well here is what I suggest. I suggest that Ruth be placed in a nursing home. I wouldn't consider her case to be an emergency, but the sooner she is placed under the care of trained professionals, the better. In the meantime, she should be fine living by herself as long as you check in on her regularly. I'll give you a list of places to call when you leave, and you can figure out which one you feel most comfortable with."

"Ok," I said. I peeked in on the room where my mother was sitting on the examination table. "Doc, are you sure she's going to be ok by herself?"

"She should be," he said, "assuming she can stay away from stress."

5.

THREE FINGERS, WE'RE SHIT OUT OF LUCK

"And this room is our Rec. Center, where our patients can do anything from watching TV to playing a board game or a game of cards with their fellow residents."

I had been following the uniformed nurse around for an hour on this tour of the Blackberry Nursing Home. This was the third nursing home I had visited in the past two days. It was just outside of Great Barrington, and so far, it looked to be the most promising.

"You can step into the room and look around if you like," the nurse said.

Across from the door, there was a wall of windows that looked out on the lake in the nursing home's backyard. On one side of the room, there were a few couches and lounging chairs positioned in a semi-circle around a television. There was one old woman crocheting and sitting so close to the TV screen that the blue light looked like it was warming her face.

163

On the other side of the room, there were a few tables with chairs around them. There were some elderly gentlemen playing cribbage. Behind them, on the wall, were shelves covered in board games. The nurse wasn't kidding: you could do anything from watching TV to playing board games and cards here, as long as those were the only two options on the spectrum.

I nodded my head at the nurse. I had seen enough. This was a fine establishment.

"All right sir," she said. "If you'll follow me into my office, we can discuss your mother's possible future here at Blackberry."

On the way to her office, we passed the dining hall. The first place I visited, "Tanner's Home for the Elderly," had a dining room that looked like it came straight out of Ken Kesey's *One Flew Over the Cuckoo's Nest* (now on sale in the Morrison Bookshop's used-books section for four bucks). There was a caged room at the back where nurses prepared the food and medication for the patients. When I asked the nurse why Tanner's Home felt it was necessary to have the cage, she replied that "Occasionally, a patient can get dangerous, and we like to take every precaution that we can to ensure everyone's safety here." Tanner's was out: any place where the nurses didn't feel safe was not a place I felt safe leaving my mother.

The second place I visited was smaller than the other two. There were fewer patients, which was good, but the building felt claustrophobic to me. And there was no real space for my mother to spend time outside, so I crossed it off the list. The price for that place was right, but I didn't want to compromise my mother's comfort because I found a deal I could only almost afford anyway.

The Blackberry nurse opened the door to her office and waved me over to a chair by her desk.

"All right, Mr. Morrison," she said. "Let's get right to it. Here at Blackberry, we charge by the month." She scribbled on a piece of paper and handed it over to me. "This is what we generally ask for."

"I can't afford that much," I said.

164

"Sometimes," she said, "we can make arrangements for those who can't afford the full price." She cleared her throat. "But we can't go too much lower than that figure there, I'm afraid. We have to cover costs and wages, at the least."

"I understand," I said. "I guess I'll get in touch with you as soon as I figure out how to get this money together."

•••

After my day's worth of looking at nursing homes for Mom, I was sitting at a table in the café. It was eleven o'clock, and we had been closed for a couple of hours. After "Blackberry," I went and ogled a few more facilities that were well out of my price range.

"There you are," Gen said. "What are you doing down here so late?"

I put down the papers I had been shuffling and squeezed the bridge of my nose with my fingers. "I've just been looking through our bank account information. I'm trying to figure out how the hell we're supposed to pay for Mom's home. It's not looking too good."

Gen stepped behind my chair and wrapped her arms around me, resting her belly on the back of my chair. She looked over my shoulder at the paperwork. "We'll figure out a way," she said. She gave me a kiss on the cheek.

I started to cry. It was the same kind of cry I had when Morty came to visit me here in jail. It was a cry of frustration, of wanting to help someone I loved but not being able to.

Gen held me closer, snuggling my wet eyes into her neck. She rubbed my head and made little shushing sounds. "What about the house? Do you think you could get a good price for it?"

"I thought about that," I said, sniffling, "but there's a couple of problems I have with that." I started counting off the reasons with my fingers. One finger: "First, I don't want to sell the house without telling Morty. I think he wants to move there at some point." Two fingers. "Second, and more important, we haven't finished paying off the mortgage yet. We still have three years to go, which means we

165

wouldn't get all that much for it in the end, with interest rates what they are. It's just a short term solution." Three fingers. "And third, I don't know how long Mom's going to need to stay at the nursing home. If they say it's safe for her to go home, I want her to have a home to come back to." I started sobbing between my words. "And I thought abou-oo-t taking out a mortgage o-on the bookshop, but the bank said-d no." I took a deep breath.

"You're a good son, Paul..." She touched my cheek with her fingertips, brushing away the tears, and used my chair to push herself upright. "...but you're not in this alone. Go talk to Morty and see if he can help out at all. I'm sure he has a little saved away that he can help with."

"I'm not counting on Morty to have any money saved away."

"Well maybe Preston can help then," she said. "He's always talking about helping the family. This is a great opportunity for him to finally back that up in a constructive manner."

"That's true, but I wouldn't bet my life on him helping out. That guy is a whole lot of hot air." I took another look at all the paper on the table in front of me, remembering that no matter how I tried, all the little shavings here and there would never add up to enough.

I thought about how I might have to consider selling the bookshop and how that was the last thing on earth I wanted to do. "You know what? That's exactly what I'll do. I'll go talk to Uncle Preston tomorrow and see if he can help us out."

6.

TALKING TO A WHOLE LOT OF HOT AIR

I got out of the car and used the knocker on the front door.

Aunt Hallie opened it up. "Paul! What a nice surprise."

"Hey Aunt Hallie," I said. "Is Uncle Preston home?"

"He sure is. Just follow me." She led me through the living room and into the "TV room."

Preston was sprawled out on the couch, staring at the flashing glow of the screen.

"Hey Uncle Pre—"

"Up-bup-bup," he said, holding up a finger.

"He's always like this," Aunt Hallie whispered at me, "when the TV's on."

I stood there until a commercial came on.

"Hey Paul," he said. "What's up?"

"Oh, the usual stuff."

"Good to hear," he said. "And how's your mother doing?"

"She's ok," I said. I scratched the back of my head. "That's actually why I came to talk to you."

"Oh?"

"Yeah," I said. "I took her to the doctor's again."

"Oh no," Aunt Hallie said.

Preston sat up on the couch and muted the TV. "And what did they say?"

I sat down on the couch next to him. "It's not looking good," I said. "She's at home right now, but I have to get her into a nursing home real soon."

"Mmm..." he mused. He put the remote control down on the coffee table. "Have you started looking yet?"

"I've seen a few places, but they're all out of my price range."

"Ah, so it's money you're after." Preston frowned and looked at the ceiling like he was pretending to think.

"I just need a little help," I said, stroking his ego. "I didn't know who else to turn to."

"Well I'm glad you came to me first," he said. He leaned back against the cushions. "Unfortunately, I don't really know how much I can help."

"Why not?"

"I just finished paying for most of Howie's law school," he said, "and I still have a few loans out there to pay for the rest. I'll give what I can, but that won't be much."

"Have you asked Morty?" Aunt Hallie asked me.

"Morty won't have any money," I said. "You know him. Money goes in one pocket and out the other."

"Hmm." Preston sucked air through his teeth, making that steam-release sound. "Another option is Fred, I guess. We can still file a lawsuit against him." I laugh when I think about how he just tossed that out there, like he had just come up with the idea then and there.

"No lawsuit, Preston! Come on!" I shook my head. "But there is an idea in there... Maybe I'll go down to his office and ask if he can help out at all."

"That's a great idea," Aunt Hallie said.

168

"Yeah," I said. "His letter said that he was doing pretty well for himself, so maybe he'll have a little dough to spare."

"I'm just saying it's not too late to sue," Uncle Preston chimed in.

"And I'm just saying that is the last thing I want to do." I went home, set on my course of action. I would go that weekend, I decided. No need in wasting time.

7.

LITTLE JACK IS CAUSE ENOUGH FOR POSTPONEMENT

Gen woke me up in the middle of the night, shaking my shoulder.

"Paul," she whispered. "Come on, wake up."

"Unghh," I said. "What is it, sweetie?"

"Come on Paul, get up," she said. "I'm having contractions. We have to go to the hospital."

"Now?" I said.

"Yeah."

So we both threw on some clothes, grabbed the overnight bag we kept packed in the closet for just this situation, and Gen headed out to the car. I poked my head into the room that was supposed to be for our baby on the way out and said, "John? Sally?"

"Mmmmuat is it?" Gen's dad said.

"We're going to the hospital. Gen's having her contractions. Keep an eye on Cecilia and I'll give you a call sometime soon?"

"Ok."

It looked like my trip to New York to talk to Fred would be postponed.

•••

Gen gave birth to a little boy. It took her a good ten hours to squeeze that little sucker out of there, but she did it. And once all of that goo was wiped off and once Gen was done holding him, I got a chance to take a close look at that little pink ball. He was swaddled in a hospital-issue blanket in a way that made him feel like a shrink-wrapped bundle in my arms. It honestly felt like I could have bounced the kid on the ground a few times. But he was so tiny and he felt warm through the layers of his artificial womb.

Gen looked over at me in a goofy, drugged up way and smiled. Her hair was everywhere, but in the front it was matted down by dried sweat. Her right ear was buried in the pillow, so her head was slightly tilted away from me. Her arms were at her sides, and she looked like she couldn't lift them again after having held the baby for a few minutes. "So," she said. "What do you think?"

"He's a keeper. Unless you want to put him back?"

"Oh-ho no. He's not 'going back' anywhere," she said.

The doctor was fiddling around with Gen's monitors and IV's, making sure everything was in order. "Ok," he said, taking a clipboard from the end of the bed. "What's this little fellow's name?"

"Huh, I haven't even thought about that too much!" Gen said. "I like the name Gregory, but I don't know..."

"How about Jack?" I said. "You know, name him after my father?"

"That sounds fine to me," she said. "Yeah, Little Jack." She looked at the baby in my arms as if looking for visual confirmation. "I can get used to that."

Little Jack said, "Eeh," like he could go either way on his new name.

I handed Little Jack off to one of the nurses. She threw him in a pushcart and whisked him away to the nursery. I swore I could see him bounce once before settling into his little stroller.

171

I turned to Gen. She was already asleep. I guess that was fair: she did do the large part of the work, and my job in the whole operation was definitely the fun part. So I stepped out into the hallway with the intention of heading towards the nursery. I remembered from Cecilia's birth that it was pretty fun to look through the glass with the other dads at the little baby menagerie. And why not? I certainly didn't want to go back home to hang out with Gen's parents.

The doctor saw me in the hallway. "Ah, Mr. Morrison?"

"Oh, Doctor." I shook his hand. "Thank you so much. You did a fantastic job." And I guess he did. Although, during the delivery, it sounded like all he did was tell my wife to keep on pushing over and over again. But he definitely earned his money when he held little Jack by his ankles like a dead duck and performed the ritual act of child abuse that accompanies all births. Little Jack started crying after the spank on the bottom, and he was officially finished being born. "I was just headed over to the nursery," I said. "Could you point me in the right direction please?"

"Well of course. Just head right down this hall," he said, pointing his finger, "and make a left at the end of the hall," he said, hooking his finger left, "and then it will be on your right." He let his arm fall back to his side. "But I was hoping that you could follow me first, and that we could discuss your bill?"

"Um...sure."

"Ok, follow me."

Gen's doctor led me to the nurses' station in the middle of the floor by the elevators. "We need to take down Mr. Morrison's billing information, so it's time for you to finally put in a little work around here, ok?" he said to the nurse behind the computer monitor.

She rolled her eyes as if she were used to the doctor's comments and began typing on the keyboard. While she prepared the bill information on the computer, the doctor stood behind her, looking over her shoulder and straight down her shirt. He looked up and saw me staring, and he winked at me and put a finger to his lips in a silent *shh* sound.

My opinion of him changed instantly. He was no longer the mastermind behind Little Jack's birth in my eyes. Now, he was the guy who had seen my wife naked on numerous occasions. No one is supposed to see my wife naked except for me, and that little wink pissed me off to no end. There was a part of me that said, "Don't worry! If you beat the shit out of him, he won't have to go far for treatment."

Lucky for him, the nurse interrupted these thoughts. "Ok, Mr. Morrison... assuming your wife stays the requisite two days with us—which is usually how long it takes to recuperate after a vaginal birth—your bill will come out to..." She click-clacked away at the keyboard for another second. "...just about eight thousand dollars. That's about six thousand for the doctor here and another two thousand for the hospital's bill."

Ouch. My fiscal disaster just kept on rolling. "Ok," I said. "I guess I'll just put that on my credit card." One of the disadvantages of working for yourself was the lack of medical insurance. That was also the big problem with getting my mom into a nursing home.

Why oh why didn't I just buy some medical insurance? That's the first thing I'll do when I get out of jail. If I get out of jail.

But that's when I decided that the sooner I could get in touch with Fred, the better. I made a promise to myself: that I would drive down to New York City to talk to Fred next Tuesday. I would probably have to close the bookshop for the day, but at least I could be fairly certain that Fred would be at his office in the Flatiron Building.

8.

THE RACCOON THAT HAD SEEN BETTER DAYS

And so I set out early Tuesday morning in the 7-YEAR OLD BUICK, bound for New York City. I had never been there before, but from the stories I've heard, I wasn't looking forward to it:

Gen told me about the time that she went down there with her parents for one of her father's business trips. After a fine dinner, they had left the restaurant to take a cab back to their hotel. They were standing on the curb when some guy ran by and took her mother's purse. He took it right off of her shoulder!

Jackson had once told me about the time he went to the big city, when he was twenty-two. He was riding on the subway when two men began screaming at each other. They exchanged blows, and the brawlers rolled up and down the subway car. They knocked over a stroller on their way!

Uncle Preston told me the story about when he pulled up to a parking lot shoved between a couple of skyscrapers. There was a guy standing on the curb. Jackson asked if he worked at the lot, and the man said yes. Preston asked how much it cost, and the guy said five bucks an hour. Preston gave him two twenties, and said he wanted to park for six hours. The guy said he would get some change and open the gate for him. He started to walk towards the shack by the gate, where another attendant was standing patiently. All of a sudden, the guy took off and turned the corner, gone forever!

Preston pulled up to the shack and said, "So, that guy didn't work here, hunh?"

"I'm the only one working here today," the guy in the shack answered, shrugging his shoulders.

So when I packed my bag (in case I had to spend the night) and threw it in the car, I made sure to chain my wallet to my pants. I left at five in the morning, hoping to beat the Hartford rush hour and arrive in New York City after their rush "hour" ended. ("Hour" is in quotation marks for NYC because, as I discovered, it was much longer than just one hour.)

I had mapped out my route carefully, memorizing it so I wouldn't have to keep looking at the piece of paper it was written on while I was driving. I would get myself on to the Mass. Pike (I-90) heading east, take that to I-84 West, take that to I-91 South, to I-95 South, and then, when I-95 turned into the Cross-Bronx Expressway, head into Manhattan. Some would say I should have taken the Taconic going south, but I liked the roomy lanes of I-90. Once I was in Manhattan, I decided, I would scramble around until I made it to the Flatiron Building—which is on 23rd Street and Broadway—and then I would find a parking spot (making sure to put the Club on my steering wheel) and find my brother.

I took the thirty minutes of empty road I had on the Mass. Pike and practiced what I would say to Fred when I finally got there. I figured I would start off with some kind of hello, ask him how he was doing and all of that, and then see if he would ask me how things were on my end. If he didn't, I would find some way to bring up mom's health issues on my own. This was the pitch I decided on:

"Yeah, Mom's been pretty sick lately. Not physically, but she's starting to lose it up here a little." I would point at my head then. "It's getting to the point where she won't be able to live by herself any more. I would have her move in with *me*," and I would accentuate that last word, "but Gen's parents just recently moved in with us and we have a new baby—a little boy named Jack—and there just isn't enough space."

He'd go into a whole act where he says something like, "Oh, that's too bad."

And then I'd say, "So I came down here to ask if you could pay for Mom's nursing home, or at least pay for part. You know, since you did sell the company behind our backs and all. Uncle Preston wants us to sue you, but I've been holding them all back from that whole messy path. And anyway, I would appreciate it all so much."

At which point I was certain that he would find it in his heart to just start throwing money at me without any further questions.

I went through the tollbooth and used exact change to pay. And it wasn't luck that I had exact change. I was thoroughly prepared for every aspect of this trip: I had spent an hour flicking myself off in the mirror so it wouldn't surprise me to see it on the road; and I had caught up on all the lingo, like "fuggedabahdit" (definition: forget about it, as in "You know how you saw me kill that man? Fuggedabahdit!"). I studied a lot, in fact, and I knew the Flatiron Building used to be the tallest building in Manhattan. I knew that the definition of a "New York Minute" was the amount of time between a traffic light turning green and the first car in line getting honked at. I knew that, for the most part, even numbered streets ran east and odd numbered west. I knew that Fifth Avenue was also called Madison Avenue; that Houston Street was pronounced differently than the city in Texas; that St. Marks Place can be found, inexplicably and inconsecutively, between Tenth Street and Ninth Street; I knew that you should never, EVER get into an unlicensed cab and only get into the yellow ones with the medallions on the hood; and that subway cars were used as public bathrooms and thus should be treated that way. I knew that in Manhattan, there was no such thing as walking; that pleasantries were best expressed through muttered curse words; that everyone thought their pizza place was the best one in the city; that doormen demand more respect than they gave to the people they hold the door open for; that it wasn't socially acceptable to start a conversation with someone you didn't know; that pigeons are a very dangerous and calculating species. And I knew that—above all else—there was no one in that city I could trust.

I pulled onto I-84. I started to think about Fred. It had been two months since we got his letter, and the last time I had seen him, he was twenty-six years old. More than seven years had passed since then. A lot can happen in seven years. A lot *had* happened in seven years. I started a bookshop and café, Mom had gotten used to life alone, Morty was married, and life had moved on. I'm sure that the same was true for Fred.

The Fred I remembered was a recluse. He would sit in his room for hours on end, just reading my books while the rest of us were downstairs, still sitting and talking an hour after we had finished eating dinner. When Morty and I would go out drinking, Fred always found an excuse to stay at home. He always said that he had to get up early for work the next day, or that his stomach was already feeling a little upset, or that he had already drank too much at dinner. The truth was that he just never felt like going out. He didn't particularly like any of us, but as long as he had a room to lock himself away in, he was fine living under the same roof as us. He was always close, but never in contact.

There were times, before Jackson had announced that I was the Morrison heir to everyone at Cristina's Restaurant, where Fred and Morty and I were almost close. As rebellious teenagers, both Morty and I were afraid of Jackson. But that fear was not translated into respect. So until we grew up and we weren't so scared of our father, Morty and I shared a common enemy with Fred.

177

We would sit around in the living room on days when Jackson would stay at the store late and when Mom was out shopping or something. Fred would turn to Morty and say, "Did you see the vein on his forehead when he was yelling at you today? I thought it was going to burst!"

"Yeah," Morty would say. "But you didn't see it as close up as I did. I saw it throbbing!"

"Oh, gross!"

"I can't believe," I would say, "that it was just because you dropped a tin of SPAM. Who would eat that stuff anyway?"

"Seriously," Fred would say. "Any one of us could run that place better than he does, I'd bet. Think about all of the wasted space that the Dr. Pepper takes up. That drink is gross!"

"He likes it, though," Morty would say. And in Jackson's voice (or our impression of it, which was just a deep, authoritative voice): "And boys, that's all that matters."

I remembered when Fred would come out on bike rides with Morty and me. We would speed around town like a group of ruffians, rebellious as we pleased. We would spit on the ground and just leave the phlegm there for someone else to deal with. When Fred was eighteen—I was fourteen and Morty was twelve—he bought us a pack of cigarettes while we were out cruising the streets. He lit one up and took the first drag. He was halfway through exhaling the smoke when he went into a fit of coughing. He tried to pass it off, the cigarette in his fingertips moving up and down with his arm every time he coughed. I managed to pull it out of his hand without getting burned and took a drag for myself. I blew the smoke out quickly and my eyes started to tear. I quietly coughed twice and passed it on to Morty. He took a drag, but when he blew out, there was no smoke. A minute later, he turned green—serious green, like the color of grass—and he clutched his stomach. He got grass-green puke stains all over his shoes, and Fred and I just had to laugh at him, so we did.

But as we got older, Morty and I found out that the vein on Jackson's forehead wasn't as scary as we used to think, and we grew to respect our father. Our time as rebellious teenagers was over, and we had lost our bond with Fred.

Because Fred never really grew out of his rebellious stage. For whatever reason, he would always hate Jackson, and as long as he hated Jackson, he hated anyone who could get along with him. And that was a long list of people, because Jackson was a very friendly man.

But I doubted that this would be the Fred that I would see. Jackson had died seven years ago, and Fred was thirty-three years old. I assumed that Fred had matured, but the truth was, I had no real clue what I was getting myself into and who I was getting into it with. Would I see the side of Fred that came to my rescue when another boy at school tried to beat me up or would I see the side of Fred that used to pin me down with his knees on my arms and slap my face with both of his hands until I cried? Or would it be some sort of strange mixture of the two?

At Hartford, I took the left exit onto I-91 South. Now, there were a couple of other cars on the road with me, and I started to think about my new baby boy. Little Jack. I wondered what his life would be like. I thought about what kind of friends he would have, and if Great Barrington would be as good for him as it seemed to be for Cecilia. And how would he and Cecilia get along? She was eight years older than him, and that would be an interesting dynamic. Would she mother him, or simply ignore him? Was it better for her to have a brother who was so much younger than her or would she have been better off being the only child? I thought about this while I kept one eye on the road.

When I left to go to New York and talk to Fred, I left my mother at her house by herself, and I left Gen with her parents, Cecilia, and the baby to take care of. I pressed down a little more on the gas with my foot, but the wheel started shaking when I hit sixty-five. The 7-YEAR OLD

179

BUICK was setting the pace of this trip, and sixty was the fastest she would let me go.

A sign overhead said it was two miles until the exit for I-95 South. I moved over to the right lane, without really checking to see if the lanes I moved into were clear of other cars. Then, a mile from my exit, an animal—I think it was a raccoon—jumped in front of my car. I quickly began to move over one lane to my left when a car honked its horn to let me know it was already in the spot I was trying to occupy. Inches from that car and still moving closer, I did the only thing I could do: I turned the wheel quickly to the right to avoid the accident.

Instead, I hit the raccoon head on with my front right tire. The front of the car bumped up into the air, and when it landed again, the car was completely out of my control. I slammed on the breaks, but this sent the 7-YEAR OLD BUICK into a roll. I held on for dear life as the pavement, which was once beneath me, became the sky, then switched back and forth between the two: sky, ground, sky and ground, the car going round and up and over itself again and again. It finally came to a stop, and at that point, the definitive answer was that the pavement was indeed the sky. My head began to pound as all of the blood in my body rushed down to my scalp. I undid my seatbelt and fell into the roof of the car. I let myself out and looked at the wreckage.

The windows had all shattered, and it was then that I noticed all of the little cuts on my body. The hood of the car had crumpled, and it was then that I felt the bruises on my knees. The car was completely totaled. It was clear that the seatbelt had saved my life, and it was then that I noticed how much my left shoulder hurt.

The right front tire was still spinning. I looked in the road and saw the raccoon. I don't think CPR could have done anything for the little guy at that point: he was pretty crushed. Upon somewhat closer inspection, one of his eyes had popped out of the socket.

Further up the road, the car I had almost hit had pulled over, and there was a man walking towards me. "Are you ok?" he shouted when he was within shouting distance.

"I'm fine," I said when he came a little closer. "But I think the raccoon has seen better days."

"Can I give you a lift somewhere? A hospital or something?"

"No, I think I'll be fine," I said. I thought about it and decided that there was no reason to turn around at this point. "Actually, I could use a lift to Manhattan, if you're headed that way."

"I have an office in the Bronx," he said, "but I could drop you off by one of the subway stations. It's a short ride on the 5 train into Manhattan."

I grabbed my bag out of the back seat and we were on our way. The guy introduced himself, saying, "I'm Ron Frankton, by the way." And we shook hands. Ron Frankton, aside from his messy hair and the five o'clock shadow he was sporting at seven in the morning, looked to be all business. He had a serious face, anyway: dark brown eyes under scrunched eyebrows, a precisely angular nose, and thin lips that disappeared when he frowned. I threw my bag in his back seat next to his thin briefcase.

"I can't believe I saw that whole thing happen," he said. "That was wild."

"Yeah, I can't believe that I'm ok." I said that even as the throbbing in my left shoulder reminded me that I might not be ok at all.

He pulled an electric shaver from his glove compartment and adjusted his rearview mirror so he could look at himself. "I mean, that was a really close call." *Bzzz...* "You might have even been better off just bumping into me." He lifted his chin up and looked in the mirror to get that really tough-to-reach place where you always get razor burns, especially from an electric. "Although I must say, all things considered, I'm glad you didn't."

He kept on shaving, not really watching the road and getting hair all over his lap and I was quiet in my seat, nodding my head and occasionally saying, "Mmhmm,"

181

whenever he spoke. Twice I was forced to speak, and both times I said, "Look out!" once when we started to drift over into another car, and once when we were approaching the tollbooth for 95 just on the other side of the New York border.

"I work at a law firm," he was saying, while combing and moussing his hair.

"I used to work as a prosecutor, but I switched over to the dark side because that's where all the money is," he said, putting some Right Guard under each arm.

"Look away," he said, peeing in a bottle.

"I still live in Connecticut, but just so my kid doesn't have to change schools—I can definitely afford the New York City lifestyle," he said through a cloud of cologne.

"Look out!" I said after we had gone over the second rumble strip, rapidly approaching the tollbooth on I-95 South.

"Relax, I do this all the time," he said, plucking one last pesky nose hair.

By the time we got to the Bronx, he looked well kempt, much different than when I first got into the car with him. The sharp business look remained, but now it was more refined.

He let me off by one of the number 5 train subway stops and said, "Well buddy, I hope your day ends better than it started. Good luck with everything!"

Instead of saying anything in response to that, I just waved goodbye to Ron Frankton and walked up the stairs to the station platform.

•••

When I got on the 5, after paying one fifty for a token, I was pleasantly surprised to see that the subway car wasn't crowded. I took a seat and checked the subway map on the wall behind me. Seventeen stops until the 14th Street/Union Square stop. From there, I could just walk north until I got to 23rd Street. There was a stop at 23rd, but the five just passed right on by. And why wouldn't it? Why would any part of New York City be simple? And so I sat and waited, counting the stops the train made.

After a while, we went underground. At that point, the subway car was completely packed with people. The whole place had the awful stench of BO. Every time new passengers got into the subway car—within two minutes—they smelled their own armpits to make sure the smell wasn't coming from them.

When we got to Union Square, I had to squeeze through bodies until I got near the door. Then I was swept out and up with the tides. I kept my hands in my pockets the whole time, wary of all the suspicious characters around me in their suits and skirts and ties and blouses.

I surfaced on the corner of a small park, gasping for the fresher air. Unfortunately, it was not to be found. There was an awful smell there, too, a strange breed of vinegar and sulfur. Honking taxis and trucks and bikers screaming. The whole place was moving and making noise. The melodic sound of a jackhammer floated on the wind. There were streets running in every direction. And then there was a park behind me.

So I did the only thing that made sense to me. I ran into the park to think for a minute and figure out which way was north.

•••

I walked around the Flatiron Building twice before I went inside. I couldn't believe that this strange building—maybe twenty stories tall by my guess, and completely triangular—used to be the tallest in Manhattan. There was an apartment building across the street that had it easily beat, by twenty floors at least.

I went through the door and was greeted by a security guard behind a desk. He stopped me as I wandered towards the elevator. "Excuse me sir," he said. "You have to sign in. Can I help you find someone?"

"Yes," I said. I took the pen he offered me and wrote my name, the time and the date down on his ledger. "I was looking for Fred Morrison? Do you know what floor he works on?"

"Oh, sure. Fred works on twelve, with the Eugene Publishing House."

"Thanks a lot." I stepped onto the elevator and pressed twelve. I was getting a little nervous. I was never good at asking for money, and it didn't help that I hadn't seen Fred since I'd last seen Jackson.

A strange soft-jazz cover of "(I Just) Died In Your Arms Tonight" was playing overhead, the trombone playing what would have been the line "It must've been some kind of ki-iss." I looked at myself in the mirror. My shirt was a little ripped and there were tiny spots of blood from where the broken glass had cut me, but other than that I looked ok. Well...I looked better than I felt, anyway.

Ding!

I got off and headed down the hall. There were rooms with suite numbers on either side, but none of them had any sort of company identification on them. I was sure that I was just going to have to try every one of them until I found Eugene Publishing House, but then I saw it at the end of the hallway. It was a door like all the others, but hanging over it was a bronzed sign engraved with the name I had been looking for. I opened the door and stepped in.

A woman was sitting behind a desk talking on the phone and she held up one finger to me, telling me to wait, and pointed at a chair, telling me to sit. So I did.

"Yeah, so Mr. Slanks said that if the book isn't good, it isn't good and there's no need to try to squeeze water out of a stone. So then we told Mr. Carmichael that we were sorry, but we were no longer interested...Mmhmm...That's what I said!...Yeah...Ok, well I'm glad that you called us before anything else...Yes, I will...Ok, you too, Mrs. Carmichael. Buhbye." She looked up at me. "Hello, how can I help you today?"

"Hi. I'm looking for Fred Morrison?"

"I'm sorry, he's not in today. Is there something else I could do for you?" She pulled out a pen and paper. "Would you like to leave a message for him or something?"

"Really?" I asked. "He's not in? I need to talk to him."

"And what is this in regards to?" she asked me.

184

"I'm his brother, Paul Morrison, and I have a family matter to discuss with him."

"His brother? I didn't know Mr. Morrison had a brother." She smiled at me now, like she was sharing some kind of secret with me. She tilted her head to one side, examining me. "Now that you mention it, I can definitely see the family resemblance."

"Yeah," I said. "Listen, do you have his address? Does he live around here?"

"No, he lives uptown somewhere," she said. She rifled through the Rolodex on her right. "Here it is. He lives at 327 West 82nd Street. He's apartment #3B. That means it's west of the park, but I don't really know uptown that well." She grinned at me again. "I think that might be by West End, but once you're on 82nd, you should be able to find it anyway. You should get off at the Museum of Natural History stop on the train, it's right around there somewhere."

So after another train ride and some walking around in circles, I found myself in front of his building. I looked at the fourteen buttons in front of me, but I didn't see Fred's name anywhere. Next to 3B was the name Kaitlin Sherwood. I took the chance and rang her bell. A few seconds later, there was a low hum from the door and I was able to open it.

9.

THE "TALK"

The "foyer" of the building, or whatever it was, was very chic. The carpeting looked like it was replaced once every few years and the wall-length mirror was the cleanest thing I had yet seen in that city. The staircase at the other end was elegant, a wooden banister hugging carpeted stairs. Everything matched with everything else, a beautiful oasis in the middle of all the craziness that made up New York.

I walked up two flights of stairs and I saw the door to 3B left open. I knocked on the door while I pushed open and said, "Hello?"

"Fred, is that you?" a woman's voice said from inside. At least this was the right place.

"No," I said. "I'm Paul. Fred's brother?"

There was the sound of some things falling over and then Kaitlin Sherwood appeared at the front door. She had her dirty blonde hair pulled back into a bun, and she wore an expression that said she wasn't up for taking any shit. "Paul?" she said. "I haven't heard about any Paul." She crossed her arms under her breasts.

"Well I'm Fred's brother, and I was hoping I could speak with him."

"He's not here right now," she said, squinting her eyes at me. "Would you like me to give him a message?"

"Well, will he be back soon?"

"Yeah."

"Can I just wait for him?" I asked.

"I don't know you," she said. "You can wait outside if you want, and if Fred knows who you are, he'll let you up... I've never heard about any brother." She squinted with suspicion. "Maybe you should just take your con somewhere else."

"Ok, ok," I said, holding my hands up in self-defense. "I'll just go wait for him downstairs. Sorry to have bothered you."

I went downstairs and sat down on the front steps of the building. So that was Fred's wife, or wife-to-be. If Fred was anything like how I remembered him, then she was perfect for him. They both shared a warm, friendly, trusting nature.

A few minutes later, a man with a beard and a cigarette walked up to the door and fumbled through a ring of keys. He paused, inhaling on his cigarette and giving a satisfied exhale. He tossed the cigarette away and put a piece of gum in his mouth.

Before he opened the door with his key, I tentatively said, "Fred?"

The beard looked at me. Then he looked at me harder, squinting his eyes. "Do...I...know you?" he asked. Then he leaned in for a closer look.

I smiled at him. "I sure hope so," I said. "It's me! Paul!"

"Paul?" he said. "Oh my God. What are you doing here?"

"I came to check in on my older brother," I said, "see how he was doing."

"Wow." He stood there with the key in his hand for a while, unsure of what to do. "Well, come on up with me. See my place."

"Ok."

We went back upstairs. He opened the door to 3B.

Kaitlin started talking from the other room. "Oh Fred, you wouldn't believe this. Some guy came to the front door saying he was your brother and he wanted to wait here. So I told him—" She froze when she came into the room and saw me with Fred. "—wait," she said. "You *do* know him?"

"Well, he *is* my brother. Take a seat on the couch," he told me.

I did, and he took Kaitlin into another room to talk to her.

"What do you mean?" I could hear her say through the wall. "Brother?"

Fred's muted voice answered.

"But you never told me about any brothers! Hell, you told me you haven't spoken to what was left of your family after your father died and you got the courage to leave that hell-hole!"

"That's true!" I heard him say back. Then he said something softer that I couldn't make out.

I tried to stop eavesdropping at that point and settled into the soft couch. The apartment looked like it belonged in the same building as the building's "foyer." Across from me on the couch was an enormous television, easily 40" across. Soft-blue drapes covered the windows, made of a sheer fabric that looked expensive. Every lamp and coffee table looked like something waiting to be appraised on "Antique Roadshow."

I examined the lamp on the table closest to me. "You see this mark right here?" I could imagine them saying on the television. "This shows me that it was manufactured by hand and that someone other than the person who made the base did the paint job, which would imply a late-nineteenth-century origin. I think this could sell for two hundred dollars, easily."

And the coffee table the lamp was delicately placed on: "Right here—let's get a close-up on this—you can see how well the wood fits together. They used some

188

sort of butterfly biscuit to hold it together. That means this table will last a lifetime. And judging from the whittled legs, I'd say it is from the early twentieth century. This could sell for seven hundred."

I felt like my chances of getting the money we needed from Fred were pretty good. It looked like he was doing very well for himself indeed.

Fred and Kaitlin returned from the other room. They stood there awkwardly until Fred said, "So this is Kaitlin Sherwood, my fiancé."

"Kaitlin," I said, standing up to shake her hand, "it is a pleasure to meet you. I'm Paul, Fred's brother."

She shook my hand in a "yeah yeah, I know you're Fred's brother now" sort of way.

"So Paul, really," Fred said. "Why are you here."

That was more of a blunt direction than I expected the conversation to take. I had to throw out all of the practice conversations I had gone over in the car. "I came to talk to you about Mom," I said. "She's been having some health issues lately."

"Is she going to die?" he asked.

"No no, nothing like that."

"Well do I have to go up and visit her?"

"You don't have to if you don't want to, but that would be nice," I said. I shook my head. "That's not exactly why I came up to talk to you." I looked over at Kaitlin, then back at Fred. "Do you mind if we talk alone for a little bit?"

"You know what?" Kaitlin said. "Take all the time alone you want. Take all the time in the world, but get out of this apartment. Go find somewhere else to talk. I have to be alone for a little while, too." Her eyes burned at me, like I was the cause of some new revelation that she didn't like.

I guess I was.

"Ok," Fred said. "Alright, everything's fine. We'll just go to the diner."

"Fine by me," Kaitlin said. "You do whatever you want." Kaitlin showed us out and slammed the door behind us. She shouted, "And you can find somewhere else to spend the night, too!" through the door.

"I hope this is important, Paul," Fred grumbled on our way down the stairs.

•••

We sat opposite each other in a booth at the back of the diner. A waitress gave us a menu and headed into the kitchen.

"So what's up?" Fred asked.

"Not too much," I said. "Gen and I opened up a bookshop and café. And we just had a little boy."

"That's not what I meant. What made you come down here?"

"I'm sorry, Fred. I—"

"What the hell could be so important that you'd have to come all the way down here?" he said. "I gave you guys my phone number. Why didn't you just call me?"

"I thought this kind of thing would be better dealt with in person," I said.

"I have a very delicate balance here," he said. "I didn't want you guys coming down here and screwing things up! How did you get my home address anyway?"

"I asked someone at your office." I took a deep calming breath, trying to settle us both down. "Listen Fred, take it easy. I'm sorry if I screwed something up for you at home with your fiancé. I wasn't trying to. I just came here to ask you a favor."

"Have you two decided what you want to order?" the waitress said, popping up out of nowhere.

"Give us another minute," Fred said. He opened up his menu in front of his face, temporarily killing the conversation.

I opened up my menu and decided on the cheeseburger with french-fries. Simple and quick.

The waitress came back with two waters and said, "You fellas ready now?"

Fred put his menu down on the table. "Go ahead, Paul."

190

"Ok, I'll have the cheeseburger with french-fries. Make the burger a medium, please." She took my menu. "Thanks."

"And I'll have a plate of the penne ala vodka," Fred said, shoving his menu at the waitress while she was still writing.

"Ok," she said. "Your food will be right out."

Fred stared at me across the table and took a sip of his water. "So?" he asked.

"Ok, here's the deal," I said. "Mom's been having these episodes where she kind of forgets what's going on."

Fred raised his eyebrow like this was not enough to make this trouble worth his while.

"What I mean is, she'll forget that Jackson's dead, and that Morty and I moved out, and that you're living down here. Sometimes she'll think everyone lives in the house with her still, and she makes dinner like we're going to show up any minute." I sighed, a complete drama-queen kind of sigh. "I spoke to a doctor, and while she is in no immediate danger, he suggests that we put her under some supervised care. Like a nursing home or something."

Fred leaned back in his seat and crossed his arms over his chest.

"And this whole time, Uncle Preston has been telling her... pressuring her into believing!... that we should be suing you for selling the store. You know, for loss of income and all that, and—"

"—You can't."

"We most certainly could, but that's not the point. We're not going to sue you, Fred. In fact, I've been the one making sure that we don't." I leaned over the booth, reaching my arms across the table to try and touch him. My arms weren't long enough, though, and my fingers just ended up grasping at the air just over the edge of the table. "The point's that Mom really needs to be put in a nursing home."

"Here's the penne ala vodka," the waitress said, putting the plate down in front of Fred. "And here's the cheeseburger with french-fries, medium." The food came out so fast that it scared me, like it had been waiting for us instead of the other way around. The waitress clasped her hands together. "You guys need anything else? A drink or something?"

"Yeah," Fred said. "Get me a rum and coke."

"Nothing for me, thanks."

"Rum and coke, coming right up."

"Food comes fast around here," I said.

"Yup," he said. He shoved some pasta in his face. "So what, you need money from me or something?"

"Well... yeah." This wasn't going how I'd wanted at all. Now I looked like some guy on his knees, begging for a handout. "You see, I'd have her move in with us, but Gen's parents just moved in and there's just no room. And with the new baby, I don't have anywhere near enough money to pay for it by myself." And then I remembered, "Oh! And I totaled my car this morning, just to top it all off."

I looked down at my cheeseburger. "It's been a long couple of months since you sent us that letter," I said.

"I don't know what you were expecting, but there's really nothing I can offer. Kaitlin and I are getting married soon, and she wants to have a baby, too."

"Come on, Fred, get off it. I saw your apartment. Things can't be going too badly for you. I just need a little money to pay for the first six months, and then after that, I'll be able to mortgage my house or something to pay for the rest."

"How much?" he asked.

"Just about five thousand dollars or so."

"Five grand?" He laughed. "Who do you think I am? None of that stuff is mine, Paul. I moved in with Kaitlin four years ago because I couldn't afford an apartment on my own anymore."

"Then tell her your mother is sick and you need the money to help her out!"

"I can't, Paul." Fred shrugged, raising his eyebrows high and sucking his lips into his mouth with a frown. "I can't."

"Why not?"

"Because!" he screamed. "Because I just can't do that. It's not all so simple, here. I never told Kaitlin about you because I didn't want her to get involved in my family life. *I* don't even want to be involved in my family life anymore! Don't you understand that?"

"I do understand that, Fred," I said. "As hard as it is to understand, I do. And I've respected that wish for as long as I could. Now I have no more options, Fred. I need to get this money from you. You're the only one left who can get Mom the help she needs, ok? We need your help. Mom needs your help... I need your help."

"I can't. I can't help," he said. "Cut the corn-ball routine. It's not my money, I can't help."

"Fred," I said. "I know you can. You have to. It's Mom! She's the one who always stood up for you, Fred. She's the one who always went and talked to you after Jackson fucked up. She's in real trouble!"

"I'm sorry." He looked genuinely sorry, slouched over and defeated.

"Listen Fred," I said matter-of-fact, "you can help. Or, this whole thing could blow up in our faces and turn into some drawn-out legal battle that ends up costing both of us more than what I need in the first place."

"Are you threatening me?" he said, spitting pasta from his mouth.

"No! Sit back down, Fred. I'm saying I want to avoid that."

"You don't threaten me, not with a lawsuit," he said, throwing his napkin down on the table. "My fiancé is a lawyer. You don't threaten me." He turned and left.

He left me alone in the booth, completely stunned.

The waitress came by and gave me the check. "Did you enjoy your food?" she asked.

"Yeah, it was great." I pulled out my wallet, and mumbled, "It looks like lunch is on me."

10.

I CONTINUE TO PULL OUT MY WALLET

I asked the waitress where I could rent a car and she said, "I don't know. In Queens? By one of the airports?"

I walked outside to a payphone on the corner and put in 50¢.

"Hello?"

"Hey Gen, it's me."

"Hey, Paul! How's the trip going?"

"Not well," I said. "There was a problem with the car, so I'm going to go rent one here."

"Oh, ok." She wasn't surprised. Of course she wasn't surprised. "And how did things go with Fred?"

"Not good. Not good at all. He didn't give me anything besides the bill for lunch."

"Oh, no. I can't believe it!"

"I am so mad at him right now. You should have seen the apartment he's living in!"

A computer voice cut in. "To continue your call, please insert 25¢." My minute was up.

"I have to go," I said. "I love you."

"Love you too."

I walked to the train station. I took the B headed downtown, then transferred at 47th-50th Street for the F going uptown. Somehow, that was the fastest way to get to Queens from uptown Manhattan.

I got out at the end of the line and took a cab to the airport. Yellow medallion, of course: I still tried to keep my head about me. The whole way, I couldn't help but stare at the rising counter, a constant reminder of how much I would owe at the end of the trip. This trip for money turned out to be more expensive than helpful. I got out, paid the cabbie and thanked him. He sped off while I pulled my bag through the still-open back door.

PART V
A TWIST LEADS TO A TURN FOR THE WORSE

LOOKING AHEAD TO THE FUNERAL AT HIGH NOON
(PROLOGUE TO PART V)

Ok, I'll admit it: I don't need to write about going to get a rental car, and telling my insurance company about the accident, which I was going to. I don't need to write about finally getting home and getting my car towed and fixed up, which I was also going to do. So I won't. Hell, I probably didn't have to write about my conversation with the secretary at Fred's office, but it's too late for that.

This is my fifth day in jail.

I can't quite force myself to write what happened with my mother when I found her, and I admit that writing this deposition helps me to forget where I am. That is probably why I am writing so much about myself, things I would never say out loud. But that is also why it's taking me so long to tell everything. Because there's a lot I need to tell to explain why my mother died, and I have to explain that before I can write what I did when I found her body.

My lawyer, when he saw this deposition, was appalled. "Paul!" he said. "For the love of God! You only need to write about what happened when you found your mother! You don't have to write your whole life's story."

But I do. And I tried to explain it to him. "The story is only completely truthful if I tell everything."

It's the only way to really explain it properly. And the rest of my free life is at stake, so I am not taking any chances with this thing. My lawyer, living on the outside, will do whatever he can, but I'll make sure that if he fails, I'll succeed.

My mother's funeral is tomorrow, so I'll finish this up by noon when I have to leave. Which means that I shouldn't mess around and that I should just get to the good stuff.

I'll jump ahead to the conversation I had with my mother, the conversation that changed everything for the worse. It happened a week after I got back from New York:

1.

THE ROCK AND THE HARD PLACE

I pulled into my mother's driveway. We had made plans to have dinner that night, and when I came into the house, she was busy in the kitchen.

"Hey Ma," I called out.

"Hello, Paul. I'm in here." She was making macaroni and cheese: my favorite dish growing up. "Just pull out some plates for us."

I started setting the table. "So how was your day today?"

"Oh, it was fine dear," she said. "First thing when I woke up I went to the library. It was nice and quiet there."

"Well that shouldn't be too surprising," I said.

"You never know," she said. "I've been there when some teenaged boys were there and they were behaving very rowdy and rude." She put the food down on the table in front of me and sat down. "But today, I felt like I was the only one there."

"That's good," I said. "And did you do anything else with yourself today?"

She pushed her food around on the plate with her fork, mesmerized by the process. "I stopped by your aunt's house."

"And how is she doing?"

"Good." She looked at me once, fast, and then back at her food. "Where did you say you went a few days ago? When you had the accident?"

I hadn't told my mother I went to visit Fred because I didn't want her to worry about it, but because of the sling I had on my left arm, I had to tell her about the accident.

"...I went to visit an old High School friend," I said. "Jeremy. You remember Jeremy, right?"

She nodded, still looking down at her plate.

"Why do you ask?"

"Oh, it's just something your Aunt Hallie said to me."

"...Ok," I said. It didn't seem like she was going to say anymore about it, and I didn't want to push it, so I let the point drop. "Well I had a busy day today. You know, Little Jack has become a handful to deal with. Every hour he wakes up crying. Not like Cecilia was at all." I put some mac and cheese in my mouth. "She was a much better sleeper than he is."

Mom put her fork down and looked at me. "I would like to check myself into a mental hospital."

She said this with such a straight face that it threw me for a minute. I sat there with my mouth hanging open, waiting for another bite. "What?"

"I think it would be for the best."

I put my fork down on the plate, the mac and cheese untouched. "And what would ever make you say that?" I asked.

"I know you went to see Fred a week ago," she said. "And I know you went and asked Preston for money."

•••

Apparently, Mom's conversation with Aunt Hallie had happened something like this:

She stopped by her sister's house on the way back from the library, like she had told me. Preston was out

199

working at the garage, and Aunt Hallie and my mother went and had some tea in the kitchen together.

They had just sat there gossiping, when Aunt Hallie happened to say, "Oh, Paul came by a week ago."

"Really?" my mother said.

"Yes," Hallie said. "He just stopped by for a while and talked with Preston. He just needed a favor. He didn't tell you?"

"No," Mom said. "What did he need?"

"He needed a little money. You know. To help pay for your nursing home?"

"Oh really?" my mom said. "He didn't tell me he was having trouble paying for it."

"I guess he didn't want to worry you. We couldn't really help out much—you know, we have our son's school debts to deal with. But Paul said that he was going to go talk to Fred in New York. I think he went a little while ago."

My mom put on a surprised expression, one that said, "Please, tell me more."

Aunt Hallie obliged, and went on to say, "But Fred said he couldn't help out either." She sighed. "So I guess Paul's back to square one."

Mom shook her head. "I had no idea that it was such a problem to pay for this."

Aunt Hallie shrugged her shoulders.

"I don't want to be a burden on my children," Mom said.

Aunt Hallie shrugged her shoulders again. "I had a friend," she said, "older than you are now. She broke her leg and couldn't really walk anymore—couldn't really do anything for herself—and she didn't want to burden her family either."

"What did she do?"

"She checked herself into a mental hospital," Aunt Hallie said. "They took care of her, and it didn't cost that much to keep herself there. It seemed like it worked out well for her." My aunt took a sip of her tea. "But there was the occasional run-in with some of the other patients. It was just occasional, but it would really bother her sometimes."

"Oh," my mother said.

•••

And that is how she had come to her decision.

I looked at her across the kitchen table. We had had countless meals there, but never had one been so catastrophic. My mother? In a publicly funded mental institution? Shivers went up my spine as I thought about what the other inmates would be like. I could imagine the guy who walked around with a knife hidden in his underwear, ready to pull it out and attack at any moment; I could imagine the woman who would bite anyone that came near her; the teenager who did too many drugs and thinks that he is on a mission from God to cleanse the world of the elderly, cleanse the world of people like my mother.

I imagined all of that and said, "Mom, I won't let you admit yourself to a place like that. It's not safe! I would never be able to sleep at night knowing you were there."

"But honey," she said. "You can't afford a nursing home for me. This is the best way out. I don't want to be a burden on you."

If Uncle Preston were here, he would have said, "There is one other way..."

"I refuse to let this happen, Mom." I pictured a man who enjoys the taste of human flesh. I shook my head. "No! I really can't let you do that, and I won't."

"Well dear," she said. "This may be one of those things you don't have a say in."

"Ok." I took a deep breath. "Well at least give me a little time before you do that. Give me a little more time to get some money together. I would be more comfortable being in debt than having you in a state-run institution. You just never know what could happen in a place like that."

We finished our food without any more talking. I helped clean up the table and Mom walked me to the door when it was time for me to go. I gave her a kiss on the cheek. "Listen Ma," I said, holding her by the shoulders and talking directly into her eyes. "I promise that I can get the money together. Please don't check yourself in anywhere.

201

Can you promise me that? That you won't check in anywhere unless we talk about it first?"

"Alright dear," she said. She gave me a hug. "Drive safe. Watch out for those raccoons on the road."

"Ha ha," I said. "Ok Mom, I will. See you tomorrow. I'll come by after we close up."

•••

That night, I was lying in bed with Gen. Little Jack was asleep in the cradle at the foot of our bed, Cecilia was asleep in her room, and Gen's parents were asleep down the hall.

"But then," I said, "out of nowhere, she says that she wants to check herself in to a mental hospital."

"What? Where did she get an idea like that?" Gen asked.

"I guess Aunt Hallie said something."

"That can't happen. Those places can be dangerous!"

"I know, but it's not like I have a whole lot of options here."

"We'll just have to scrape some money together. We'll cut a few corners here and there. Buy some cheaper coffee. No big deal."

"That still won't be enough," I said. "I'm afraid to say it—I'm afraid to even think it!—but I don't want to sell the bookshop, I can't sell it. I can only think of one way out of this."

2.

I THOUGHT ABOUT MY MOTHER AND I COULD IMAGINE

The next day, I decided that I would go around and talk to everyone—Morty, Preston, then yes, even Howie—about what to do next. I got into the car—which was still running thanks to some mechanical magic gratefully covered by the insurance company—and drove off before anyone else in the house was awake.

First, I drove over to Morty's house. Morty lived a few miles from Mom on the outskirts of Marborough, in an apartment behind Grangers's Liquor Store. It wasn't huge, but it had two bedrooms, which was more than enough space for a bachelor like him.

I knocked on the front door.

Morty called out, "One minute," from inside. I heard his wheels squeaking a little before the knob turned. The door opened an inch, and Morty squeaked backwards. "Come on in, man."

I pushed the door the rest of the way in. It opened immediately into a short hallway that was the width of the

203

doorway. "Hey Morty, how's it going?" I closed the door behind me and followed him into the living room.

"Hey Paul," he said.

I sat down on the couch. "So how have you been?"

"Oh, you know," he said. "Things are going." He rolled into the kitchen. "You want a drink?"

"Jesus, it's eight o'clock!" I said. "That's way too early for me." I looked down at my folded hands. "Maybe a little too early for you, too."

"Oh come on, Paul," he said. "It's Sunday! The Lord's day. The day of rest. I'm just trying to maintain my religious nature and relax."

"Ha ha." It was a very forced laugh. "Ok, whatever gets you through the day."

He rolled in next to me on the couch with a Bud Light. He saw the face I made at it, and said, "I have to watch my weight."

I nodded and looked down at my hands again. "I talked to Mom yesterday."

"I saw her yesterday too. She didn't look very good, did she." Morty said that not as a question, but as a fact.

"Yeah, well, she's got a lot on her mind."

Morty nodded while staring off for a moment. "What did she say to you?"

"She'd gotten wind of the trouble of paying for her nursing home."

"Wow, that's trouble."

"I know. That's like the worst thing that could have happened in this situation. With her condition, you know?"

He took a sip. "Yeah…"

"Anyway," I said, "the worst part is that she has decided to take matters into her own hands at this point."

"What does that mean?"

I told Morty about Mom's talk with Aunt Hallie and her plan. "So basically," I concluded, "we have to get the money together before she has a chance to check herself in."

"So what can we do about it?" he asked. It wasn't a hopeless question: he genuinely wanted to know what he could do to help out.

"Well I do have one idea," I said. "But, considering Mom's condition, I think we should try to keep this as quiet as possible around her, if you know what I mean."

"I do," he said. "I'll keep it to myself, I'm no blabber mouth."

●●●

That was always true: Morty was never a blabbermouth.

When we were growing up, Fred would always tell on us for the stupid things that Morty and I did. One time when Mom and Jackson were out of the house, Morty and I took a wedding tape that one of our cousins—a fourth cousin five times removed or something ridiculous like that—had sent us. We had made our plans and had the tape drawn and quartered: Morty grabbed the thin tape with all of the video information on it and I grabbed the thick plastic case. Then (and this was the brilliant part of our plan) we ran in opposite directions with it. We ran all over the house, passing each other occasionally with the thin tape of memories streaming behind us. The house was completely covered with the translucent, black streamers, but we had it all cleaned up and had hidden the damning evidence in the trashcan out front well before our parents returned. Plus, this was a fourth cousin five times removed and they wouldn't miss the tape. We figured that we were in the clear.

Mom and Jackson came into the house and slammed the door behind them. Fred came out of his room and walked downstairs to where all four of us were standing. He turned to our parents, and the first words out of his mouth were, "Morty and Paul ruined Jean's wedding tape. It's in the garbage can out front."

To say the least, this put Morty and me at odds with our older brother many times. No one really likes a tattletale, and that's what Fred was in our eyes.

But then there was this one time when the tables were turned and we had caught Fred in the act. He was home with a couple of friends after school one day when he was fourteen. So ten-year-old Paul and eight-year-old Morty walk into his room to see what's up with the older kids. And what did we find? Beer! Everywhere! And those fourteen-year-olds were drinking it! Fred pushed us out and slammed the door before we got too far inside.

I turned to Morty, rubbing my hands together. "Ooh, we got him now," I said. "Mom and Jackson will flip when they hear about this."

But Morty, that non-tattletale bastard, talked me out of what would have been the best revenge ever.

●●●

No, Morty was no tattletale.

So I didn't worry about him spilling the beans to Mom, or anyone else, for that matter. "I have one idea," I repeated. "Mind you, it's not a great one, but it's the only one I've got."

I thought about my mother and I could imagine a woman who spat at nurses and gnawed on the arms of other patients.

I cleared my throat and told him what I had in mind.

"It'll be just like the good old days," Morty said.

"What do you mean?"

"Well," he said, "it was always Fred against the rest of the family when we were growing up, so why should it be any different now?"

●●●

Then I took the drive over to Preston's house. He opened the front door, which was a rare occurrence. "Hello Uncle Preston."

"Hey, come in." He led me into the TV room and sat down on the couch. Then straight to the point as ever, he said, "So what's on your mind?"

I sat down. "I don't know if you know about it, but Aunt Hallie and my mom had a conversation recently."

"Yeah," he said. "Your mother was over here not that long ago. They had tea together or something."

"Well do you know what they talked about?"

"No."

"Ok." I blew out and massaged my cheeks with my hands. "Apparently, when they talked, the end result was that my mother had come to a decision."

He started picking at his teeth; he was losing interest. "And what was that."

"She decided," I said loud enough for him to pay attention, "to admit herself to a public mental institution. To save us money."

"Oh," he said like that might not have been a bad idea.

"Uncle Preston!" I said. "We can't let that happen."

"Listen, I already told you that I don't have any money to help out. Fred didn't give you the money. Maybe this isn't a bad idea."

I thought about my mother and I could imagine a man who foamed at the mouth and shouted at the nurses because he thought they were demons.

"It's a terrible idea," I said. "Who knows what the other patients will be like? It's not worth the risk."

"Well then I think that we are running out of options," he said.

"There is one other option," I said.

He sat upright. "Do you mean...?"

"Yes." I paused because it all felt so dramatic. "I'm ready to sue Fred. I'm ready to do it."

"Oh Paul!" he said. "I'm so happy to hear that!"

"Make no mistake: this is a last-resort decision on my part. I'm going to do this because I've run out of other options."

"Well you're doing the right thing," Uncle Preston said.

"That has yet to be seen." I scratched my neck. "But if we're going to do this, there's a favor I have to ask you."

He spread his arms wide. "Anything."

"Do not, under any circumstances, talk to my mother about what's going on. Don't tell her what's going on at the trial, don't tell her that things are looking good, don't even tell her we're suing Fred. I want to be the one to talk to her about this. It's a delicate subject and she's in a delicate state right now. Are we clear?"

"Sure, Paul, sure." He held up his right hand. "I promise."

"I'm really counting on you to keep that promise."

"I will, I will." He started rubbing his hands together. "So what's the next step?"

"I'm going to talk to your son to figure that out."

"Oh good," Preston said. "I know Howie was looking forward to taking this case on. He passed the bar exam a month ago, you know."

"Well thank God for that, at least."

•••

"Paul!" Howie opened his front door. "My dad told me you were coming by. How's everything going?"

I stepped into his apartment. It was small, but like Morty's place, not bad for a single guy. The floors were pretty clean, but unlike Morty's place, there were only a few half-full beer cans lying around. There was the kitchen, there was the living room, there was the door leading to the bedroom. It was pretty standard, albeit a little crowded.

The drive over from Preston's was short—Howie had not moved that far away from home. He was still in the same town, in fact, just on the other side of the local Main Street. The ride was no more than five minutes, so Preston must have gotten on the phone with Howie pretty quick after I left if my cousin knew to expect me.

"It's going," I said, "it's going. Things are a little hectic around my house right now with the baby and Gen's parents and the business and all that, but it's going fine."

"Glad to hear it. Listen. I know why you're here, and I just want you to know that I am very excited to get started on this project. I've already done quite a bit of research on everything—you know, before we talked and you said you didn't want to do it—so we'll hit the ground running." He paused, took a second to breathe. "Take a seat. Does Fred know what's going to hit him yet?"

"Well no," I said, falling into his couch. (It was a very soft couch, really quite nice.) "Not really. When I saw him, I mentioned that we could sue him if we wanted to, but I told him it wasn't something we'd really do. Actually, he got pretty pissed off right after I mentioned it and stormed out on our lunch. It was quite a scene."

"Ooh," Howie said, sucking air through his teeth. "Ouch. The old walking-out-on-the-lunch move, hunh?"

"Yeah... Well I guess lunch would've been on me, anyway. He didn't look like he was about to pull out his wallet or anything."

"Ok." He stood up. "Give me one second, Paul. I just have to pull out a couple of papers for you to sign."

He left me alone in the living room and went into the bedroom, shutting his door behind him. I could hear the shuffling of papers and the opening and closing of metal, probably filing cabinets.

He came back in with the papers in his hand and shook them in the air at me. "Here they are!" He was giddy as a schoolboy jock participating in the beat-down of the local nerd. He slammed the papers down on the table and pulled a pen from behind his ear. "I'm going to need your signature here," he said, making an "X" on the paper. "And here," with another "X," "and here. Also, I need your initials here and here and here and here." By the time he was finished marking it up, the papers looked like a misguided treasure map.

I started signing left and right.

"And I'll take these down to the courthouse—get them filed and what have you—the next chance I get. We should have this case looked at within a couple of weeks if I explain the necessity of a speedy trial to the judge on duty."

"That sounds great, Howie." I stood up and shook his hand. "Ok, I'll get out of your hair now. Give me a call when you get any information on anything."

I thought about my mother and I could imagine a man who ripped out his own hair and shoved it down the throats of his fellow patients while they were sleeping.

"Oh, and do me a favor," I said. "Don't mention this to my mother. Ok?"

"Sure thing, Paul. See you later."

3.

THE NEXT BEST THING

And while Howie got to work, I went home to get back to some work of my own. I had not been doing my fair share lately, both at the bookstore and in the bedroom, where Little Jack kept Gen and me awake.

"Ding ding ding!" The doorbells announced my entrance into the bookstore. I walked back to the café and was surprised to see Gen's mother behind the register, a place I'd never seen her before. She was talking to a customer, and as I got closer, I heard her say, "You can wait, but I can't do anything about it. I don't even know how to begin using this contraption."

"Here, Sally," I said. "Let me show you."

She looked over at me. "No, I'd rather not. I think you should just do it." And then she walked back into the kitchen.

•••

After the bookshop was closed and all the customers had found their way out, I walked in on Sally, alone, drinking a glass of wine in the kitchen. It was eleven o'clock at night. "So how have things been lately?" I asked her. Sally and I had only spoken a handful of times since she had moved in with Gen and me, and this was the first time I had the chance to speak to her alone.

She took a sip of wine from her glass and smacked her lips. "Aah." She put the glass down on the table. "How do you think things have been?" She laughed to herself. "My husband is passed-out-drunk upstairs and I've been living with my daughter and her family in a bookshop." She picked up the glass and took a big gulp that time. "This is not the life I envisioned for myself, to say the least.

"You know, Paul," she continued, "the truth of the matter is that it's my fault. Or at least partially my fault— certainly there were outside forces that had their effects as well." She looked down at the glass on the table. She thought about it for a second, then picked it up and had a sip. "Certainly I should have seen this coming, at least. John was in a downward spiral at work and I knew it. Why didn't I get a divorce then? Half of our money back then would have almost meant something. Now it's too late: half of nothing is nothing." She sighed. "There'd be no point in that, anymore."

She picked up her wine glass and finished what was left—about half of the glass—in three swallows. "Did you ever feel like you could have prevented a disaster in your life, but instead you just...didn't?"

I thought about my mother, preparing herself—at home, alone—to check into a publicly funded mental institution. "Yeah," I said. "I know what you mean."

I got up to pour myself a glass of water. When I turned back from the sink, Sally was asleep on the kitchen table. She was snoring.

I took a second and thought about what I should do. I thought about waking her up, but I noticed the two empty wine bottles and figured that would be pretty difficult. I tried anyway. I shook her, saying, "Sally. Hey Sally. Come on, you should go upstairs."

Nothing.

I thought about leaving her there at the table, but that didn't seem right. So I hooked one arm under her legs and cradled her head with the other and I carried her upstairs like we were crossing the threshold for the first time. I was careful not to bump her body on the doorway, and laid her down in the bed next to John. I closed the bedroom door behind me, and I was careful to be quiet even though there was no way either of them could hear a thing over the sounds of their own snoring.

•••

I opened the door to my room. Gen was in bed under the blankets, but still awake. She held the blanket up to her chin and smiled when I came in.

Little Jack, who was never awake except at the most inconvenient of times, was in his crib. I peeked in on him while he slept, resting a hand on the sidebars of his literal bed-chamber. "Eeh," Little Jack said in his sleep, indifferent to my watchful eye and indifferent to his own dreams.

"Why can't we all be like Little Jack here?" I asked Gen. "Wouldn't it be great if we all just went with the flow?"

"Yeah, and it would also be great if there were people to clean up after us all the time." Gen raised an eyebrow at me. "But I don't see that happening any time soon. So until then, we should probably pretend we're adults."

"Mmm." I stripped down to my boxers and got into bed. "How unfortunate for us."

I started kissing Gen's neck. "Paul!" she giggled. "The baby's in the room."

"Oh, like he's going to know what's going on." I kept kissing.

"I gave birth like five days ago!" she said. "I wouldn't even be able to feel you down there I've been stretched so wide."

I started touching her down there.

"And it's still sore!" she said. "Paul!"

I grinned at her. "What?"

"Stop that."

212

"Ok, ok, fine. You win, I'll stop."

She straightened out her nightgown under the blankets and gave me a look. "So you told everyone today?" she said. "About suing Fred?"

Ah, talking about lawsuits: the next best thing to sex. "Yup."

"And what did they think?"

"Morty, Uncle Preston and Howie are all for it," I said. "Of course, Uncle Preston and Howie were a little more excited about it than I would have liked. I swear, those two completely forgot they knew Fred at all. They talk about him as if he were just a sum of money. A means to an end. Fred lost his title of 'nephew' and 'cousin' in their eyes a while ago."

"At least everyone's behind you on this one," Gen said.

"I still don't know how to tell Mom, though. Or if I should tell Mom. I mean, I don't really see how it can be kept a secret from her, but I really want it to be. I know someone will say something to her, and the truth is, it's probably best if she hears about it from me. Definitely better for her to hear it from me than from Uncle Preston or Howie."

"Then I guess if you think that one of them will spill the beans, you should just get it over with and tell your mom now."

4.

TELLING MOM WHAT I HAVE TO

The next day, around noon, I left Gen and Cecilia in charge of the bookshop and drove over to my mother's house. I had given it a lot of thought, and decided that I would sugarcoat the situation for her. There was no need to alarm her with the facts at hand—that I was suing Fred to help pay for her medical bill—and as long as she was taken care of, she didn't need to know exactly how we came across the money.

I pulled into her driveway, right behind her car.

"Hey Ma," I said after I let myself into the house.

"Hello dear! I'm in the living room!" Mom was sitting on the couch reading a magazine. She held up a finger when I walked in. "Hold on, let me finish this paragraph first."

"Sure thing. Take your time."

"What a terrible world we live in," she said when she was finished reading.

"What's the article on?"

"Oh," she said. "Just some old thing on the Civil War. An article on how barbaric it really was, family members sticking each other with bayonets and everything. It gives me chills just thinking about it."

How appropriate.

"So how are you?" she asked.

"I'm fine. Things are going well at home with the baby and with Gen's parents and everything," I was lying a little, at least about Gen's parents. I put my hand on her's. "I wanted to talk to you about the nursing home thing."

"Yes?"

"I think we should be getting enough money to pay for it soon."

"That's good," she said. "You're not going to be in debt because of this, though. Right?"

"Not too bad," I said. "No."

"Good. Because if you would, I still haven't given up the other option."

"Don't even think about it."

"Where is the money coming from?" she asked.

"Fred."

"Fred?" she said. "Really? I thought he already said he couldn't help."

"He did."

"He changed his mind?"

"Yeah, something like that."

"That's good news," she said.

"Yeah, it's a relief for me, knowing that you won't have to go to a public institution." I paused and thought of the best way to say it. "But there's a little catch."

"What's that?"

"It might take us a little while to actually get the money from Fred. Some sort of legal issue with transferring that much money or something. We have to go to court, and it could take a couple of weeks."

"That's ok," Mom said. "I can stick it out." She repositioned herself on the couch. "The truth is, I feel absolutely fine."

215

"That's good." I smiled. "I hired Howie to deal with the court stuff."

"Oh!" she said, beaming. "That's great news! Your uncle Preston and Aunt Hallie must be so proud of him. He just passed the bar and already he's working. What a bright young man he turned out to be."

"Yeah, Uncle Preston was real happy when I told him about it." That much was true, even if the rest of my report was a little glossed over.

Mom stood up. "Since you're here anyway, why don't you stay for lunch?"

"That sounds great," I said. "But we have to make it a quick one. I have to get back to the bookshop kind of soon."

"Of course."

•••

When I got back after lunch, Sally told me that there was a message for me. "You have to ask Gen who it was," she said. "I can't remember."

It turned out that it was Uncle Preston, so I gave him a call.

"Yes. Paul. Gen told me you were over at your mother's place?" I could hear the banging sound of metal on metal in the background, the music of Preston's garage serenading me over the phone.

"Yeah, I just stopped over there for lunch."

"Did you mention the lawsuit to her?"

"Yup. I told her all about it so you wouldn't have to. Everything's all squared away. Now we just have to wait for the money to come rolling in, I guess."

"Ha! I like your attitude." There was a particularly loud thump in the background, followed by some yelling. "Ok Paul, I have to run. My guy Marcello just crashed one of the cars while he was pulling it in."

"Ouch. Ok, I'll talk to you later."

Ah, Uncle Preston. Ever so clever! I'm sure you found some way to charge your customer for your guy Marcello's mistake.

5.

HERE I COME, FRED, BAYONET IN HAND

Howie was working hard to get the lawsuit to trial as quickly as possible. He would check in with me every day to let me know how things were going. He spent a lot of time on the case, either because he wanted to make a first good impression with the legal system at large or because it was the only work he had.

We were having one of our regular check-ins over the phone:

"So, Howie," I said. "What's the scoop? How are we looking?"

"Things are lookin' good. At this rate, we can start the preliminary hearings as early as next week. And that's no small accomplishment, either! Sometimes, it can take months just to get to the preliminary stuff."

"Well good. We don't want this thing to drag out too long. Just remember. We only have one goal in mind here, and that's to get enough money for the nursing home as

217

fast as possible. We don't need to be cleaning Fred out or anything."

"I know it," Howie said. "Although, we could if we wanted to. We could take him for all he's worth, if we wanted to."

"It's a good thing for him that we don't want to do that, then."

"You bet it is."

There was a pause in the talking that stretched out into a silence. "Ok," I said. "I guess I'll talk to you tomorrow and see how things are looking then."

"Sounds good," he said.

I hung up the phone.

Gen poked her head in the kitchen door from the café, carrying a tray of dirty dishes. "What's the story?" she asked me.

"It sounds like things are going smooth, although I'm still nervous about Howie's attitude towards the case. And his experience. He actually used the term 'preliminary stuff' when he was talking to me. I mean, I understand that he feels comfortable enough around me that he doesn't feel the need to use professional terms, but I hope to God that he at least knows them."

"I'm sure he does, hun." She put the dishes in the sink and started cleaning them.

I stood up and walked over to help her. "He'd better. We can't be screwing this up at this point. If this doesn't work out..." I winced. "I can't even think about this not working out. This has to work out."

"It will." She leaned over and gave me a kiss on the forehead. "It will."

One cup needed a special amount of cleaning attention because of some gunk stuck to the bottom. I sponged hard. "I was thinking about inviting everyone over for dinner," I said. "You know, before we really get into this lawsuit."

"That sounds like a good idea," Gen said. "Yeah! We could set it up in the café, no problem. Get a nice big table and everything. It'll be nice."

218

"That's what I was thinking."

She dried her hands off on a towel next to the sink. "Who would you invite?"

"I was thinking that we could get my mom, Morty, Uncle Preston, Aunt Hallie, and Howie over here. You know, the whole gang. Cook up a nice big dinner and just relax together before the trial starts. One last chance to just kick back and relax."

"Sign me up," Gen said, walking out into the café. "I'll be there.

•••

When Gen told her parents about the dinner, her mother was unenthusiastic about the idea, to say the least.

"Do we have to do it?" Sally asked Gen.

"Yes, Mom. You do."

"Your father and I could just go out for dinner for the night," Sally suggested, "let you and Paul have some alone time with his family."

"No! I want you guys to be there. And it's important—for Cecilia's sake if, nothing else—that you at least pretend to like Paul's family. For once. I've had enough of you spending the whole time drinking in a corner whenever his family comes over. You need to be more social with them."

"Dear, you're asking a lot. The reason I don't talk to them when they're over is I'm afraid of what I might say to one of them. You of all people should know that I have a tough time holding my tongue. And when Paul's family is involved, it's even harder. They just have no class whatsoever. I swear it! I've never met such a boorish group."

"Well you better learn to hold your tongue, in that case. I don't want you saying anything embarrassing. Ok?"

"I'll do my best," Sally said. "But I certainly won't be making any promises to that effect."

"Mom!" Gen yelled. "Just don't do it! If it would help, I would suggest that you take it easy on the drinking."

"I don't know about that one," John mumbled.

"Oh, not you, too, Dad. It's just one night, for Christ's sake! It's not like I'm asking you for a real favor here, guys. I'm just asking you to show Paul and me a little respect. It's the least you two could do."

John and Sally looked at each other.

"I mean," Gen continued, looking to hurt her parent's feelings a little bit, "we have taken you into our home and fed you. All you guys do around here is spend our money on drinks..."

I can only imagine Sally's face after that doozey from Gen. It must've been priceless.

"...I don't think it's too much to ask of you guys. You just have to sit at a table with us for an hour and carry on some kind of a conversation with Paul's family. It would mean so much to us if you could do that. Just that. That's all I ask. And then you two can get back to drinking and passing out anywhere you please."

"Where are your manners?" Sally said, turning on her daughter. "Who do you think you are talking to, young lady? We're not just two people you picked up on the street and took in to your home. We are still your parents. And I, for one, will not sit by and be spoken to this way. John, say something!"

"Your mother's right," John said. He hadn't been listening to the women talking, but life with Sally had taught him how to be in the conversation without being in the conversation.

"Well I don't care," Gen said. "You two are coming to the dinner, and that's the end of it. Paul wants everyone to get together one last time before that Fred thing goes to trial, and I don't want you to ruin it for him."

"Alright," Sally said. "Alright. We'll be there."

"Thank you!" Gen said, exasperated. "That wasn't too hard, now was it?"

•••

Morty and Mom showed up first, at five o'clock.

It's funny to me how people who live the farthest away always seem to show up first. It was true of the kids at school when I was growing up, too: out of the five guys I hung out with most, it was always Bobby—who lived a mile away on Halemburgh Street—waiting on the steps for the school doors to open while Junior—who lived right across the street—was lucky to walk into the classroom only fifteen minutes late.

Morty and Mom "ooh"ed and "ah"ed when they saw the big table Gen and I had set up (with minimal help from Gen's parents). It was a big table that we covered in a tablecloth and candles and plates and napkins and silverware.

"Do you guys want anything to drink?" Gen asked. "I have to go check on the ham anyway."

"Sure," Morty said. "You got any beer, Paul?"

"Yeah. I got a six-pack of Rolling Rock and Sam Adams. Whichever you want is fine."

"Is it Summer Ale?" Morty asked me.

"I don't know. Winter Ale, I think. Does it make a difference?" I asked.

"It most certainly does."

"Well come check it out with me," Gen said, "and you can figure it out."

Gen held the kitchen door open for Morty and he rolled in.

I looked over at my mother. She was still standing by the door, holding on to her purse so tight that each of her knuckles looked like tiny, snow-capped mountains. She was looking down at her feet, but she smiled when she looked up and noticed me staring at her. "Sorry," she said. "I was daydreaming."

"That's ok. Here. Why don't you sit down?"

She took the chair that I offered her.

"Are you feeling ok, Mom?"

"Oh." She waved her hand around in the air. "I'm perfectly fine. Don't you worry about me one bit."

She smiled at me again. It felt like she was trying to convince me.

I put my hand on hers and gave her the worried smile: a half smile combined with scrunched eyebrows. I used it to let my mother know that I knew she wasn't telling me everything, but also that I could see she didn't want to be pressed about it.

Morty came back into the café with a Rolling Rock in hand.

I sucked air through my teeth. "Not the right kind of ale, eh?"

"No," he said. "But that's ok. I'm a sucker for the Rock."

"I know. That's why I bought it."

He raised the green bottle towards me then took a few forceful chugs.

"Paul?" Gen said, poking her head out of the kitchen. "Little Jack just woke up from his nap. Will you go up and get him?"

"Sure thing. I'll be right back, guys," I said to Mom and Morty.

I walked through the kitchen and up the stairs. I didn't hear Little Jack's crying until I reached the landing. Sometimes it amazed me that Gen could hear the baby from anywhere in the house.

"Hey there, little guy! Oh, you like it when you get picked up, hunh?" It worked every time: whenever Little Jack was crying, you just had to pick him up and he would stop immediately. It's not like he was starved for attention, or anything. Between Gen and me, Gen's parents, and even Cecilia, this kid got more than his fair share.

I brought him downstairs. In the kitchen, Gen said, "It's probably time to feed him."

That's the other thing. Little Jack never cried when he was hungry, either. So for us, feeding time was more like guesswork than a science. He would cry at night and one of us would pick him up and he'd stop crying and we'd try to feed him, but he would only eat half the time. That didn't mean he didn't eat enough; it just meant that he woke us up twice as much as Cecilia did when she was a baby.

"Ok," I said. "Will you bring out a bottle for us? I'm going to go sit with Mom."

Gen opened up the oven. "Yup. I'll bring it out in just one minute."

While I'd been getting Little Jack from upstairs, the rest of the party arrived. Howie, Uncle Preston, Aunt Hallie, Mom and Morty were all sitting around in a circle.

"Hey guys," I said. "How's it going?"

"Things are better than ever," Preston said, grinning like a fool.

"Oh, what's that you've got there?" Aunt Hallie asked.

"Would you like to hold him for a while?"

"Why yes. I would," she said, taking the infant. She cooed in Little Jack's face. "Oh Preston, when are we going to have another baby?"

Preston's eyes went wide.

Aunt Hallie looked at him and laughed. "I'm just pulling your leg."

"Oh thank God." Uncle Preston took out a handkerchief and matted his forehead. "What are you trying to do? Give me a heart attack?" He bit his lip right after he said it. Even with Jackson's death so far in the past, heart attacks would always remain a somewhat taboo subject. Everyone felt the sting of those words: "heart attack."

"Well," I said. "I want a beer. Can I get anyone else something to drink?"

"I'll take another Rock," Morty said, shaking his empty bottle.

"Anyone else?"

•••

Gen came out with the food, her parents and Cecilia in tow.

I put Little Jack into his "baby bouncer," a metal-framed baby holder with two bungee cords upholding a soft harness. He would push off the floor with his feet and bounce up and down. It usually got a smile out of the little guy.

"Hey Grandma!" my little girl said. They hugged. "Woah. Two grandmas in one room is funny. Ha ha!" And with that she started to run into the kitchen.

"Hey hey!" Gen said. "We're ready to eat now!"

"I knooooooooow, Mooooooooom! I'm going to wash my hands. Jeez!" The door slammed behind her.

"When did she become a teenager?" Gen asked me. "Ok, everybody! Food's ready! Come grab a seat and dig in."

Through no choice of my own, I ended up at a corner of the table, sandwiched between Howie and Uncle Preston. John and Sally dominated the far corner of the table, both of them already a little tipsy. Morty was sitting next to John, and my mother was between Sally and Aunt Hallie.

"Gen!" Morty said. "This food looks amazing!" Morty was the only one at the table with a pre-assigned seat. But that was just because he always brought his pre-assigned seat with him. Cecilia grinned from her chair directly across the table from me.

"Thank you," Gen said. "I can never get enough compliments." And then she looked over at me. Did I deserve that?

"So," I said, raising my beer. "I think a toast is in order."

"Why not," Morty said.

Once everyone raised their glasses, I said, "To family." As soon as I spoke, Cecilia made out to take a sip of her juice. So I took her hint and sped up the pace of my toast. "To family," I said again, faster, "and keeping close those we hold dear.

"I look around this table and see everyone I love, but I can't help looking around this table and noticing those that are missing. Jackson, my father, should be in our hearts as we eat. And Fred, who is away in New York. My love is with him, too, and I hope he will come home soon and see that we forgive him for everything he has done. Even though we continue to have our problems to this very day, I still love him. He's always my brother, and I can't help but to love him always." I took a sip from my beer.

"Here, here," Morty said. "Or, as Fred would say, total cornball."

"Yes," Uncle Preston said, "and he will always be my nephew. And that is precisely why I am proud of all of us here." Preston the orator stood up. "Proud of all of the people who love him. Proud that we can see past the pain that our immediate conflict creates and see that—once restitution is made—Fred will be a better person for it."

"Restitution?" my mother asked. She turned to Aunt Hallie and raised her eyebrows.

Hallie looked over at me and I opened my eyes wider, using my body language to tell her she should cover for me; make up a half-truth for me.

My aunt got the message loud and clear. "Preston meant that it'll be like Fred is paying you back for the General Store when all this legal stuff is cleared up. You know, when he helps to pay your bill for the nursing home."

"Oh," my mother said, clearly not convinced.

I laughed a nervous laugh—loud and lunatic—to blow past my mother's uncertainty and talk about something else. "Ha ha! Look at Little Jack in his bouncy chair. His feet barely touch the ground!"

"Yeah," Morty said. "Me and Little Jack have a lot in common."

"Ha!" Sally said loudly before covering her mouth with a hand.

"Honey," Mom said to Morty. "It's not polite to draw attention to your disability." She took a look at Sally out of the corner of her eye. "It makes some people uncomfortable, including me."

"Sorry Mom." Morty turned and grinned and winked at me. "I'll try not to do it anymore."

Gen asked, "Will you pass the greenbeans, please, Preston? Thank you." Gen shoveled some onto her own plate, then loaded up Cecilia's plate.

"Hey!" my daughter said.

"Young lady," Gen said, giving Cecilia a look that would turn a dandelion white. "You need to eat your vegetables. Don't make that face at me—it is not an option."

"That's how we should deal with Fred," Preston mumbled.

"What's that?" my mother asked.

"Ha ha!" That loud, nervous laughter from me again. This time, however, it drew the attention of everyone at the table. "Uh," I stammered, "...ah...I could just stare at Little Jack all day and just laugh. I still can't believe he will be a person someday. Just like my little girl here." I smiled at Cecilia across the table.

"Just make sure to give them morals while they're young," Uncle Preston said. He looked down at his plate and mumbled, "Just look what happened to Fred, how he turned out."

"What did you say?" my mother asked. She laughed. "Everyone says your vision is the first thing to go, but at this point, I feel like I can only hear what someone says when I read their lips!"

"Well Uncle Preston isn't helping you out, Ma." I stared at him, and said, "He sure is mumbling a lot."

Preston continued to look down at his plate.

"Anyone need something more to drink?" I asked. "I know that I could go for another beer right about now."

Sally shook her glass, splashing around the little bit of orange screwdriver left at the bottom. "Way ahead of you, Paul. Another round for me."

A beer for Morty, Howie, and John; juice for Gen, my mother, and Cecilia; nothing for Aunt Hallie.

"And I guess I'll have a beer, too," Uncle Preston said.

"Ok. Will you help me bring everything out, please?"

"...Sure," Preston said.

The door to the kitchen swung behind us and I waited for it to settle closed before I spoke. Preston, on the other hand, went straight for the fridge.

"What are you trying to do?" I asked his back.

"Get some drinks," he said into the refrigerator. He chuckled. "What does it look like?"

"That's not what I mean and you know it."

Preston closed the fridge, the remainder of the two six-packs in each hand, and faced me. "What do you mean then?"

"I asked a favor of you before you came here. Before we even decided to sue Fred. It wasn't a big favor. I just asked that you wouldn't talk about the legal stuff around Mom. Is it really that hard to shut up about Fred?"

"Paul," Uncle Preston said, reaching out to me with the six-packs. "It wasn't my intention—"

"—Wasn't your intention? It's very simple, Preston, to not mention Fred and the lawsuit."

"I mumbled because I was trying to be discreet. I was making sure your mom couldn't hear."

"Well you did a great job of that," I said. "She couldn't understand you, but she did hear you. And now she's a little edgy. I think she can tell something's going on, that there's something we're not telling her."

"Well I think you should tell her everything, anyway. Either way, whether she knows or not, you're being very paranoid and over-protective."

"Good!" I screamed. "I'd rather be paranoid and over-protective than make my mother worry by letting her know about what's going on with Fred."

Gen came into the kitchen, saying "...just make sure everything's going alright in there" over her shoulder. The kitchen door swung behind her and settled to a close. "You guys want to keep it down? We can hear you yelling in the other room." She looked back and forth between us. "What's going on here, anyway?"

I looked at Uncle Preston, repeating Gen's question with my eyebrows.

"Nothing," Preston said. "Paul and I are just a little high-strung about the lawsuit."

"Ok. Well why don't you bring the beers out and I'll get the juice." Preston headed for the door. Preston passed Gen and she turned around. "Oh, and Preston?"

"Yeah?"

"I don't want you mumbling about Fred in my house. Especially not in front of Paul's mom. Ok?"

Preston pursed his lips together and went back to the table.

Gen came over and hugged me, resting her head on my shoulder. She had begun to lose the weight she'd put on during her pregnancy with Little Jack, but her belly between us made our hug slightly awkward. We released each other.

"Hang in there, tough guy," Gen said, first pinching my cheek, then playfully slapping my face.

I smiled. "You know I will, but that man..." I shook my fist at Uncle Preston through the swinging kitchen door.

"Don't let him bother you. The more you let him get to you, the more your mother will worry that there's something wrong." She pulled out four glasses and the bottle of vodka, and opened the fridge for the juice. "Now here: bring out my mom's screwdriver so I don't give it to Cecilia by accident."

I took the glass from her hand and kissed her.

•••

I took one last bite of ham, then pushed my chair away from the table and rubbed my belly. "I can't remember the last time I ate that much."

"And I can't remember the last time you had four beers in a night," Gen said.

It was true. Ever since I had started drinking, I've had a low tolerance, which meant that I could get pretty tipsy off of a couple of beers. It was both a blessing and a curse: it was good because I could go out drinking for a night and spend half as much as anyone else on alcohol, but the problem was that I always tried to keep up with my friends and I would end up kneeling in front of a toilet.

"That's nothin'," Morty said. "I had four beers when I woke up this morning."

There were some chuckles around the table.

"Stop laughing," I said. "He's serious."

"So what does everyone have planned for tomorrow?" Aunt Hallie asked.

"Well," Howie said, the first word he had spoken all dinner. "I'm heading in to court early in the morning."

"Oh! How exciting!" my mother said. "Is that for the problem Fred's having with sending the money to us?"

Howie looked at her, confused. "No," he said. "There's no 'problem' with Fred sending money. I'm going to the preliminary hearing for the civil suit tomorrow."

Mom turned to Sally and said, "What's a civil suit?"

"It's a trial case where the defendant would have to pay money to the plaintiff if found guilty. You should ask John over there. He's lost a few civil suits to the bank. He knows all about them. Don't you, dearest?"

John pretended to ignore his wife.

"Basically," Sally continued, "Howie here is in charge of suing Fred for lost income from the sale of the General Store."

My mother's jaw dropped like she was going to say something, but all that came out was "...ah..."

My jaw dropped and nothing came out. I wish I hadn't had so many beers because that would have been a great time to say something comforting to my mom.

Gen, Uncle Preston, Aunt Hallie, and Morty all looked over at me: Gen looked concerned; Preston had a look that said, "Well, what can you do?"; Aunt Hallie looked interested in where this was going; and Morty looked like he didn't even know how to respond.

Sally picked up her glass and shook it at me, a big smile on her face. "Paul! Refill over here!"

•••

When Uncle Preston, Aunt Hallie and Howie headed back home, I had the chance to talk to my mother alone. Mom, Morty and I were sitting at the table, and Gen and Cecilia were clearing the dishes.

"I gotta go pee," Morty said.

"Use the one over there," I said.

"Well, duh. It's not like I'm going to go upstairs." Morty turned himself by holding his right wheel tight and pushing his left wheel forward. "Be right baaaack," he sang.

Mom was holding her hands in her lap. Since Sally had dropped the bomb, my mother had become very quiet, staring off at a wall while everyone else made Smalltalk around the table.

"So Ma. Did you enjoy the food?"

She slowly looked over at me, her eyes fixed on the wall until her nose was pointed right at me. "Yes, dear," she said. "I always enjoy Gen's cooking."

"Good."

Mom looked down at her lap.

I bent my head over, trying to catch her eye. I smiled at her. "Is everything ok?"

She started knitting her fingers together and rubbing her hands.

"Ma?"

"I just don't understand what's happening," she said. "What's happening?"

I sighed. "I don't really understand it myself."

Morty came out of the bathroom and saw the serious looks on our faces. "Uh," he said. "I'm going to go help Gen in the kitchen if I can."

I gave him a nod and grimaced.

"Yup, just passin' through to help out in the kitchen." He mouthed the words "good luck" to me. The swinging door slapped the back of his chair before he made it through.

"Listen, Ma," I said. "Here's the story." I told her about my visit with Fred, how he'd basically blown me off. I told her about how it seemed that Fred wanted to help—that he would have helped—but that somehow, his pride had managed to get in the way. I told my Mom about my long nights in the café, pouring over financial records and trying my best to make ends meet. I told her how I went to Uncle Preston in my hour of need and how the television had taken precedence over my dilemma. I told her how Preston and Howie had been trying to pressure us into this for so long and I told her about how, eventually, I caved in.

I told my mom how I would imagine her potential fellow patients at a public mental institution: the guy who walked around with a knife hidden in his underwear, ready to pull it out and attack at any moment; the woman who would bite anyone that came near her; the teenager who did too many drugs and thinks that he is on a mission from God to cleanse the world of the elderly; the woman who spat at nurses and gnawed on the arms of other patients; the man who foamed at the mouth and shouted at the nurses because he thought they were demons; the man who ripped out his own hair and shoved it down the throats of his fellow patients while they were sleeping.

"With the situation the way it is," I concluded, "I had no choice but to sue Fred for the money. Doing anything else would be gross negligence on my part and I want you to be taken care of. I want to take care of you. It's the least I can do to repay you for bringing me into this world."

My mother continued to stare at her hands in her lap, but I kept talking at her, hoping some of what I said would help her to understand that this was the only way out.

"Ma, say something to me. I'm worried about you."

She looked up at me and her wrinkled face felt the pull of gravity. The corners of her mouth sunk down with the loose skin of her jaw line and her eyes began to tear. "What could I possibly say?" she asked me. "Once I became a mother, I gave my whole life to you kids. To all three of you. Now, thirty years later, I see you destroying each other. Morty can't walk and he drinks all the time; because he doesn't want to help, Fred is hurting you; and you are suing your brother for money to put me in a nursing home."

I moved my chair closer to her, so that my knee touched her thigh. "But Ma," I said. "I don't have a choice!"

"Helping me like this is killing me."

If Oedipus were here, he would've said, "Take it from me: sometimes whatever is meant to happen will happen, no matter how hard you try to avoid it."

"It's the only way I know to save you from yourself," I whispered so she couldn't hear.

"Paul, ever since your father died, there has been one disaster after another. If he were around to see what's happened since he's been gone, he would be devastated."

231

"We're doing our best, though," I said. I put an arm around her, rubbing her shoulder, trying to console her like she used to console me when I got hurt as a kid. "We're going to get through this just fine. In a little while, we'll remember this and think about how funny it was."

"There's nothing funny about this." She looked down and away from me. She moved her lips a couple of times, almost starting another sentence, then said nothing. She took a deep breath, and said, "Paul. Do you remember when you asked me about the promise Jackson made to Fred?"

That'd been over seven years ago. For someone who would forget her husband was dead, my mom had a very good memory. "Yeah, I remember, Ma."

She kept looking away from me and down at the floor when she spoke. "Well, I think that's why we're having all of these problems now. After Fred was born, your father decided that it was the right time to start the business..."

6.

A TRUST LEADS TO DESTRUCTION

And this was the story that my mother told me.

A couple of years after Fred was born, after four years of marriage and menial jobs, Jackson had decided that it was time to take a chance and start his own business. He had decided on opening a general store because he figured that if you sold things everyone needed, you would always have customers. Jackson had a strong sense of family—he always did, even if he did a poor job of expressing this sense—and he figured that a family business would be a great way to make sure that his family would live better than he did when he'd been growing up. So he took out his life savings, and, with a mortgage on the house from the bank, bought up the plot of land on Marborough's Main Street and began construction. Jackson had to do a lot of the work himself to save on costs, but he managed to open the place up with the amount of money available to him.

However, before he could even think about opening the store, he had to have a sit-down with a lawyer, who explained the ins and outs of commercial land ownership.

One of the first things Jackson told the lawyer was, "I'm a family man, Mr. Levinson. I want to make sure this store is here for my family when I retire. I'm worried that there may be some problems down the road, and I want you to make sure that the store will be there for my children."

"Well Mr. Morrison, I can help you out," the lawyer said. He proceeded to give Jackson a couple of options. Jackson listened carefully, and decided on a course of action.

"Thank you, Mr. Levinson. You've eased my mind." The lawyer took care of all of the paperwork so Jackson's plans to ensure his children's future would be complete. He came home to his wife and two year old son, happy and confident.

It was almost a full year later that Jackson let Fred in on what was, in Jackson's mind, a masterpiece of financial planning. They were sitting in our house—the house they had bought a while before the General Store opened, the house that Mom still lived in—in the living room after dinner one night. Fred had gone in to work with Jackson that day, helping out as best as a three year old could. Jackson was proud of Fred. At that age, Fred was not the lazy bum that he slowly grew into, and there was nothing that Jackson liked more than a go-getter.

So they were sitting around the living room when Jackson said, "Fred? Come here. Sit down for a second."

Fred came bouncing over. "Yeah, Dad?"

"Son, I want to let you in on a little secret. I'm proud of the work you did today."

Fred grinned big, and Mom looked on the father-son scene proudly.

"Thanks!"

"I opened the Store so our family would never have to worry about money. I wanted to make sure that my children would always be taken care of."

Fred was only half-listening, since that's the most that a young child can do.

Jackson smiled at Fred. "When we opened up the Store, I spoke to a lawyer. I told him that I wanted my children to have the Store when I retired. So he suggested to me," (and this was one of the things that was so great about Jackson, that he would speak to a three year old about important and complicated things, assuming they understood much more than they ever could), "that I put the deed to the land and the store in your name in Trust until you are eighteen. This way, we won't have to pay any gift or estate taxes when the store changes hands."

Even Jackson could recognize the fact that Fred didn't understand a word he was saying. "What I'm saying, Fred, is that when you turn eighteen, the Store will belong to you."

Fred beamed. A three year old may not have been able to understand the specifics of what Jackson was saying, but he could still feel proud that his father was putting trust in him.

"But son," Jackson continued, getting more serious, "I'm a little nervous, and I'll tell you why. I had to work hard to get where I am today, and I want to make sure that you have some sort of drive in your life. The store will belong to you when you're eighteen, but I want you to know that you are going to have to work hard for it. If I think that you aren't putting in the effort, I won't hand the Store to you on a silver platter."

"Ok, Dad." Fred's attention span had run out of fuel and he was ready to be done with the conversation.

"So I promise—if you work hard for it, and if you put in the effort—the Store will be yours."

•••

Mom was crying when she finished telling the story, sobs cutting her off when she said, "So you see... Paul... Fred..."

"It's ok, Ma. It's ok." I kept rubbing her shoulder like I'd been the entire time she'd been talking. She calmed down to the point where she could speak again.

"It wasn't until you and Morty were teenagers that your father put your names on the deed, and since he never went to a lawyer after doing that, the whole place still legally belonged to Fred. If only... your father had been... been... more..." She trailed off in tears again.

"It's ok, Ma. I understand."

She looked down and away from me again. She really seemed to love looking at that spot on the floor.

"We can't un-do what's been done already," I said. "We just have to try to pick up the pieces and get on with our lives."

"I know that," she said. She held herself with one of your arms. "I just remember all of the promises your father made and think about how—if he'd just thought about what he'd been saying to you boys—things could be so different now."

"Of course they could. But that's not the way things turned out. You can't keep going back to that and worrying. When I saw Fred, he seemed much happier than he'd ever been at home. He had a fiancé, for Christ's sake! Who would have ever guessed that Fred would find a girl he liked and liked him back."

Mom smiled. I'm very glad for that smile when I think back on the whole night. That one smile was one small triumph in a night of failures. I'd failed to provide my mother with the care she needed, and then, on top of that, I'd failed to keep what should have been secret from her. But that smile is what I like to remember, that smile on my mother's face lit her up in a way I hadn't seen for a long time, probably since Jackson's death.

"I know," she said. "The way he talked about girls, I never thought he would find the right one for him." That one smile slowly dissipated. "I'm sorry, Paul. I'm sorry all of this is happening. I'm sorry that I'm causing so many problems. I'm sorry—"

I held up my hand to cut her off. "Mom, I don't want to hear it. I should be the one apologizing. This whole mess is my fault. I could have put the bookshop up for a mortgage or something. I'm sorry I—"

This time Mom held up a hand to cut me off. "You're doing your best, and your best is very good. I'm proud of you, Paul."

My mother hugged me, and it made me feel real good.

PART VI
BURIED OUT AT AN
ODD SEA

DEADLINES APPROACHING
(PROLOGUE TO PART VI)

My lawyer stopped by this morning to remind me that my mother's funeral is today. Like I could've forgotten that. "Paul," he said. "You have to be ready to go at twelve sharp. One of the cops will escort you from your cell here to a van that will take you down to the church. I did my best to give you some private time with your family, but the judge said that the cop has to be within an arm's reach of you at all times. So don't give him a hard time and stay close. Once the services are over, the van will take you to the cemetery, where you will have one hour. After that, you have to come back here: no party, no going home for a while, you will come right back.

237

"I had to pull a lot of strings to get you out of here for this event, so don't screw around. Follow every instruction that the officer gives you."

I told him that I would.

"Oh. They also said that you would have to wear an ankle bracelet. It works like the lojack system—you know, the anti-theft system they have in cars—so they know where you are. They make people who are under house-arrest wear them all the time. They are a little big, but not too uncomfortable. You'll barely notice it."

I thanked him, then quickly got back to work writing. The deadline of my mother's funeral is quickly approaching. It's finally time to tell what I've set out to tell, or else remain silent and leave my children without a father and my wife without a husband.

My story begins to end the morning after the dinner; my story ends the day after I saw my mother alive for the last time.

1.

THE LAST CHANCE TO SAY GOODBYE

"So basically, we're on the fast track," Howie continued. "The judge has said that we will start the jury-selection process next week, and the trial will start directly after that."

"Well you know that for us it's the sooner the better," I said.

"You don't know how right you are. Oftentimes, when a case is rushed to trial like this, the defendant will be intimidated by the jury and will look to strike a deal with the prosecution. If we're lucky, this thing may never go to trial at all and we'll have the money for your mother in no time."

"It sounds like you're doing a great job down there at the courthouse, Howie. Keep up the good work."

"You bet. Alright, I'll talk to you later."

"Bye bye."

I hung up the phone. After Morty took Mom home, I spent the rest of the night trying to fall asleep. There was too much on my mind, however, and on the few occasions where I was close to sleep, Little Jack would wake up and cry.

But when I got out of bed that morning, I felt a little better about everything. The sun was out, and it was always easier to be afraid at night when the darkness feeds your imagination.

Howie's call had put what was left of my fears to rest. He seemed fully confident that this would be a speedy trial whether they decided to settle or not, and it was an infectious confidence. I was sure that my mother would be able to hold out long enough, and then we would be able to put her under the care of trained professionals.

"Good morning, John," I said as he stumbled into the kitchen.

He had a hand over his eyes and he looked pale. "Turn that damn light off," he said. "It's burning a hole in my retina."

"A little hung over, eh?"

"You don't know the half of it," he said.

Sally and John had gone upstairs almost immediately after Sally opened her mouth and told Mom about the lawsuit the night before. They spent the next couple of hours getting drunk in their room, so I wasn't surprised that John was just getting up at ten o'clock and that Sally was still asleep.

John poured himself a glass of water and sat down at the kitchen table.

I flicked off the light switch. "Did you enjoy the dinner last night?"

"Yes, yes. I had a fine time." He held his head. "No offense, Paul, but could we not talk right now? My ears are ringing."

"That's the phone, John. I'll get it, don't worry."

He whispered something to himself and drank the rest of his water in one gulp.

"Hello?" I said.

"Hello, dear. It's me."

"Hey, Ma. How are you feeling today?"

"Good," she said. "Good."

"I have some good news."

"Oh? What's that?"

"I just spoke to Howie. He's down at the courthouse right now."

John looked over at me. When he thought I wasn't looking, he refilled his glass with vodka and ice.

"He said that things are going faster than any of us thought it would. There's a very good chance that the case won't even have to go to trial."

Mom said something that I couldn't quite hear. "What was that?"

"I said that would be nice."

"Yeah. So he said that sometimes, just by seeing the jury in the box, the defendant will try to cut a deal. So there's a chance that this whole thing will be over by next week. Isn't that great?"

"That would be lovely, dear." It sounded like she didn't believe that that was great news.

"So," I said after a pause.

"Well I was just calling to check in," Mom said. "Just to make sure everything is going ok."

"Are you sure you're doing ok? Because I can take a ride out there right now, if you want. We can have some lunch or something."

"No, don't bother yourself," she said.

"It's no bother."

"I was just about to go up for a bath."

"Ok," I said. "Well I'm always a phone call away. If you change your mind."

"Thank you, dear. You've always been so good to me." I thought I heard some whimpering, but my mom quickly said, "Well I'll talk to you later, then."

"Take care, Ma," I said. "Maybe we can have dinner together tonight?"

"We'll see. Goodbye, Paul."

She hung up before I got the chance to say goodbye.

I wandered into the café, where Gen was standing behind the register. Little Jack was in his baby bouncer. "Eh," he said.

Gen smiled when she saw me. "So what did Howie say?"

"Things are looking up. We may not have to go to trial, depending on Fred. Hopefully, he doesn't see this as a personal attack. Otherwise, we'll just have to let this thing run its course. Either way, I think that we can ride it out until the money comes in."

Cecilia came running over to us from across the café. "Hey Dad!" she said. "Can I do the register? That man over there said he was ready to buy a book."

"Sure thing," I said. "You know how to do it better than I do at this point."

She smiled at me. One of her K9 teeth was missing.

"Woah," I said. "When did you lose that tooth?"

"God, Dad," Cecilia said. "I lost it like three days ago."

"Yeah," Gen said. "Where have you been? The tooth fairy already stopped by and everything."

"Really?" I asked.

Gen raised her eyebrows and nodded at me.

"Wow," I said. "Well I guess I've just had my head in the clouds, lately. How much did the tooth fairy give you?"

"A dollar!" Cecilia said, triumphantly holding out the picture of George Washington.

"A dollar?" I asked, looking at Gen. "When I was a kid, the tooth fairy used to give us a nickel."

Gen shrugged. "I guess inflation caught up with her."

"Did you find everything you wanted?" Cecilia asked the man she had pointed out before, the one who was ready to buy a book.

"Why yes I did, young lady," he said. He handed her the book.

"That's three dollars and fifty cents."

I looked at Gen and tilted my head towards the kitchen door. She shrugged and nodded.

"Ok Cecilia, be good to your customer here. I'm going to go talk to Mommy in the kitchen for a second."

"I don't think you have to worry," the customer said, pulling out his wallet. "Your little girl here is more polite than most people you find behind a cash register."

I smiled at him politely, giving him the once over. It made me feel guilty, but any time a stranger said anything about my daughter, I always became over-sensitive and found myself wondering if this was some sort of pervert or child molester. I must watch the news too much. I followed Gen into the kitchen. John had disappeared with his glass of vodka, presumably making his way back upstairs and into bed.

"A dollar, Gen?"

She looked surprised. "Yeah, Paul. A dollar. Your daughter lost her tooth, so I gave her a dollar."

"You know how tight things are with money right now."

"It's just a dollar. At least one of us noticed that she lost a tooth at all, hmm?"

That stung.

I gave Gen a glare that instantly softened when we made eye contact. I looked down at the floor, feeling the shame that her soft brown eyes threw at me. "I'm sorry. I've had a lot on my mind. It's not like anyone told me or anything."

"I know, tough guy," she said, punching me in the arm, "but it's also kind of hard to miss a missing tooth."

"I'm sorry."

"It's fine," Gen said. "But don't start giving me trouble because I gave Cecilia a dollar, ok? She deserves at least that much. Between the trial coming up and all the attention we've been giving Little Jack, I was worried that our girl was falling through the cracks. You should've seen how excited she was when she woke up and found the dollar under her pillow."

"Where was I for that?"

"It was the morning after you decided to sue Fred. When you were out talking to Morty and Preston and Howie. I was going to tell you to come wake Cecilia up with me, but you were already gone by the time I woke up."

"Wow. I'm sorry, honey. I wish I'd been there." I felt terrible. I mean, here I was, missing out on my daughter growing up, and she was slowly becoming a teenager right before my eyes.

"Well I wish you'd been there, too." Gen started to cry.

I went over and put my hands on her shoulders, making her look at me. "Hun, it's ok. We're all going to be fine."

"I know. I just want all this to be over. You've been so preoccupied lately with Fred and your mother." She tried to calm herself down. "I want my husband back and I want the father of my children back."

I hugged her to my chest. "It'll be over soon," I said, stroking her hair. "I know that I've been slacking on my family duties, but you understand."

"Yeah," she said. "I understand. I just wish there was something I could do to help make this go away faster. I just want this to be over with."

"It will be soon. It will be. I promise."

2.

A FINAL RESTING PLACE DEEMED INAPPROPRIATE

I hung up the phone. For the past hour, I had been calling my mother every five minutes without success. She had said she was going to take a bath when I last spoke with her, but that had been earlier that morning, almost three hours ago. I was starting to get worried. There was a chance that she couldn't hear the phone, or that she couldn't find it, but I was still worried.

I went into the café. "I'm going to run over to my mom's house," I said to Gen.

"Still haven't gotten through?"

I shook my head no.

"Well I'll see you when you get back." She kissed me. "Come back soon!"

"As quick as I can," I said. I gave Cecilia a high-five on the way out. "You be good for Mommy, ok? I'll be back soon."

"Where you going?" she asked.

"I'm going to check in on Grandma. Just to make sure that she's doing ok and see that she's not too lonely in that big house all by herself."

"K! See you later, alligator!"

"In a while, crocodile," I said, finishing the rhyme.

During the car ride over to my mother's house, I turned the radio on as loud as I could. Turning the volume up diminished the quality of the sound, but it drowned out my voice while I sang along. Truth be told, the grinding of the speakers was a more appealing sound than any that ever came from my mouth.

"By the hand now, take me by the hand, pretty mama," I said, harmonizing with the Doobie Brothers. "Come and dance with your daddy all night long. I'd like to hear some funky Dixieland, pretty mama come take me by the hand."

Nothing relaxed me more than turning up the radio in my crap car and screaming along with the lyrics. There was something about the way singing made me feel. I could get completely lost in it and really push everything else out of my head. It had a very Zen quality to it. Music truly is a wonderful thing.

I pulled into her driveway and saw her car.

"Hey Ma," I came into her house screaming. "Are you home?"

I looked on the first floor, yelling into all of the rooms. No answer.

I started to climb the stairs, getting nervous. I started questioning myself. Had I seen her car in the driveway? Part of me hoped that I hadn't, that I just thought I had. I started to convince myself that maybe I'd been mistaken. That my mother wasn't answering because she had taken a drive; gone shopping; visited her sister; anything.

When I got to the top of the stairs, I looked right, down to the end of the hall. There was the room I had lived in for most of my life; the room I had lived in with Gen for a year and a half after we got married; the room that I brought my darling Cecilia home to after she had been given life.

"Ma?" I asked scared, my voice cracking.

Down the hall from my room, there was no light coming from my brother Fred's old room. There was no light from my brother Morty's old old room next door. There was no light from my mother's room, the room she used to share with Jackson.

I turned around. Behind me, there was a little light sneaking between the bottom of the bathroom door and the carpet of the hallway.

I opened the door.

There was the tub that Mom had overfilled, spilling water down the stairs; there was the radiator in the corner that always made a loud banging sound, even in the heat of New England summers; there was the medicine cabinet, the mirror replaced after that time Fred smashed it; and there was the radio that had always been on the edge of the sink, plugged in the wall.

Except now, it was in the tub. In the water. With my mother.

I slammed the bathroom door shut and slumped to the carpet. I began to squeeze the soft beige of the floor between my fingers, staring at the closed door in front of me. She was dead, I'd seen. Her skin had been a very pale white, and the misplaced radio dispelled any illusions that she'd merely fallen asleep.

"Why did this happen? Why did this have to happen?" I asked the closed bathroom door. Was it an accident? Or did my mother do it on purpose? I didn't know. I don't know.

I pictured my mother, when she and I were much younger: *we are in the park. And so are Morty and Fred, and Jackson. It's New England Spring, which means that it is warm in the sun, cold in the shade, and freezing everywhere when the wind comes through. Mom and Jackson are sitting on a picnic blanket, and I am running around with my brothers. We are tossing something around—a Frisbee, I think. I run to make a catch, trip over a root that is sticking out of the ground, and skin my knee.*

"Mom!" I scream, and run over to the blanket. "I got hurt!"

"Let me look at that," Jackson says. He gives me a look that says, "Suck it up." Then he actually says, "Oh, that's not too bad."

"Ow!" I say when he touches the cut.

"Get your fingers out of there. You're going to infect it."

"It's not going to get infected, dear," Jackson says.

"If it does," my mother says, "then we're going to have to pay for the hospital bill. Isn't this just like that quote you like so much? 'A stitch in time saves nine?' Who says that."

"Ben Franklin did."

"Well this is just like that. Now go on, go get some antiseptic and a Band-Aid for your son."

"The boy's fine," he grumbles as he gets up to get the goods.

She cradles me in her arms and tells me, "It will be fine, the cut will heal up real quick."

Sitting on the carpet of the hallway on the second floor of my mother's house, I could picture her younger face perfectly on that day in the park. *I look up at her, and the light filtered green through the tree branches above, surrounding her head.*

"Don't coddle the boy, Ruth!" Jackson says to my mother when he returns. "If you coddle him, then he won't ever leave the house."

I took a deep breath and collected myself, and decided on a course of action. There were a few things that needed to be taken care of. For starters, I couldn't let someone find my mother like that. So, with resolution, I opened the bathroom door.

"Bang!" said the radiator.

First, I unplugged the radio and pulled it out of the tub, trying to avoid looking at my mother and praying that I wouldn't hurt myself in the process. I put the radio under the sink to get it out of the way, making sure I wouldn't trip

248

on it later. I crouched there for a moment, breathing hard and trying to calm myself. I was scared.

I forced myself to look back at the tub and my mother, both dead and wet and porcelain white. I walked to the tub and put a hand down on its edge to balance as I slowly bent to my knees. I pulled the drain and listened as the water started to gurgle down.

My mother's face was calm, but it was an eerie calm. It didn't look relaxed. Rather, it was devoid of anything. I put a hand to her face, cupped her cheek, and felt the cold, wet flesh. There was some hair cemented by moisture to the corner of her mouth and I brushed it away.

I picture my mother again, when I was in High School: *she is in bed. I'm back home after a day at school and working at the General Store.*

Mom is really sick. She has a fever and her hair is flat on her head, cemented by sweat. She went to the doctor earlier that day, driving herself since the rest of us were busy.

"Don't come any closer, I have the flu," she says.

I go downstairs for a while. Jackson picked up some food from Cristina's Restaurant for us since he doesn't know how to cook.

"Here, bring this tea up to your mother," he says.

I bring the tea up to her.

"Thank you," she says.

I sit on the edge of her bed and talk with her for a while, about nothing in particular. I wipe some sweat off of her face with the back of my hand and feel good about myself, knowing that I am helping the woman who devoted her life to helping me.

I recall feeling strange that, after her death, my mother's life would flash before my eyes. I'd always heard about that happening when someone jumped off of a building—about how when a person knows they are going to die, they see their whole life like it's a movie or something—but I felt it was strange that someone else's life would come to life in my mind.

I rested my head on the edge of the tub and looked at my mother's eyes. They stared at the ceiling with a blank intensity that could have been confused for a sign of life. I sighed and stood up again. The tub was half-empty.

I reached under her body and pulled her out, holding her to my chest like she held me when I was a baby. Her skin was prune-ish from the water, and—aside from her face—her skin was warm when I first picked her up. I started to cry while I held her. The tears fell from my face and mixed with the condensation on her naked body, already evaporating and cooling.

I carried her to her bedroom slow and careful with lopsided steps, one arm hooked under her knees and the other under the small of her back so that her head and arms and feet all hung loose. Her limp limbs were heavy, and while I tried to keep everything balanced, her arms flew all over the place and she began to slip out of my arms. I almost dropped her, the arm under her back slipping up and up and up, but I managed to catch her body by the neck and, with a heft, I regrasped her and retained my grip.

I passed through both doorways carefully, trying not to hit her head. It was not easy to carry her body. I mean physically, although it was no easy task emotionally, either. By the time I laid her out on the bed, her skin was cold and dry. I arranged her body so that her arms and legs fell straight, all pointing to the foot of the bed.

I made sure that her body was well placed. I didn't want my mother to roll off the bed while I went to her closet and pulled out one of the dresses. I picked out one that I knew she liked to wear. It was plain, a yellow pastel. I struggled with her body—pulling at her head, shimmying the yellow past her torso. I left the dress there, bunched up just above her hips for a moment, and left her while I found a pair of underwear in her closet. I put her feet through the white panties and slid them up her legs, lifting her body from under the small of her back with one hand when the underwear reached her hips so I could pull it over her butt. I kept crying, but I found the will to continue by remembering the care this woman must have given to me as a child,

250

changing my diapers and cleaning vomit from the shoulders of her clothing.

Her underwear was in place, and I tugged the yellow pastel around her thighs, smoothing the dress out over her legs. I grabbed her a pair of red shoes and put them on her bare feet. I was finished.

I stood at the foot of my mother's bed and watched her for a moment. She looked like she was at peace. She looked like she was at peace for the first time since Fred had sent that horrible letter home, telling us where he'd been.

Again I wondered why this had to happen, why the woman who took care of us brothers had to lose her life. My mother always said she had given her life to us boys, but now, this phrase — meant to be cute — took on a whole new meaning.

I waited until my mother's hair dried, then I went to call the police.

EPILOGUE

WHAT COULD BE AND WHAT SHOULD BE

And now it will only be a little while before my police officer comes by to escort me to the van. Most of my being is dreading the funeral. Even though I found her body—saw it with my eyes—I still deny her death. Going to the funeral will be a final affirmation of what I already hate to know.

At the same time, a part of me is looking forward to the funeral. For starters, I'll be able to get out of jail for a little while. But more important, a small part of me sees this as one final opportunity. I can only hope that that is true and that we can take this chance to make amends.

When the officer escorts me to the van and the funeral ceremony, I hope to find everyone I love waiting for me, waiting to comfort me. Here is how I have played it out in my head at night, over and over again, while trying to sleep in my jail-cell-cot:

•••

When I arrive at the funeral, Gen and the kids will be waiting for me right inside the church doors. Gen will hug me and remind me that everything will be ok in the end; Cecilia will show me how to be resilient; and Little Jack will show me that sometimes you just have to say "Eh" and get on with your life.

I'll walk into the church and everyone I care about and everyone who cares about me will be sitting in the pews already. They all offer their condolences while I make my way up the center aisle to my seat up front. Morty will be there, of course, creating a fire hazard with The Chair, trying to make the best of a shit situation. If there's one thing he's practiced in, it's making the best of a shit situation.

In fact, the only person who isn't there is Fred. But don't worry, he'll show up later.

Reverend Sommers, the same man who lead the services for Jackson's funeral, presides. He would give a speech about loving mothers, making the point that the Virgin Mary is exemplified in the care that all mothers give to their children. He would say, without irony, that my mother in particular was a wonderful caregiver, that she gave her life for her children. He wouldn't know how right he was.

Morty and I would go up to speak as well, repeating each other and the Reverend in praising our mother. Uncle Preston would probably say a few words as well, reminding us that he is there to take care of us all, that he can be counted on to help out if there is any trouble even though he already proved he should be counted on for nothing.

When it's over, I'll help to carry my dead mother — for the second time — out to the waiting hearse.

It is a wonderful service, everyone agrees, and they'll tell me so when I'm standing in the church lobby. They'll all say, "Hang in there," or, "See you over at the cemetery," or, "She was a wonderful woman."

After almost everyone has headed over to the cemetery, the police officer will tap me on the shoulder while I'm standing with Gen and the kids and politely say it's time to get in the van and head over to the cemetery.

When the van arrives at the funeral plot, I'll get out among the endless sea of grass and marble. There's the hole, a perfect fit for the box containing my mother. Reverend Sommers would be there to speak once again, doing his whole "ashes to ashes, dust to dust" routine. Then my mother would be lowered into the ground. I would be the first to shovel some dirt on her coffin.

Everyone else will wait their turn to throw some dirt in the hole while Gen holds me. I'd be sobbing hard—I'm soaking the shoulder of Gen's black dress—but I would feel no shame. I'll be proud to show the world just how much my mother meant to me.

I'll be standing off to the side of my mother's final resting place when Morty will wheel over and say, "Look!"

I turn in the direction he's pointing and I see exactly what I wanted to see: no more than thirty yards away, a man is standing among the tombstones with his hands in his pockets. He seems wary, watching the whole procession from afar. While I watch him, he looks like he's going to come over—he starts coming over—but then he turns back and continues to merely observe.

I turn to Morty and say, "Come on."

I grab Morty's chair from behind and push him through the marble and grass towards the spectator. The man notices us coming and for a minute I think he is going to turn and run. But instead, he holds his ground and waits for us.

"Hello Fred."

"Hey Paul. Morty."

And those are the only words that will be passed between us three brothers. We'll continue to stand there—watching the funeral from a distance—because that is always the easiest way to observe death, to distance yourself from it.

Everyone down by the gravesite has finished burying our mother and the crowd will slowly disperse. I'll put an arm around Fred and a hand on Morty's shoulder, and we'll stand there like that until the officer comes to take me back to jail, quietly remembering the woman that brought us all into the world, remembering that no matter how different we brothers are, we always have a connection with each other that is completely unique, a connection that—now that our mother is gone—we will never have with anyone else again.

•••

It may not be a realistic end, but it certainly would be fitting. At this point, it is too late to save my mother. But I hope that her death will not be in vain. While she was still alive, she desperately sought to keep her family together. While she was still alive, she always reminded us three brothers that we would always be responsible for one another. While she was still alive, however, she was fighting a losing battle. And it was the feeling that her goal was unreachable that killed her in the end, I think, whether her death was intentional or not. In her death, at least, I think that we three can remember her lessons and find a way to come together again, once and for all, as brothers. It's the least we can do, at this point.

I picture my mother when we were all younger: *she's running us boys through our bedtime routine. We are all in the bathroom brushing our teeth and listening to the radio. She is dancing with us and we are all laughing and having a great time. When we finish brushing, we all head off to our rooms.*

Starting with Morty, the youngest, my mother makes her rounds and reads to each of us in turn, giving us a hug before we close our eyes and she turns off the lights in our rooms.

That is the connection that Fred and Morty and I will always have. We know more about each other than we know about ourselves because we have spent our whole lives observing each other, because we know things about each other that we don't want to know about ourselves.

But now the police officer is here and it's time to find out what will really happen at the funeral. It's time to put on my ankle bracelet (which, by the way, is very noticeable) and it's time to find out if we brothers can turn our mother's death into something positive.

God, I hope Fred shows up.

THE END

Made in the USA
Charleston, SC
11 June 2011